8 Rooms

by eight authors

Fourth in the acclaimed 'Short Story Reinvented' Series

Independent Book Publisher

Legend Press Ltd, 3rd Floor, Unicorn House,
221-222 Shoreditch High Street, London E1 6PJ
info@legend-paperbooks.co.uk
www.legendpress.co.uk

British Library Cataloguing in Publication Data available.

ISBN 978-1-9065580-9-3

Set in Times
Printed by J. H. Haynes and Co. Ltd., Sparkford.

Cover designed by Gudrun Jobst
www.yellowoftheegg.co.uk

Legend Press

Independent Book Publisher

Contents

The Short Story Reinvented Series

Legend Press' unique short-fiction series, The Short Story Reinvented', is designed for today's busy, but discerning, reader. Short fiction is a perfect answer in a world where everyone wants things to be easily accessible, sleek and tailored to fit their needs.

High-quality, thought-provoking short fiction can perfectly fill what before may have been an enforced gap of 'dead-time' in a daily routine. Dipping into short fiction is not as daunting as delving into a thick novel on a commute or during a lunch break, when you know that you might soon be interrupted mid-chapter, yet the subject matter in this popular series is weighty and meaningful, providing something new to think about and feel inspired about for the rest of the day, week, month and year.

Legend Press receives hundreds of submissions for the collections, from all over the UK as well as from all around the world. The successful entries for each book are chosen so that all stories combine and contrast compellingly to make the most varied, yet at the same time the most cohesive, collection possible.

1

C.J. Carver

The one good thing about this journey is that I'm travelling in a vehicle my daughter might term a convertible. The truck has no roof, no canvas top, and I can stand in the fresh air and look around. Not that the air could be called fresh, it's incredibly polluted and I can taste chemicals at the back of my throat. There's a faint blue haze hanging over the streets but it's nothing to do with mist or fog or anything natural, it's the city's hangover from burning coal. Some cars have their headlights on the pollution's so thick, and I know that when I sneeze, my snot will be speckled with black.

That said, it's a big relief to be outside and despite the dirty air, I can't believe the colours; the red of that woman's dress, the bright white of that schoolgirl's socks. Even that man's overalls aren't a normal brown, but conker brown, mahogany, nutmeg. The intensity after seeing nothing but monochrome inside the camp makes my eyes ache.

The truck turns right at the traffic lights and down a broad street, wide enough for our truck to turn full circle if the driver so wished. The knot below my ribs immediately tightens as I search for the stadium, but thankfully I can't see it. I breathe deeply and try to enjoy my surroundings, but the knot won't loosen. I'll have to suffer from it.

We are, I realise, driving right through the centre of town, parading us criminals for all to see. It's supposed to scare the general public into behaving themselves but nobody seems to be taking much notice. Everyone's busy shopping, haggling over everything from kitchen mops to plastic tulips. We pass a dental surgery, then a shop devoted to women's underwear – mostly utilitarian white cotton and as titillating as a bath mat – and a stall selling goldfish. A waft of frying noodles floats past. I am amazed when my mouth instantly salivates, my stomach contracting with a growl. I didn't think it was possible to feel hunger on a journey like this, but it shows how instinct can overcome even the strongest emotion.

Little wonder I'm hungry. For the past five years I've been fed with just enough food to keep me alive. Hunger has dogged my every thought. For a man who loves his food, living on runny corn gruel in the morning and a bowl of weak vegetable soup in the afternoon has been torture. It didn't help that I refused to acknowledge my criminality when I first arrived. The prison commissioner promptly accused me of *denying guilt and resisting reform* and cut my meals to one a day. I thought that type of belief had gone out with the proverbial Ark, but not in my camp. It's like being back in the sixties. And there was I thinking the effectiveness of thought reform and political education had decreased since Mao Zedong kicked the bucket. Fat lot I know.

A radio attached to a rickety-looking shutter blares pop music as we trundle past. The smell of noodles intensifies and I wonder if the military policeman standing next to me is also salivating. From the aroma I guess the noodles are being cooked with garlic and chicken, the music . . . I'm not sure what group it might be. I've never been into pop. I'm more an opera man. My daughter hates Chinese opera. Says it gives her a headache.

I wonder what Li's doing right now? Whoops, I mean Lia. She changed her name when she joined the Hong Kong police force, said she wanted something more Western, as if her Chinese name wasn't good enough. Apparently Lia is Italian, although why she wants an Italian name is beyond me. Does she think it'll help her career? I don't think so, but who am I to protest? I'm just her father.

The truck swerves around an army jeep and the policeman beside me is caught unawares – he's gawping at a girl wearing spangly heels and a mini skirt that barely covers her sex – and he crashes into me. The board hanging around my neck whacks him under the chin. He makes a brief, surprisingly high-pitched noise of pain and hurriedly stands upright, dusting his uniform down, looking embarrassed. I feel sorry for him until he catches my eye and curls his lip into a sneer. I wink back. It always disconcerts them, this conspiratorial gesture and this policeman's no different to all the others. He glances around to make sure nobody else has noticed, terrified he might be reported as having an inappropriate relationship with a prisoner, or some other claptrap. I sigh inwardly and turn my gaze away. He's just another drone.

There's another prisoner on board, a woman, and most of the stares we attract go to her. She's young and pretty, and I wonder what the authorities trumped up for her. Wife of Soldier Negligent in her Marital Duties? Mistress of High Official No Longer Required? I feel sorry for her because she's too young for this. She should be at home bringing up her one child and caring for her husband. It's alright for me, I suppose, as I'm in my fifties. Still pretty fit too, even if I am as scrawny as an underfed chicken, but at least I can feel I've lived a little. Seen a bit too, and although I'd rather not have experienced the last few years in a *laogai* – Chinese gulags are particularly unpleasant places to be – life hasn't been all bad. I've been pretty lucky really.

A woman shaped like a giant brick and dressed head to toe in black shouts something, I don't catch what, but the policeman next to me shouts back, telling her to shut up. She's pointing at me, and still shouting. She's either mad or an idiot. You don't yell at the police. You're likely to end up where I am if you do. Curious, I ask the policeman, "*What did she say?"*

"She was complaining she couldn't read your board."

I can't read what it says either, especially since it's upsidedown and written by what I can only assume was a blind orang-utan. I ask him, *"What does it say?"*

He sends me a pitying look. *"Don't you know why you're here?"*

"Not really."

He glances away and for a moment I think he's not going to respond, but then he says:

"Active Falun Gong member, subversive planning violence and disobedience against the State."

"Thank you."

I sigh, ignoring his probing, curious look. How could they say I'm planning such rubbish? I couldn't plan a trip to the zoo. I'm hopeless at planning. I try, Miahua kindly assures me, which makes me realise how bad I really am. Take Lia's fourth birthday party. Half the people turned up on the wrong day, including the magician, and Miahua's mother, Fang Dongmei, a bent twisted old hag with a permanently sour expression, who never let me forget it. When I admitted I'd clean forgotten to invite some wasterel friend of hers she stared at me – she's got a creepy stare, that woman, her eyes are so dark you can't see where the pupil starts and the iris begins – before she spat on the ground. Her gob of spittle missed the tip of my shoe by a hairsbreadth. It was impressive. I wish I had such a good aim.

Luckily Lia didn't care my organisational skills weren't up to scratch. I'd bought her a puppy, just as she wanted, and to see her face light up like that . . . Oh, how I wish I'd taken us to the mountains like I wanted, but Miahua wouldn't hear of it. She started by saying I'd make more money as a doctor in the city, which was true, but the real reason was that she didn't want to leave her mother behind. When I suggested bringing the old hag with us, maybe find her somewhere to live nearby – no way did I want her actually living with us – Miahua was really pleased and everything was looking rosy until she put it to her darling Mama. Mama promptly responded by saying she wasn't going to leave all her friends behind. All her contacts, her herbalist, her hairdresser, her chiropodist, her favourite shops. Why should she move to somewhere strange at her age? I can remember her stubborn look as though it were yesterday. Mules have nothing on the old crone.

Why didn't I put my foot down? Why didn't I insist we go without her? Because I'm a soft touch, and look where it got me!

Banged up for teaching my patients callisthenics. For improving their blood pressure, lowering their cholesterol, building stronger bones, helping diabetics, helping Mei Ting overcome her terrible nerves, helping Zhi Peng lose weight – heavens that man was fat! – and boosting Ri Feng's self-confidence. And what about Miao Tian? She'd been bent double with arthritis, barely able to hobble to the park, and after doing barely ten-minute exercises each day for a month she could move more easily and her energy levels were through the roof.

I'm an old fashioned doctor, the type who happily spends a full hour listening to a patient if that's what is needed. I've found that questioning patients not just about their symptoms, but other aspects of their lives, helps build a picture of what's really happening. Take Xui Li, for example. A friend of a neighbour, a once handsome woman in her mid-twenties who ran a grocery store on the end of our street, Xui Li came to me with a headache. It was the first time she'd visited my surgery since she left school and she kept looking over her shoulder, jumping at the slightest sound. She was a nervous wreck and nothing like the strong, confident woman I knew when she was eighteen.

Xui Li insisted all she needed was some strong painkillers. I surreptitiously studied the yellowing bruises through the makeup she'd pancaked on her face. Indicating vaguely, I asked her, *"Did you fall"*

She looked away, *"Yes."*

"Do you fall very often?"

"Yes. I'm very clumsy."

I nodded, and made a note on my pad. Everyone on the street knew her husband beat her, but there was no point in mentioning it. She'd be terrified I might report back to her husband, and that he'd reprimand her with yet another beating. That's what wife beaters do. You step out of line an inch and you get belted. You soon become like Xui Li, afraid of your own shadow. I said noncommittally:

"Your headache may well ease if you try a little light exercise."

She looked startled. I continued, *"SuLyn Peng has benefited enormously."*

SuLyn was the local beauty that every woman wanted to be like and every man man wanted to sleep with. She was also a pop star, a bit of a celebrity, but thankfully as yet it hadn't gone to her head. *"I don't know if you know, but she used to suffer dreadfully from headaches."*

This was a complete lie, SuLyn had only seen me because she'd been petrified she was pregnant, but I'd learned over the years that the odd white lie invariably outweighed the sin it was supposed to be.

Xui Li blinked several times. She gulped before saying, *"Really?"*

"She'll be at the park with the rest of the group on Thursday. I know she'd love to meet you."

Xui Li's expression changed. It was no longer stiff with nervousness, embarrassment or fear, and it took me a long time to recognise what it was, long after Xui Li had met

SuLyn and they became friends, giving Xui Li a social life and re-born confidence that eventually eked to sweeten her bitter marriage. It was hope.

Miahua tells me I should be proud having helped so many people, that I should feel gratified having spent my life doing something so fulfilling. But do you know what gets me through the day? It's not thinking of my patients, believe me. It's thinking of those mountains, the clear-running streams, and air as clear as ice.

I'm a young man again and Miahua has the bloom of youthful beauty, her hair long and glossy and not cut into that hideous bob she says is so easy to care for. I can see our little stone house, the sheep grazing the grass. Wildflowers are sprinkled everywhere. And there's Lia. She's playing with the puppy, teasing him by hiding his ball, and suddenly she looks up and sees me . . . and she leaps to her feet and she's running towards me, her face beaming, yelling, "*Papa!*"

I scoop her up and swing her high before pressing my face against her neck and breathing in her scent – fresh grass with a hint of ginger, a sprinkle of cinnamon. She must have been cooking with her mother earlier. The puppy is still playing with the ball, pouncing and growling at it, when Miahua steps outside. She's smiling that lovely smile of old, carefree and joyous. She puts an arm around my waist, and with Lia's chubby arms around my neck, we go into our little stone house. While Miahua prepares our evening meal I sit on the stoop drinking green tea, gazing at the jagged peaks cutting into the purple evening skies. I breathe in the clean air.

"*What are you smiling about?*" The policeman has whispered the question.

"*I don't suppose you get many people smiling.*"

"*You're the first.*"

I won't tell him about my home in the mountains because it's none of his business.

"I was recalling the second stage of my rehabilitation."

He looks startled, so I add with a shrug, *"I found it particularly hard, that's all."*

In fact, I'd found it almost impossible. I was supposed to recognise my crimes, and ruthlessly censure myself while at the same time expressing gratitude for the magnanimity of the Democratic Socialist Party. I told you this place was out of the Ark. But when I heard the revered son of the same man who'd seen the massive influx of prisoners during the Anti-Rightist Campaign in the late fifties ran it, everything made a strange kind of sense.

An uncle of mine was arrested back then. He might even have been sent to my camp. It's a cruel story, and one that gets my goat every time I think of it. It was the time when the good old CCP – the Chinese Communist Party – decided to be a bit magnanimous and encouraged everyone to offer helpful criticisms of the Party, apparently without reprisal; ha ha. My poor uncle, under immense pressure from a Party secretary to voice his views, tentatively suggested that during the 1955 political movement the CCP was responsible for the deaths of hundreds of innocent people. His remarks were duly published, and three years later he was arrested as a rightist and sentenced to life imprisonment.

The truck bounces over a pothole and I grasp the metal bar in front of me. My minds eye can picture my uncle quite clearly. I try and recall my father's face, but it's blurry and indistinct. Disconcerted, I look over the bonnet of the truck and watch a man with a soft face like a doughball sitting on a stool outside a tool making shop. He's got his flask of green tea with him – I can see it steaming in the cool air – and he's lighting a cigarette. Another man joins him. He's brought out his flask as well. They're both wearing greasy blue overalls and I guess they're taking a break from work. The first man glances at me, then at the woman prisoner, all without a flicker of interest. He doesn't even appear to read our boards. I feel as though ice water has been poured into my veins. He doesn't care. He has obviously seen this many times before; two prisoners on their way to the stadium to be executed.

A shout builds in my throat. I want to yell at him, make him see me, hold my gaze, recognise my plight, my fate, but I'm prevented at the memory of Xu Guan. He was a patient of mine back at camp, who was known for chanting anti-government slogans. Before he was paraded through the streets he had his larynx cut out. Which sounds pretty bad, but when you consider it was done without anaesthetic . . .

I say a quick prayer for Xu Guan who was executed two weeks ago, and try not to dwell on the fact that I'm following in his footsteps. I might even die on the same spot as he did for all I know. It's the same stadium after all, and I can't imagine they're going to execute us anywhere but right in the centre, giving the crowds an unimpeded view. A wave of nausea fills me and I hurriedly turn my thoughts aside, fixing my concentration on watching the men drinking their tea. The second man has pushed back his armsleeves and loosened the overalls around his neck. To my relief the nausea recedes. Glancing up, I can see the sun struggling to get through the polluted mist. If we weren't burning so much coal the sky would be clear, a bright blue Autumnal day.

Despite my efforts, Xu Guan's face edges into my mind's eye, his bright button eyes alive with humour, his mouth slightly curved on one side as though he was perpetually smiling at a secret joke. He was only nineteen when he was arrested for hacking into the PSB's – Public Security Bureau's – system. He did it for a dare. What a waste of a young life. Will he be there to welcome me when I die? Will we be in heaven or hell, or nowhere at all? I've never quite known what to make of religion. My mother was baptised a Catholic when she was twelve years old, and attended a Catholic high school which was eventually closed down by the CCP to force Catholics to abandon the Vatican. My father leaned towards Buddhism, but since religion is outlawed in China, neither spoke of their beliefs. Not even in the privacy of our own home – that's how paranoid Mao has made the older generation.

Will I see my parents again, I wonder? As I picture my mother on her deathbed, her breath getting horribly short, her eyes turning pale and distant, another wave of nausea washes over me. I put my shoulders back and take several deep breaths. I really must get a grip. I couldn't bear the ignominity of being sick in the truck.

Still, there's a part of me that can't quite believe I'm going to die today. The other part of me, the one that's chattering away at the moment, taking deep breaths and making sure I stand here with as much dignity as I can when I'm handcuffed and shackled and paraded to the public, has to be in denial. I keep thinking a miracle might happen, that Lia has pulled some strings, and at any moment a police car will rocket along the road and screech to a halt in front of the truck and halt the proceedings.

I'm not going to be rescued. I know it, but I can't stop hoping. And cursing too, for being such an idiot. I should never have forgotten what happened to my uncle. However, as Miahua said time and again, I only got into trouble because I was trying to help.

A vibrant cheeping chirping makes me look down. Sparrows are hopping in the gutters looking for food. I love sparrows, their busyness, their happy chattering. I used to feed them on my balcony. I crane my neck to give the two workmen a final glance. They're slurping their tea, puffing on their cigarettes seemingly without a care in the world. I want to scream: *you try and do some good, and you get executed for your trouble!* But of course I don't. I want to maintain my decorum right until the end. I've heard of people weeping, falling to their knees and begging, shitting themselves, and I'm determined not to become one of them. Come what may, I'll hold my head high, even if I do take the prize for being the most stupid person on the planet.

What was I thinking, I wonder? It all started when another doctor recommended callisthenics to me, along with some deep breathing exercises. I was, I admit, somewhat overweight – Miahua's a great cook and I hate to leave even a single grain of rice on my plate – and despite my reservations, he was so persuasive about the benefits that I gave it a try. Within weeks I found not only had I shed several pounds, but I was so much more clear minded and energetic I got Miahua to give it a go. Every morning, before our porridge and before I headed to the surgery, Miahua to the office, we'd move the living room table aside and begin. Lia thought we were hysterical when she came and visited. I can remember her standing there in her cream silk pyjamas, shiny black hair hanging to her waist, clutching her sides with laughter. She looked so like her rmother at that age I nearly lost one of my Indian Squats and fell over backwards. Between chortles, Lia managed to say, "*What on earth are you doing?*"

Miahua stuck her nose in the air. "*What do you think?*

"*Whatever it is, it looks painful. Wouldn't you be better off doing yoga or something?*"

Miahua sniffed dismissively. "*I hate yoga.*"

It was true. Miahua had never got on with yoga, saying it was too slow, her mind too busy, but she took to callisthenics really well – the fact that she could do the exercises at home was a major factor – and she was delighted when not only did the exercises improve her muscle strength and tone, but like myself she felt a zillion times better. Even I recognised the difference her, she looked younger, more animated. She seemed to have lost ten years in the same amount of weeks.

This was why I took callisthenics to my patients. I started with the top eight I knew would benefit the most. I wanted them to share my and Miahua's newfound vigour and perhaps spread the word to others. All but one agreed to test callisthenics out. When I mentioned it to Chen Zhengsu – a lugubrious man with a penchant for hypochondria – he looked as though I'd offered to ram a melon up his backside. He practically galloped out of the surgery; apparently petrified I was going to make him start exercising right away. Before then, I had no idea there were some people out there who were so opposed to exerting themselves, and from the look on his face when I suggested it, I wasn't surprised he never came back.

So, there I was with seven patients all signed up and ready to start. Somewhat foolishly, I thought that once I gave them a practical demonstraton – showing them how to work on their muscle groups, how to mix and match the exercises to suit them – they'd get cracking. But I hadn't taken in one of the most important factors about exercising. Motivation. I'm not sure how it happened, but I have a sneaking feeling it was probably Ming Rong's idea. As head of a valve company that exports to foreign countries, he thinks he's smarter than everyone else and is always coming up with what he thinks are bright ideas. This one was for all of us to meet once a week in the park where I'd lead a half hour exercise class and make sure everyone was working their muscles correctly.

It's not uncommon to see people practising Tai Chi in public spaces, but of course they're doing it solo, not in a group. Groups – unless they benefit the Party, of course – are anathema in China, they threaten the system, so it was little wonder we eventually got arrested. It didn't help that SuLyn's apartment held a shrine to Bodhisattva, or that Mei Ting admitted to dabbling with Buddhism. Branded subversives, all seven of us were carted off, interrogated, and chucked into jail.

Lia flew in from Hong Kong. She tried to call in favours as a cop, but nothing she tried did any good. All she got for her trouble was a demotion and a transfer out of the prestigious banking area, where she was investigating fraud, to some stinking dump on the outskirts of Macau. She was lucky not to lose her job. Having a subversive father apparently planning on toppling the government isn't the best recommendation for a fast-track route to the top.

That was the last time I saw my daughter. She wore her uniform on purpose, hoping to gain me some leniency, and for a moment I didn't recognise her. She stood so rigid, so tall, her bearing so military, I thought she was one of those obsessive robot-women who's entire being was wrapped up in toeing the Party line. It was only when the man from the PSB was forced to go outside to answer a phone call when the daughter I love so much appeared, shining from her eyes. I had trouble holding back my tears.

"I'll get you out, Papa."

"I don't want you to."

"I'll do everything I can, I promise."

Her voice choked. She was trying not to cry as well. I took her hand in mine. It was cold and I rubbed it, trying to warm it. *"Do you know what I want the most?"*

"No. Tell me. I'll do anything."

"I want you to hug me and promise you'll return to Hong Kong. That will be the greatest gift you can give me, because then I know you're safe. I'll be able to picture you in your city apartment, cooking dinner for friends, maybe cooking for your husband one day. If you stay here, you'll get implicated. You know how things work."

She shook her head. *"No."*

"Come. Hug me."

She squeezed me tight. Told me she loved me. I kissed her

hair and told her she was the apple of my eye. Then I told her to go. It took every ounce of self-possession to look at her for the last time, and smile. No way did I want her tarred with the same sordid brush as me. The further she stood from me, the better, and although it just about killed me to watch her walk away, I didn't have any doubts that what I was doing was one hundred percent right for my beloved, cherished, glorious daughter.

The PSB officer was surprised when I said I no longer wanted to see Lia. I told him I was ashamed to let her witness me doing so poorly in the camp. I told him I would only lay eyes on her when I'd completed my sentence and been redeemed. Both of us knew this would never happen. Not that I couldn't be redeemed, I hasten to add, but that I'd get to complete my sentence. There's no way the system would want to lose someone as valuable as me, not unless they wanted to make an example of them.

Take Wen Zhang, one of my patients at the camp. He was a big man, very strong, and despite the appalling diet, one of the camps best workers. He'd build walls, break up concrete, dig holes you could bury a bulldozer in while barely breaking sweat. His release date was the twenty-fifth June, and on the nineteenth, out of nowhere, he was subjected to a beating due to his *poor work attitude* in feeding the pigs – his favourite job at the end of the day. His letter writing privileges were revoked, along with his family members' visiting rights, and his sentence extended by three years. He could have made love to those pigs, sang to them joyfully while he shovelled their shit and the outcome would have been the same, because good prison camp slave labour results in good profits for the government.

Us slaves spend our last drops of sweat, our last drops of blood, supporting the national economy. It's not just that we produce stuff to export around the world – the ubiquitous T-shirts, rice, cotton, etc. – but prison camps are encouraged to be part of the competitive market like any other businesses. A camp that earns foreign money is considered a real success. My camp's teamed up with a European car manufacturer who supplies us with equipment in return for cheap labour. Wen Zhang's previous camp produces wine that's sold from Los Angeles to Berlin. I bet the liberals in the West wouldn't quaff half as much of the stuff if they knew where it came from.

Don't get me wrong. I'm not having a go at China. I love my country. Well, I hate it too – how could I not considering where I'm headed? – but I have to admit it's one of the most extraordinary places on earth, with one of the richest civilisations. I just find it amazing that we're the first nation with a prison system so extensive and well organised that it constitutes an integral part of the economy. Not that your average man on the street realises it. They might suspect it, but with all prison camps being given corporate names it's impossible to know whether the box of Golden Dragon tea you've just bought was produced by slave labour or fully paid employees.

They're clever, though, these camps. They make sure they know exactly what your skills are, and then use them. Dressmaker, chef or cow herder, it doesn't matter, your particular skill will be utilised one hundred percent. An architect came in a few weeks back – the idiot used one of those protest parks the government created for the Olympics, needless to say anyone who actually used them won't see the light of day again – and already he's designing the new kitchen block. As a doctor, I spend just about all my time in the infirmary. This is the reason why I know so much about the system. Doctors listen. It's their job.

I heard so many horror stories in the first six months I'm amazed I got any sleep. There were too many to count. The worst atrocities appeared to be in the *laogai* based in the remote Qinghai and Jiangxi Provinces. It seemed the further the camp from the seat of government, the more the use of violence. I heard of prisoners routinely beaten to death for stealing food. Others foot-shackled with twenty-kilo weights for taking too long in the latrines. One prisoner was late for roll call and had his back broken. He was left lying on the ground with no help, no medical attention. He was dead by morning.

The thought of being in one of those isolated border camps made my heart turn cold. I found I could stand the snakes, the lice crawling over my body, the flies, fleas and bed bugs. I could ignore the fact that we were never allowed eggs or meat, or that we were supervised every minute of every day. All I had to do was picture one of those places. I knew I was relatively lucky living just a day's train ride from Bejing meaning Miahua could visit me – once a month for twenty minutes – bringing me vital things such as underwear, warm undershirts and socks, food, and occasionally the odd book; all strictly controlled needless to say. I would do pretty much anything to stay put. So when I was told I was to be transferred to a camp in the Xinjiang Autonomous Region, you can imagine my reaction.

I can remember the shock of Miahua's face when I told her. She tried not to show any emotion, but her face spasmed into a rictus, emphasising her delicate bone structure and giving her the appearance of a bird's skull, a death's head the colour of curdled milk. If I ever doubted she loved me, I didn't any longer.

That said, I still went through a stage of wanting to blame her for my misfortune. The same refrain rattled around my head for days: if only she hadn't put her old bag of a mother first . . . if only she'd forced Fang Dongmei to join us in the mountains . . . if only her mother had dropped dead . . . I don't want to think about those shameful, bitter-dark thoughts now, there's no point, but at the time I found Miahua's visits almost unbearable. I wanted to throttle her, I wanted to hold her. I wanted to scream at her, I wanted to weep in her arms.

On the day of departure, around eighty of us were shuttled to Beijing's Yongdingmen Station and forced into a train already crammed with other prisoners. It was mid-summer, and while it was baking outside, inside the train is was almost unbearable. There were no seats. They'd been removed to make more space, but there still wasn't enough room for everyone to sit, so we took turns. There must have been fifteen hundred people, I reckon, being shunted out west. At the end of the train was a carriage of armed guards, and more guards were stationed throughout the train. They took shifts watching us, making sure nobody jumped through the windows when the train slowed – a tempting thought except for the gunmen waiting for the chance to practise their marksmanship on our fleeing figure.

I managed to squeeze a space for myself and Xu Guan at the end of the second carriage and beside the doors, which had their windows wide open and, once we got going, offered a breeze. Unfortunately, this position also meant we were outside the toilet. This normally wouldn't bother me, but since it had no door and just a hole in the floor where to aim your effluent – and a lot of prisoners didn't care if they missed – it wasn't the best place to be. It stank, but we both decided it was worth it to be next to a window.

I don't know how many hundreds of miles the journey was, but it took three days. We rattled through pollution-choked cities where everyone wore white masks and the acid rain ate its way through anything metal – lamp posts, bridges, cars – gradually travelling north-west, all the time moving through towns and villages, but eventually they began to change, becoming smaller and smaller, until they were just collections of rickety shacks.

Finally we emerged on to a vast plain flooded with light and colour. We were on the edge of a yellow and green sea of grass stretching in every direction. In the distance stood a spine of snow-capped peaks. They looked tiny but I knew they had to be massive. I had never seen such distances before, and I stared, for a moment breathless with awe. The clarity of the air was astonishing. I felt as though I'd had both eyeballs removed, thoroughly washed, dried and then polished. Behind us lay towns and cities, bustle and noise, ahead was an immense space empty of humans. As the train ventured across the plateau, I felt we were as exposed as a millipede on a freshly laundered bed sheet.

In all actuality, the plateau was deceptive. It wasn't uninhabited after all. After a couple of hours I saw a huge building, a great slab of grey misery appear in the distance. As we approached, I saw it was belching great gouts of thick black smoke into the air. Again, I stared. I felt the shock of it like a fist against my heart.

It was like being offered a glass of fine wine and then your host spits in it. I'd never thought about pollution before, I'd just lived in it, breathed it, knowing it was a fact of life, but *this*. It hurt to see such a brilliant, beautiful wilderness befouled.

I counted seven gulags that day, all pumping a variety of filthy clouds into the atmosphere – one coloured vivid orange. I dreaded to think what they were making that produced such evil looking vapour. There were no villages or towns in between these places, nothing but grasses and rivers. Each gulag was entirely self-supporting, supplied by the single railroad that the inmates had built years before. It's always puzzled me why people become prison guards, so I say to the policeman next to me, "*What made you become a policeman?*"

He jerks slightly in surprise. "*Why do you ask?*"

"Would you humour me?"
"My father was a cop."
Was it really that simple? I don't think so. Both my family nor Miahua's had any police or military backgrounds, and there's our daughter, the cherry on the cake of our life, a full-blown sergeant. Miahua's a secretary. You can't get much further from being a policewoman than that, surely? Besides, why should you inherit the same profession of your parents? It smacks of a lack of imagination to me. My father wasn't a doctor. He was an accountant, a bean counter for a national manufacturing company that made robots. Not the type of robot you see in science fiction stories, but the kind that sit on an assembly line putting other machines together, like engines. By all accounts it wasn't exactly thrilling work, but we lived comfortably and had enough money not just for my education, but for a few luxuries also. My background didn't help when I was being sentenced, needless to say. Even though Mao's been dead a long time, should you get anyone from the old school listening to your case, those who are born into wealthier families invariably incur harsher sentences.

Amazingly, Miahua made the journey to visit me in my new camp. I'd told her not to but here she was, the fifth visitor to the camp in a month, the second relative to visit in two. The other three visitors had been officials. Families didn't visit relatives out here. It's too far, too expensive, and far too devastating. I didn't know whether to laugh or cry when I saw her. *"Whatever are you doing here?"*

"Visiting my husband."

Her voice was firm, her expression stout, and if I didn't know her well, I would have thought her unmoved. There were no tears, but in the depths of her eyes I caught a shadow drifting, like a dying fish.

"Oh, Miahua . . ."

She'd aged, as I suppose I must have, and silver threaded

her hair. She wanted to hold hands, but I didn't want her to see the dirt engrained in my pores, or feel how my skin was dry and flaky like the empty husk of a cicada. She insisted. Her skin felt incredibly soft, her hand as small and delicate as mouse bones. When I raised her fingers to my mouth, I caught a dift of her fragrance, and the next second I was at home, sitting on our balcony at the end of a long day as I usually did, unwinding with the newspaper, some tea, and a lot of grumbling about our neighbour's too-loud TV. The sun was a heavy pink through the pollution, the buildings soft-edged grey in the haze. Traffic was growling outside, horns honking and beeping, the stench of diesel fumes mingling with frying rice, steamed greens, garlic chicken . . .

The vision was so intense that for a couple of minutes I couldn't speak.

"*Are you okay?*" She immediately turned her head away, biting her lip, "*Sorry, stupid question.*"

"*No, I'm fine. I was just wondering how our neighbours are.*"

She rolled her eyes. "*Nothing changes. I mean, of course things do, I'm sorry, of course I didn't mean . . .*"

She was flustered and I put a finger up to halt her, saying gently, "*Shhh. I know what you mean, okay? I'm glad nothing changes.*"

It was impossible to have a normal conversation, although we tried. She told me Fang Dongmei had managed to find someone to take on my practise, a cousin of hers who'd been displaced from Fuling – one of the towns that had part of it purposely flooded in order to create the Three Gorges Dam – and although my patients missed me, they were quite taken by the new doctor. I felt a stab of jealousy. Knowing I'd want to menatally stick pins into them later, I said, "*What's their name?*"

"*Hui Zhong.*"

I was startled. *"It's a woman?"*

"Yes."

I wondered if she lived up to her name. Hui Zong meant beautiful on the inside and smart on the outside. I didn't dare ask. I didn't want to be outshon by a woman. I'm not a misongynist, but I'd much rather have had a nearly blind old man with halitosis than an intelligent, bright young thing that would make everyone forget I ever existed. I can't help myself. *"Is she pretty?"*

Amazingly, a sparkle of humour enters Miahua's eyes. *"What if she is?"*

"Nobody will remember me, the ugly bloke from Xining."

When Miahua left, my heart broke. I couldn't see her again. Not like this. It was an inhuman thing to do to her, and although she's my wife, my only love, I hated her being there. I loved her for coming, don't get me wrong, but I hated her to see me losing weight, to see my greasy hair, my blackening teeth and filthy fingernails.

Although I tried to be upbeat, I'd seen how it tore at her. I had no news, nothing to tell her except our dreary routine: up at 6:00 a.m. for a slice of cornbread and if we're lucky, some salted carrot. Before the prisoners are marshalled into the factory at 7:00 a.m., I authorise any sick prisoners to either remain in barracks – the place is run like a military camp – or go to work. Our camp has barely any safety measures or barriers, and the prisoners often get hands or fingers crushed. I spend the day caring for them and any guards that are ailing, before a fifteen minute break for lunch, during which we slurp whatever pathetic slop we've been given. Then it's back to work until 7:00 p.m., after which you're locked back inside your barracks to sleep as best you can until you awake the next day to go through the whole dreary routine again.

I wrote to Fang Dongmei and told her I didn't want Miahua to visit again. I didn't give a lengthy explanation as I knew my mother-in-law would grab this with both hands to ensure her precious daughter wouldn't sully herself any longer with her no-good husband. All I said was that Miahua needed to move forward with her life and that she couldn't do that with the millstone of me hanging around her neck. I also wrote to Miahua saying the same thing, and adding that if she did come out again, I wouldn't see her. Just as I never saw Lia any more.

It makes me sound holier-than-thou, doesn't it? Being supposedly so unselfish? But the simple fact is it made me feel better doing the right thing. It almost absolved me, in a peculiar way. I won't lie and say it wasn't hard, because after sending those letters my blood seemed to drain away, my heart begin to atrophy. I had terrible dreams too, of Miahua and Lia in terrible danger and needing me and I'm unable to help.

They wrote, though, both of them, week after week. I almost rescinded my decision on several occasions, but as my physical condition deteriorated, my hair falling out, my teeth loosening, my skin sagging over my bones, I knew I couldn't let them see me like this. Far better for them to have the memory of when I had a chubby face and a roll of fat over my belly from good eating.

After Miahua's visit, I didn't expect to see anyone from the outside again. So you can imagine my surprise when a month later I was escorted to the visitor's room, a damp space with no windows wedged between the guard's office and a row of storerooms. I just about fell over to see the bent figure swathed in robes of black sitting waiting for me. Her expression was as sour as usual, as though she'd just swallowed a pile of rotting fish intestines. If I'd expected any sympathy from my mother-in-law, however, it was banished the second she opened her mouth. I gave as good as I got, needless to say. Worse, in fact. I had no idea I had so much rage in me. Once I started, I couldn't stop. The vitriol poured out of me like a rushing tide of black filth. I was frenzied, almost frothing at the mouth, shouting, blaming her for everything. It was, I yelled, entirely her fault I was here.

If it hadn't been for the guard standing over us, I might have hit her, strangled her, bashed her head against the wall. I know I'm a doctor, supposedly incapable of causing harm, but at that moment I honestly felt as though I could happily kill the witch. I hated her, and I had no doubt it showed. I looked into her cold black eyes while I ranted, cursing her to hell and back, and couldn't see a drop of emotion, let alone any empathy for my plight. Impassive, she sat there like a big black bat.

Eventually I ran out of steam. She didn't say a word. We spent the last five minutes of the visit in silence. When the guard said our time was up, she got to her feet and shuffled off without a backward glance. I reckoned that would be the last of it. But no. The old harridan visited me every four months, come rain, hail or shine. Oddly, I even came to look forward to seeing her, especially since I didn't have to make any effort. She'd be rude to me, and I'd be rude back. She'd tell me I was a useless good-for-nothing and I'd tell her she was an ugly old bag. I'd moan about the food and she'd grumble about her bunions. I didn't waste valuable energy trying to hide my misery. It wasn't as if she could give me a hard time about it over the next family dinner.

During one visit, I remember her banging on about Lia, how it was my fault she lived abroad, miles away from her family. For no reason, I drifted off, picturing Lia and her smile. Not as she is now, but when she was four or five years old and I could tickle her, lift her in the air, hug her and tell her stories that would leave her wide-eyed and bursting with questions. Fang Dongmei got annoyed that I wasn't listening to her diatribe and demanded to know what I was thinking. So I told her. She said, *"Miahua was the same at that age."*

It was the closest she ever got to admitting she might love

her daughter as much as I loved mine.

We've reached the end of the main thoroughfare. I sneak a look at the policeman's watch, which isn't a cheap rip-off copy like most cops' but a shiny chrome Seiko, the real thing – I wonder if his parents bought it for him? Or his girlfriend? – and when I see it's past eleven and that we're nearing the end of our journey, I feel that same crushing weight on my chest I've felt for the past few weeks. My legs weaken and my breath falters. My mouth dries up. I want to fall to my knees and sob and howl and bang my fists against the wooden planking, but I don't. Instead, I close my eyes and haul air into my lungs. I've taught enough patients to know that breathing fully and deeply right into the bottom of your belly helps calm you, no matter what's happening around you. What did I use to say? *When you relax the body, you relax the mind.*

I haul in another breath, right down to my toes. Then another. I can feel the policeman's eyes on me but I don't turn to look at him. If he looks at me with contempt it wouldn't be a problem, but I couldn't bear to see sympathy. I'd collapse if I did.

I try not to think where I'm going. Instead I force myself to concentrate on the vibration of the truck's engine from the floor and into the soles of my shoes, up my legs and through my spine, to the top of my head. I'm reasonably tall for a Chinese, which, Miahua told me, gave me an advantage over the other doctors. My height apparently made me more authoritative, but in camp, being taller means I attracted more attention, most of it the unwelcome type.

I can see the stadium. My blood pressure goes into free fall and I know I'm as pale as chalk.

I wish I had a faith, someone or something to pray to, but I have nothing really. My faith is in my family, Miahua and Lia. I told Fang Dongmei to make sure they didn't know about today, until it was all over. I'd given her letters to hand to them, long letters of love, tenderness, warmth and devotion, and as many jokes as I could remember. I took a long time writing those letters, multitudes of drafts; until I believed I'd struck the right balance. I imagined them reading and re-reading them and I didn't want a single word to drag my girls down.

I can feel every shake and judder the truck makes through my whole body, right to my fingertips. I can see the pale outline of the sun, still struggling with the blanket of pollution.

I force myself to look at the stadium. It isn't that big. It looks as though it was built forty or fifty years ago, and the concrete has great cracks running through it. The whole place is shabby and dirty and if I was a spectator I wouldn't feel very safe, the building looks as though it might crumble at any moment.

I try and swallow but I have no saliva. It's as though I've got cotton wool balled in my throat. How long have I got? Minutes now, not hours. I begin to tremble.

Then I see the other trucks. Six of them, diverging to the stadium. I count fifteen prisoners. The trucks, like my own, are stuffed with military cops and bristling with guns. No chance of anyone making a break for it. As we close in, heading for the stadium's entrance, I stare at a skinny man with almost no hair. He stares back. He looks defiant, almost cocky. My blood slackens and I feel lightheaded. It's almost as though I'm looking at myself.

Two more trucks join us, three prisoners in each, and for a moment, my brain stalls. I look away, desperately hoping I'm seeing things. I can feel my blood humming in my ears and an oily snake writhing in my stomach. I swallow drily and look back.

It's almost five years since I've seen them and although their appearances have changed – they're wearing pale blue smocks and, like myself, are pale and thin – a doctor never forgets a patient.

There's little Mei Ting, who had trouble with her nerves, Zhi Peng – not an ounce of fat on him any more – and Ri Feng, who is silently weeping. Miao Tian is also crying, but Xui Li has her chin held high. She's holding SuLyn's hand.

Their boards all say the same as mine.

Active Falun Gong member, subversive planning violence and disobedience against the State.

They're here because of me. They're going to die because I introduced them to callisthenics. My chest tightens so much I can barely breathe. I can't stop looking at them, their skeletal frames, their gaunt faces coloured like a frog's underbelly. I hear someone making a deep, agonised groaning noise, like an animal that's been shot and is in its death throes, and realise it's me. Tears are pouring down my face but I'm not sobbing.

The trucks turn into the stadium. Our truck follows them. People are still gathering inside, ushering one another into their seats. It's half full. The grass is scuffed and half starved. The sky is the colour of dirty pearls.

The trucks pull into a line and switch off their engines.

My breathing turns shallow.

I hear the tailgate drop with a clang. The military cops jump out, taking the woman prisoner with them. The policeman next to me says, "*Out.*"

I have to hold the side of the truck to stop myself falling. My legs feel soft, boneless. I look into his eyes. They're an unusual soft, pale brown, like unprocessed sugar. I have to work my mouth before I can ask him. "*Will you be the one?*"

He looks away, then down at the ground. He shrugs. I glance over at the neighbouring truck. SuLyn tries to smile at me but her lips are trembling so hard it's nothing but a grimace of fear. Zhi Peng is sobbing. Mei Ting is trying to comfort him.

My pulse is thudding, roaring in my ears.

A woman in the crowd is shouting something but I don't hear what she says. I'm trembling head to toe. She shouts again, screaming so hard her voice cracks. The policeman says, "*Look.*"

I turn to see an old woman in the front row, dressed head to toe in black. She's waving her arms. For a moment I think it's the mad woman from the street who couldn't read my board earlier, but then my brain catches up. I can't believe what I'm seeing. It's Fang Dongmei and she's shouting so hard to gain my attention her face is swollen red, her black eyes alive and urgent.

She's holding up a poster, a cheap toothpaste advertisement that shows a line of snowy mountains in the background, and in her other hand is a dress Lia used to wear years ago, when she was a little girl. Miahua made it for her and its pink and white, with daisies dotted all over it. It was Lia's favourite dress until she grew out of it.

Fang Dongmei has stopped yelling and is standing there, sobbing, rivulets of tears pouring down her face, pooling into canyons of wrinkles.

I'm filled with a rush of love for my mother-in-law that's so strong I nearly topple over.

She shouts again, telling me to concentrate. I do as she says and I look carefully at the picture of snowy mountains and then fix my gaze on Lia's pink and white dress and suddenly I'm no longer in the stadium. I can't feel the policeman's hands on me, urging me out of the truck to kneel with the others because I'm no longer here. I'm in the mountains and walking home, tired after a day's work. Sheep are grazing and there are wildflowers sprinkled everywhere.

Lia's running towards me, her face beaming, "*Papa!*"

I scoop her up and swing her high before greeting Miahua. She puts an arm around my waist, and with Lia's chubby arms around my neck, we go into our little stone house where Fang Dongmei is preparing our evening meal. I grin at my mother-in-law and she scowls back. Miahua joins me on the stoop to sip tea. Lia comes to sit on her lap. I lean back and gaze at the jagged peaks cutting into the purple evening skies. I breathe in air as clear as . . .

2

Rebecca Strong

It all started a few months ago. For a long time – in fact, for all the time that preceded – I had no thoughts at all. And then, in the darkness, a whisper of a thought sparked and I was moving, on a wave, further into what now seems like eternity. Something carried me beyond any control I could conceive: air, wind, liquid, and motion, colluded to push me where they wanted me to go. Aside from these factors, these natural conspirators, nothing, and no one, was aware that I was here.

I heard, and felt, and saw nothing. No conscious thought had yet invaded me, but from within this nothingness, I knew what I must do. That has been my mantra: if I am here, ipso facto, I know what to do. I floated, for a while, deciding what to become, or indeed, whether to become at all. Never in my fleeting life had I had so much power, and never shall I again.

I was intrigued as to where this was going, so I took the plunge, and before long I was stuck fast, stuck to a surface that in time I came to both love and hate. I waited, confused and immature, to see what would happen next. There was, and remains, only me in this environment, this chamber that I am magnificently affecting. It was dark but expansive, yet I remained bound, and after a while the immobility became a comfort. I christened myself "I", for then I became.

I heard nothing but the rush of blood. I began to feed off my environment, growing bones, organs, cells dividing and multiplying, DNA and chromosomes and blood that coursed through me, awash with life. Over the weeks I became stronger, able to turn my head and seek out this newness that surrounded me, this great plain that was mine to explore. I curled and uncurled, clenched and retracted, flexed and unflexed until I became fully aware of my limits, pushing the boundaries of my physical capabilities until I was satisfied I could do no more. I took command of my space, floating hypnotically in a liquid so unique it became my water and my waste, my pool and my drowning. I could not see myself, or even feel my parts, but I used them all the same. I was caught in a rhythmic trance timed with the constant drumbeat that metered my growth.

It took a while before I became aware of anything – or anyone – outside my own chamber. The constant gurgling and machinations were a daily comfort to me; even the wrenching and tugging of the walls above me in the early days. My heart and mind literally grew to love these things and sought comfort in their physical ruminations. I had all that I needed, connected to this space by a cord that brought me everything. I could ask for nothing more, except as time passed, I began to want more, to wonder more, to crave external stimulation. The rumblings around me echoed within my own body for I was a miniature version of my own environment, a Russian doll. And before long, I got what I wanted – I realised She was there.

In this room I remain both alone and with Her, trapped and protected, somebody in Her body. I am closed off yet exposed so, gradually, Her world becomes my own. We control each other, She and I.

I remember when I first heard Her. I think She was crying. There was a slight shuddering that lasted quite a few minutes, and high-pitched sobs that just about carried through to my ears. I felt awash with sadness, but I didn't know why – aside from the disruption, the new sensation was interesting. I opened and closed my mouth in response, liquid spilling in and out, in and out. Still, I made no sound – but for Her muffled squeaks and bodily processes my world was silent. After a while, the sound diminished, and all was calm again. I began to feel exhilarated – so I was not alone, I was part of something greater, something more powerful. Perhaps I, too, would progress to that state, for I appeared to be changing every day, developing ceaselessly towards something greater than myself. I began to wonder if She knew I was there, if I could communicate with Her in any way. I moved my limbs and tried to punch with my fists, but I was feeble and weak, and received nothing in return. "I'm here!" I wanted to cry, "I can hear you!" but I had no way of getting the message through, or so I thought at the time. Instead I waited until I could hear Her again, and that's when the voices started to come. Clearer and clearer each day until I knew we were not alone, She and I, but *he* was there too.

We have a routine, the two of us. We wake fairly early in what I have come to know as a period of light, and head straight for the water. It is the most quiet and peaceful time of the day. Sometimes She hums to me; there's one particular tune I find very comforting, and some days it sends me back to sleep, content that all is well. I am usually woken again by the water cascading over my enclosure as if I'm cocooned inside a waterfall. When the water is turned off, She becomes silent. We move more quickly, bending, tucking, darting, and all the while silent so as not to awaken *him* early. Once we are ready, we move away and I hear faint bangs and crashes, tinkling and gathering until once again we are back where we started, with *him*. This is when *he* wakes and I feel Her whole being tense.

She takes something to *him* and sits with *him* a while. *His* satisfied grunts fill the void, and She waits patiently until *he* has finished. Perhaps this is when they are happiest together and there I am, in the middle, contentedly waking and sleeping at intervals. Sometimes they must talk about me, because I feel one of them pressing gently down on top of me and I try to push back, to let them know I know. Then She gathers again and retreats; She does not speak unless *he* speaks to Her, and I cannot always catch their words.

This is when they separate, and we are not near *him* until the light has once again fallen. Instead we go outside, She and I, where the world brushes against Her skin and She wraps us up protectively. Sometimes a glimmer of sun shines through a gap and I stretch toward the bands of red that dance before me in ribbons. She walks for a while and I am rocked to sleep, my dreams indistinguishable from my cosy reality. I dream that I am here, and when I wake, here I am. Yet now I am being thrown about, first one way, then the next, and I am unsettled. I hear constant rumbling and we are travelling again, moving further and further away from the place we start out from and where we shall return. I hear other voices, strange sounds, conversations we are not part of and people we cannot touch. In this place, I am Her secret, even as I grow. I twist and turn, trying to get comfortable to no avail until suddenly it stops, and we are moving alone again, away from the strange turbulence I love to leave behind. We are outside for a short while before we go into the whispering nest where we remain for a long time, at peace.

We are here most days, with Jean. Jean has a gentle voice just like Her, but huskier. Amidst the beeps, the clicks, and the comings and goings, we remain near to Jean, who She likes to talk to. Just as I seek comfort in Her, I think She seeks comfort in Jean.

"How are you?" Jean asks.

"OK." She replies. She never says too much. When She is

silent, Jean talks unless they are interrupted.

"Everything alright at home?"

"Yes, fine. For now." I can feel Her shift about in discomfort. She does not like talking about *him*.

"And the little one?" Does she mean me? I kick my legs up in response.

"Ha-ha, doing well I think. In fact, she or *he* is moving now – maybe it heard us?" She presses down on top of me again and I turn my head towards Her.

"You'd be surprised how much they're aware of," says Jean. "Pregnancy is always more magical the first time around, but even then, after it's born you tend to forget how it felt to carry this person around inside you, day in, day out, for nigh on nine months. They must absorb a lot more than we realise. This woman was in here the other day with a screaming newborn. She said it was because *he* hated the car – she'd driven to work in a foul mood while she was pregnant because she hated her job, and she must have passed on the negative vibes. Now her little boy cries every time she starts up the car, which is unusual – they usually love the motion."

"I hope they're not that intuitive," She says, with a wobble in Her voice. "God knows what this little one has picked up on already."

"You need to be careful," says Jean, "you're influencing the baby already. And you tell that oaf the same – it's not just about the two of you any more. When *he*'s...not treating you properly, *he*'s affecting the little one too. They say that a woman becomes a mother as soon as she's pregnant, but a man only becomes a father once the baby's born. They don't understand that this little person already exists – it has emotions and thoughts. Who knows how much of our personality develops in the womb. I mean...oh love, no need to cry. Sshhh. I shouldn't go on; I know you're doing your best. Look, go into the back and make us a cup of tea, eh?"

I could feel the slight shuddering as Jean's words had taken effect. She's scared, I know, scared of *him* but also scared of me. I want to tell Her I'm ok, I'm being taken care of, but I can't. She stands up and moves away, and before I know it the motion is pushing and pulling me, side to side, and I drift off...

When I wake, we are back seated, and strange voices come and go. I don't know where Jean is. I hear snippets of conversation, words like books, returns, stamps, dates and numbers. There are odd screeches followed by reprimands, little thumps running low down, the clicking and clacking of objects being moved, taken and brought back. I rest, and wake, and rest again. I can tell that the more noise surrounds us, the more She forgets about *him*, and the more we are OK.

Later on, someone else arrives. I think *his* name is George. *He* has a low, friendly voice and *he* asks how we are.

"Well, thanks", She replies, with a slight squeak in Her voice, "how are you?" I can feel the whoosh that thrums constantly in my ear speed up.

"Oh, I'm fine," *he* says jovially, "and how's this bun coming along?"

She giggles.

"He or she is doing fine. We have another scan the day after tomorrow."

"Aha. Is this the one where they can tell you if it's a monkey or a donkey growing in there?"

She laughs, and I feel happy. I think it might be my favourite sound. "I was hoping for a puppy actually!"

"Well, maybe you'll get your wish. I once knew a woman who was hoping for a lamb, and it turned out all she had was an oversized goldfish swimming around in there."

"Ha-ha, well, you never know..." She falls silent.

"You can go home now, you know," George says, breaking

the pause.

"Oh, right, course. Actually, I was going to ask a favour."

"Which is…?"

"Would you be able to do my shift, the day after tomorrow? Jean will be here, and it means I can take the day off without having to rush to the scan and back."

"It'd be my pleasure."

"Are you sure? I know it'll be a really long day for you, but –"

"Sshhh, really it's fine. You shouldn't be rushing about any way; you need to look after both of you now. Look at that bump, it's really coming along!"

"Yeah, sometimes I think it's getting bigger by the day, but it's meant to be a centimetre a week I think." There's a lengthy silence, I don't know why. "Well, I'd better get home; I think I've missed my usual bus already."

"Take it easy, OK?" is the last thing I hear George say as *his* voice fades and then *he*'s gone, or rather we've gone and She's out but I'm still in.

When it is good, it is very, very good, but when it is bad it is horrid. I suppose that's why we're still with *him* – the good times, I mean. I know *he* must be something to me, and to Her, but I'm not sure what. I feel no connection to *him*, other than through Her.

We move, slowly and tediously, back to where *he* is. I fidget, restlessly, as I am shaken about, just like in the mornings. There are more sounds towards the end of the day, more conversations I cannot quite make out, sometimes cheering and shouting coupled with ting after ting until the voices diminish and we too move away from them.

I am rocked, gently, for a few minutes until we pause and I feel Her breathe in deeply before taking the last few steps. We have arrived. *He* is there, of course. *He* always seems to be here and I do not know what *he* has been doing while we've been away. She greets *him*, briefly, before moving around Her confined space. I am stuck in this room, this warm enclosure, but when we are with *him*, She too is stuck, rattling around like a defunct pinball trying to avoid any conflict. She walks a few paces, stops. Walks back, stops. Things clatter and hiss and sometimes I drift away until *he* shouts:

"Bring me a drink!" But She does not reply; I wake to feel Her moving around still and I miss Her voice. I think She forgets about me more when we are with *him*.

After a while, they sit down together. And this is when it goes one of two ways: the good way, meaning She has made *him* happy and *he* grunts and snuffles contentedly until we move away, She and I, and *he* is left with the indistinguishable voices that seem to come from nowhere. Or it goes the bad way, and I am afraid for Her, for us. It starts with something small.

"It's cold," *he*'ll say, or "Why do you put this crap in front of me?"

"I'm sorry," She'll reply, "I haven't had time to –"

"Same old rubbish. Day in, day out, your pathetic excuses. I don't ask for much from you, just that you're a proper wife. A proper wife who makes a decent meal." Sometimes *his* words are…blurry, more muffled than usual. I strain upwards to hear them, because I don't want to leave Her alone.

If She remains silent, on occasion, it all goes away and we are OK. Other times, it enrages *him*, and even I've come to learn what will happen. I suppose the thing I have most in common with *him* is that we're both creatures of habit, though in here I have no choice in the matter. I can see how the consistency comforts *him*, makes *him* feel in control.

"I've been at work, and I make you a meal every day." She mumbles.

"What the –? How dare you put this shit in front of me and then complain. You and your shitty library job. Haven't I taken care of you for years? You've got it so good and you're never happy. You get to do whatever you want, and all I ask is that you treat me with some respect when you get home, make me a meal, keep the house tidy. Is that too much to ask? Is it?"

"And what have you done all day? Drink yourself silly with the small amount of money I bring home."

"Oh, as if I haven't brought enough money home. I told you, there's a job coming up soon – I'm just waiting for the details. And don't you talk to me like that. First you get your own job, then you start answering me back, then it's 'the baby this, the baby that'."

"As if you care about the baby!" She screams. There's a loud screech and suddenly *his* voice is higher, towering over us. We're jerked forwards and then *his* voice changes, becoming lower, calmer.

"I'm sick of hearing about this baby," *he* mutters, "if I had a decent wife, maybe I'd care about her damn baby" and then *he* drops us and She flops down, Her hand circling this chamber.

The distant voices start up and mask Her sobbing. It makes the room shake around me, and I push back in response. Waves of sadness envelop me, and the disquiet lasts for a while. When She finally falls silent and starts to move around again I know She is alright and I allow myself to leave Her.

When I sleep, my dreams include only Her. My eyes flit from side to side as the thrumming continues, my own little beats racing at twice the speed of Hers. I feel myself inside Her, and I hear Her voice. When I wake, She is there, and I don't know how much time has passed. Sometimes, the room is smaller, more compact. Yet sometimes it is bigger and I'm as insignificant as a bunch of cells that may never actually come to be.

Later, when it's dark, I hear *him* close to us again. She does not say very much. She lies flat, and I am rocked for a while, amidst *his* grunts and shoves. It is the only time *he* is close to Her and gentle, and I am not afraid. Afterwards, She and I lie awake whilst *he* must be sleeping. I do not like it when She lies still – I need to feel Her with me. I push and kick until She strokes this cocoon and eventually I am forced to lie still with Her in the darkness. There is always the hope that tomorrow will be different, but I know it will most likely be the same.

The sound of water has haunted me since the day we had our last scan. I could hear it falling all around us as we left home. This liquid chamber is compact, different, whereas the water outside is free-flowing and dangerous, I've learnt that much. She was shivering as we walked, and there was a different type of shaking as we travelled to a strange place I don't remember being in before. We were safe though, I knew that much. We're safe anywhere that *he*'s not.

We spent extra time at home with *him* that day before we left. *He* stayed at home, of course. I think She wanted *him* to come with us, but *he* mentioned something about waiting for a phone call about a job and She didn't ask *him* twice.

The scan days are special, and they're something to do with me. She hums all morning and speaks to me when we're alone. "I get to see you today!" She tells me, though I don't quite know what She means.

We go to a special place that feels bigger, and even though we are inside She walks and walks, and twists this way and that until eventually we come to a stop. All the voices I hear are softer and gentle, and I stay fairly quiet, content to wait and listen.

After a while, a voice calls out and She gets up again. We go somewhere darker, and She lies down, which makes me feel slightly squashed. I push back, trying to get Her to move a bit.

"How are you doing today?" says a voice at a slight distance.

"Alright thank you." She answers.

"Baby active?"

"Yes, fairly."

"Right, well today we're going to take a look at the organs, measure the head, the fundal height, and generally make sure the little one is developing well. Just relax."

And then, before anything else is said, my internal beats are magnified for Her to hear and I have surround sound, my lifelines projected inside the room and out.

"That's amazing!" She says, but there is no response. Instead the walls are being poked and prodded, and I shift around trying to avoid the compression.

"Do you want to know the sex?" says the voice.

"Um…ok then" She answers, and Her own beats speed up.

"Bear in mind it's not 100% accurate though," warns the voice. "But it looks to me like you're having a little girl."

"That's fantastic" She says, though I feel a certain sadness wash over us and I feel a little afraid. I am pushed around a while longer before She moves upwards and I am free again.

"Would you like a picture?" asks the voice.

"Oh, yes please!" She replies instantly, and then after a pause, "Hello you." I think She's talking to me again, and I push with my hands.

"Does everything seem alright?" She asks, Her words tainted with apprehension.

"It all seems fine. You need to have some routine blood tests too, and they'll let you know if there are any problems. But that's it for today, your little girl seems to be developing well and I've noted the measurements down on this card!"

"Thank you," She says, and then there is some shuffling before we are moving again, away from the voice and back into the red light.

I am hoping we're not going straight back home to *him*, but we do. *He* doesn't seem to have moved, though when we get back *he* turns the other voices off and asks,

"So?"

"Everything seems fine."

"That's it? They didn't say anything else?"

"Not much, really." Except they did, and She is not repeating it.

"It's taken you three hours, but that's all they said?"

"Well, they measured the organs and made notes on a card. The baby is developing well. I...I have a picture." There is a moment's pause as She moves closer to *him*, and I hear *him* clear *his* throat.

"I can't tell which bit's where" *he* says dismissively. We move away again. "I don't suppose they told you the sex?"

"No...um, I didn't ask."

"Shame. It'd be nice to know my little boy's kicking around in there. Eh, do you hear me son?" *He* shouts loudly, *his* voice too clear in my head. I stay quiet and *he* laughs.

That's when the phone goes. I know the sound now – a high-pitched series of beeps that often causes Her to rush about or *him* to shout "get the phone, will you?" Then one of them will start speaking to someone who doesn't seem to be here with us, unless they have suddenly arrived; I am not sure. The beeping doesn't last long this time.

"Hello," *he* grunts, and then "who is this?" *He* doesn't sound pleased. "It's for you," *he* says, slowly, and then there is a whoosh and something hits Her just above me.

"Hello," She says, hesitantly. "Oh, George!" It's George,

but I don't think *he*'s here because I cannot hear *him*. We move away from *him*, a couple of twists and we're alone. She is still speaking to George, sounding happy and afraid at the same time.

"It went alright thanks. The baby's fine. I can show you the picture next time…Yes…Yes…Well, it's nice of you to call, but you really shouldn't…I mean, I'd prefer it if you didn't…Yes…I'll see you tomorrow." And then George has gone altogether.

"Who was that?" *he* asks calmly when we get back to *him*.

"George, um…from the library. *He* covered for me today and *he* just called to ask how it went."

"George. I see. And when the phone rang two nights ago and you left the room was it George then too?"

"No…I told you that was –"

"And when you come back from work late which, by the way, I have noticed you doing lately, is that because of George?"

"No! I just walk a bit more slowly now. Sometimes I miss the –"

"Don't give me your crap! You think you're so much better than me, always have done. Well don't forget you jumped at the chance to marry me, I didn't force you. Your father was grateful I took you off *his* hands, even *he*'d had enough of you."

"That's not true, *he* had no idea what you're really like. I had no idea…please, just stop! George is nothing, nobody, just a colleague." She's crying now, and I'm shaken with the convulsions. I brush my hands against the walls, to calm them, but in this moment I am powerless.

"Well that's what you would say, isn't it? That's right, turn on the waterworks again. I've seen how you skip off to work, eager to get away. I've even followed you once or twice – oh, you didn't know that did you? At least you haven't been lying about where you're going, though I wouldn't put it past you. Why do you think I've been home a lot lately, eh? Why do you think I haven't been able to work?"

"Haven't been able? You haven't worked for weeks, you're just drinking all the time, that's nothing to do with me!" She sounds shocked, confused.

"Nothing to do with you? It's because I have to keep an eye on you! I can't trust you, not like the other guys whose wives behave properly. Don't you think I'd love to be out there working without a care in the world? Jim called the other day with a job and I had to turn *him* down, had to tell *him* I already had work. And you know why that was? Making sure you're not shaming me is turning into a full-time job. I was thinking about working again this week, even called Jim back and left a message, but now I see I won't be able to yet again."

"You're being ridiculous! You don't have to watch me, I haven't done anything wrong!"

A smacking sound makes me jump, and causes Her to step aside. The volume drops, and I stir in my pool, expectantly.

"How dare you call me ridiculous," *he* spits out close by. "If you haven't done anything wrong, how come no one else from work calls you, if your colleagues are all so concerned? How come the lovely George is the only one who has your number?"

"They all have my number, it's in the staff log book" She sobs, "and Jean calls sometimes, you know that. *He*...George...he only called today because of the scan, because I told *him* about it and asked *him* to do my shift."

"Aah, isn't *he* nice? So caring. So interested in the scan...I wonder why that is. Could it be *he*'s more connected to this baby than I know?" *His* voice is louder now, and I think *he*'s standing over us. I can hear *his* breath, heavy and menacing.

"What, what do you –?"

"How the fuck do I even know this baby is mine?" *He* says,

defining each word slowly with the sharpness of *his* tongue. And then I'm back in the picture, the main focus. I feel Her body snatch upwards sharply, and the crying ceases.

"It couldn't be anyone else's." She replies, slowly and definitively. Her beats speed up, and so do mine. The whooshing intensifies in my ears, and I feel dizzy.

"Is that because you were more careful, with George?" *He* laughs, a horrible sound. Not like when She laughs, not like when we're happy. I don't know who *he* is to us, but I want Her to take us away. Instead, She screams, a sound that terrifies me, and we are jerked forwards until She is lying down and I am squashed.

"Ah, my hair! Let go, please...the baby –!" She cries, but then She starts moving without standing up. The walls are pushing in to me, and I cannot move.

"Get upstairs, you bitch," *he* instructs, and after a few seconds She manages to lift herself and I am relieved though I stay quite still. I hear scrambling, and I know *he* is behind us and we cannot get away.

I hear water running in between Her shrieks, and *he* is muttering to us but I don't know what *he*'s saying. Then the whole room flies forwards and She screams again before it warps into a gurgling sound. Water gushes, and then I can hear *him* again.

"Don't ever think you can get one over on me," *he* shouts, "Don't ever think you can trick me, because I'll know, and I'll be waiting." More gurgling, followed by gasps. The walls go in and out, rapidly, freeing then squeezing me. The beats rush in my ears and my head is spinning. Another splash, and then calm. The room is still shaking, but I hear nothing, and after a while I cannot take this any more and I start to drift away, gently slipping until I know nothing more.

When I wake, we are alone. My head is hurting, and I feel

extremely tired. Something is pushing gently on the walls, and I muster up a little strength to squirm against it.

"Oh, thank goodness!" I hear Her say quietly. I stay still, in case *he* is there, but *he*'s not. She lies flat and I push back a little more as She presses down gently on my head.

"I'm sorry," She whispers, "I'm sorry baby, please forgive me, I'm sorry." I can't respond too much, but She seems appeased. "Shah, my little girl, I'm here." She whispers again, "we're OK now." I let myself wallow in Her gentle tones and again I sleep, dreams of rushing water making me twitch from time to time.

The next day, everything was silent until we went out. She went through the usual motions, but there was no interaction with *him* and I couldn't even tell if *he* was there or not. I felt much better; almost back to normal, though I'm not sure She did.

"What happened?" Jean asked, as soon as we got inside.

"I don't want to talk about it." The first time I had heard Her voice that day, always reassuring.

"You'd better get in the back. I'll be there in a minute, I'll just get Noel to look after things." Noel was someone else who'd been around lately gaining 'experience'. *He* had a voice like George's, but squeaky. She moved off before I could hear Noel's reply, and within a few seconds the door swished and we were alone until it swished once more and Jean was with us again.

"I'll put the kettle on," she said, "you sit right there." I liked Jean. More than anyone, she reminded me a little of Her.

"Thank you," She said, and we sat.

"Did *he* do this to you?" Jean asked tentatively as something near to us bubbled, hissed, calmed down and then tinkled.

"Does it look that bad?"

"No...not that bad. But what happened? I've seen you with puffy eyes before but you look like you've caught the sun badly too. And what's happened to your hair?"

"He...he..." yet She cannot finish, and I am shaken once more as She cries.

"Sshhh, it's alright. Let it out. Here, look, take this tissue."

"Thank you." I can hear Her inhale and exhale deeply a few times.

"That's it – have a sip of your tea too."

"George called, yesterday, when I got home."

"Oh Lord. Where did *he* get your number? From the log? I've told everyone those are there for emergencies only."

"It's not George's fault, *he* was just being kind. But when I got off the phone, my husband went mad. Accused me of all sorts. I just don't know what to do when *he* gets like that, if I stay silent it enrages *him* and *he* does whatever *he* likes, but if I protest *he* gets furious too."

"So *he* was angry about George calling?"

"George only called to find out how the scan went. It was nice of *him* really, but *he* shouldn't have. We only spoke for two minutes but that was enough. *He*...no, I can't, I don't want to say any more. I'll only cause more trouble, I mustn't –"

"None of this is your fault! You don't need to protect *him*. And I'm not going to tell anyone, don't worry, I just want to help you."

"You promise you won't say anything? Because I know you want to help, but that would make things so much worse."

"I promise. But you can't go on like this, not now you have a baby to think about."

"Well, that's another thing. *He* was ranting about the baby, whether it was even *his*, and then *he* –" Her voice dropped low, so quiet I could only just hear it. "He dragged me up the stairs by my hair, ran hot water into the bath and...and held my head under it."

Jean gasped. "The bastard! *He*'s a piece of work. You need to report *him* to the police – you're carrying *his* child and *he*'s treating you like that?"

"No, please, you promised. It wasn't for long, I think I was just scalded."

"Relax, I said I won't say anything and I won't. But that doesn't mean that you shouldn't."

"I can't, I can't...I'm sure *he* won't do it again, it was just a misunderstanding. *He*'s been on edge because there hasn't been much work, and *he*'s been at home a lot."

"Drinking again, no doubt?"

"Sometimes...but *he* doesn't mean to hurt me, *he*'s just anxious with the baby and everything. You know how men get when they feel out of control, like they're not the head of the household."

"I can name a damn few men who would never treat their wives like that, I can assure you."

"Please, can we just leave it? I don't want any more upset, not for the baby. She's been really quiet since it happened and I just want to get back to normal."

"She?"

"Yes, I found out at the scan! But keep it to yourself – *he* asked me when I got home and I told *him* I didn't find out. *He*'d be disappointed."

"He wants a boy then? There's a surprise. Well, you make sure that little one's still active, and if not you go and get checked out. Don't want to be taking any risks. With *him* behaving like that, you're the only one looking after that baby and you owe it as much care as you can manage."

"I know. I just hope this never happens once she's born. I'm sure *he* wouldn't –" She sobs again and I feel Her pressing down on me, so I lean towards the pressure.

"Come on," says Jean, "let's take a look at your face. I have some foundation that should cover up most of the redness, and if we take your hair down it'll cover that patch.

"Thank you...I don't know what I'd do without you."

"Nonsense, you'd cope fine. But if anything like this ever happens again...if *he* so much as threatens you, I want you to tell me, alright? And if you need to get away, at any time, you just call me and you can stay with me. You can't just think of yourself any more, you need to make sure you're both safe."

"Thank you. I really do appreciate it you know. But I'm sure we'll be fine. I won't let anything happen to this baby."

I fall into the ensuing silence, and wake to hear George's voice. It makes me happy, so I kick a little. I have less room now, and it's harder to bounce around in here; even my back is pressed up against the wall.

"I'm sorry," *he* was saying, "I just thought I'd see how you got on."

"It's OK, it was nice of you, really. It's just that...my husband's a little..." She stops, Her voice breaking a little.

"It's just that those phone numbers are for work emergencies only, and you shouldn't refer to them for personal calls." Jean interrupts.

"Right, I'm...er...sorry." George stutters.

"I have to go," She mumbles, and then we're off, without so much as a goodbye.

Sometimes, I'm awake whilst they are asleep. There's not a lot I can do, in here, but I'm slowly coming to understand my purpose. As much as I am part of Her, it seems that I may be part of *him* as well. I know Her, but *he* and I are still strangers to each other. In the dark, I can hear *him* make a long grunting noise, and it's become almost comforting to me now. I like it when *he* is here, but asleep.

When it's dark, I am swimming in their dreams. The thrumming in my ears is always there, but all else is still. She breaths, in and out, calm and contented. Sometimes She turns and I am tossed in a loop, rocked momentarily, our bodies charged with current. Then She is still again, and my own jerks cannot wake Her; She has a break from me whilst I watch under Her, encompassed in a chamber tailor-made for me.

I think my purpose is to stay here as long as possible, and not let *him* get to me. She and I are meant to look after each other. I don't know how long it will be for, but things are changing in here, or rather in Her. She is more tired now, and I think it's because of me. I am getting bigger, and stronger, and if this continues I won't be here much longer because the pool is not infinite and soon it won't be enough. I understand more by the day, and I want to fight back. I dictate more of Her actions now – She sleeps longer, consumes more, breathes deeply and walks more slowly. She speaks of me to others, and they ask how I am. I am Her main focus, though we are separated by these walls. She is tired, but never tires of me, of displaying Her voice, Her tunes, when we are alone. She provides the stimuli to all my senses; the light to my eyes, the sound to my ears, the barrier to my touch. I feed off Her body, and Her thoughts. She grows as I grow, and I move as She moves – each in control of the other. I am at Her mercy, and She is at mine.

He cannot get me in here, I think. *He* can get Her, but She won't let *him* get me, and I feel safe from *him*, accepting of *him*, even. She needs *him*, too, else we'd be away, away with one of the others with whom bad times do not exist. But the good times, with *him*, bring Her comfort. Deep inside, where I remain, I think She cannot take me away from *him*, because I am *him*, too.

I call myself 'I' but they call me 'baby'. When they are

happy, they call me to perform, to dance for their amusement and I willingly oblige. They push down on me to get my attention, not realising they have it whenever I am awake. They make plans together; trips and shops, paint and furniture, clothes and toys all smattered about their talk. They stay close together, and I hear their breathing, faithful and synchronised. I wade in the middle, biding my time. And I understand more each day, how She and I may be something, but the three of us are whole.

The next few weeks passed fairly peacefully. *He* even took a construction job that came up, so *he* ventured outside when we did each day, sometimes before. There would be a great rumbling when we got outside, and they would say goodbye to each other before *he* disappeared. Sometimes when we returned *he* wouldn't be there. Those other voices only surfaced late at night, and not even every day. I grew into this peace, infringing Her activity and inciting Her to rest.

One day, She told *him* in the morning that we were going for blood tests and might be back late. *He* barely paid any attention – the idea of me excites *him*, but I am not real for *him* yet. We remained inside much later than *him*, and when we ventured out we took a strange trip again to the large, twisted space full of unfamiliar sounds about which I'm unsure how to feel. There was a lot of sitting, waiting, and drifting away, before a voice addressed us briefly and then we were moving again, through the coils of this space and back into the open.

There were only two places we could go now, I thought: back to the whispering nest, or back to the dwelling place where *he* too would return. But, as it turned out, we headed to neither. Instead, something strange happened. We dove into another world, which made me realise I haven't understood very much at all.

She walked steadily to a new place that shifted my bearings because there were no beeps or clicks, but there were whispers with a voice I knew. A voice that didn't belong in this unfamiliar place.

"Have you been waiting long?" She asked, just after She sat down. I shifted a little, positioning myself so I could remain comfortable and within earshot. Her beats thrummed steadily, threatening to drown out the conversation.

"About half-an-hour," said George, "but I don't mind. Did you get the tests done?"

"Yes, sorry, you had to take a ticket and there was a bit of a queue. Anyway, I'm here now, or rather, we're here." She presses down upon me, and I turn my cheek towards Her.

"Yes, you are. Bigger by the day! How are you feeling?"

"Good. Tired. Better for seeing you. Finally."

"How long do we have?"

"A couple of hours at least. I told *him* I had an appointment later on and would be late."

"I can't tell you how good it is to be with you. Without anyone else around, I mean. How long has it been, three months?"

"You know it's been impossible."

"What can I get you?" asks a sudden twang that makes me jump.

"Two teas please. And a couple of slices of that cake over there," replies George. At the sound of *his* voice I lie still again, though I'm still confused at *his* presence.

"Thank you," says the twang, before fading away.

"So, how's the baby?"

"She's fine."

"Oh, she's fine? You found out it's definitely a girl then?"

"Yep, but I've only told Jean...and now you."

"What about *him*?"

"He doesn't know. *He* wants a boy."

"Well, *he* doesn't know *he*'s not getting either, does *he*?"

"Of course *he* doesn't. Look, we need to work out what we're going to do. We need a plan. Because I can't risk being around *him* once she's born, it's too...dangerous."

"I know. But wait...oh, thank you," *he* pauses, as something tinkles around us. "Look, I've been meaning to ask you, are you sure?"

"Sure we should be with you? Or sure this baby is yours because if you're asking me again, I –"

"I know we've been over this, but it's been a while and I just need to hear it again."

"She's yours, I've told you. *He* was in a drunken stupor for practically the whole two-week period I got pregnant – *he* can't even remember that *he* was too drunk to perform." Her voice softens. "Trust me, OK?"

"OK. So, what are we going to do? Do you want to move some things in to my flat, so they're ready?"

"We can't live with you, not there; we need to go away. Don't you understand? If *he* finds us...you saw what *he* did just because you phoned, once. If *he* finds us, *he*'ll kill you. Maybe even me...or worse."

"I wouldn't let that happen."

"You don't know *him*, you might not be able to protect us. No one knows *him* like I do. *He*'s...he's not normal. Things are black and white in *his* world. *He* knows what *he* wants, and nothing will stand in *his* way. If it's all going according to *his* plan, *he*'s kind, considerate even. But the second some small element of *his* life veers off course, *he*'s... unpredictable."

"Then we'll go away. I have an aunt, in Wales. I'll ask if we can stay with her for a few weeks, get ourselves on track, and I'll get a job there. It'll be fine...listen, leave it to me."

"If you're sure. There's not much time. And nobody else can find out."

"It'll be fine. Your turn to trust me." Her beats have slowed now, and She is calm. I sense She is happy, but not in a way I've felt before. There is a sense of comfort with George that no one else brings. *His* words, and *his* voice, are soothing to us both.

"Now," *he* instructs, "tell me more about this little one. How many weeks are left?"

"Six," She answers, "six weeks and you'll be a dad. How does that feel?"

"Amazing" I hear George say, as I slip away and leave them to their intimacy.

I can no longer tell how well I know any of them, not even Her. She is my protector, my provider, but She is no longer enough. I was meant to also look to *him*, but now I'm not so sure. Despite *his* rage, *he* fulfilled our needs, but a void has been exposed and She is filling it with George. Whilst George is fleeting, *he* is there every day. And although *he* frightens us, George has no influence at all. I think I have underestimated Her power to protect me, to maintain this haven I've come to love. Perhaps I'm meant to remain here after all, in this room without a view; I'm increasingly aware that I cannot.

They don't know much about each other, he and George. I hear one, and then the other, never both at the same time. I think She'd like to be with George, more than we are with him, but I sense something is brewing, and She is biding Her time. At least She includes me, whomever She is with, though the more we switch between the two, the more I feel distanced from Her. It's as if our bond is thinning, and we are ready to be apart; I need more than this chamber, and She will not attempt to convince me otherwise. The beats thrum on with a steady pace, like a countdown to some end I cannot fathom.

We no longer go to the whispering nest, with its beeps and clicks, nor converse with Jean and the others. I don't know where they've gone, these familiar sounds that brought me comfort for so long.

At first there was only I, but then I realised She was there too. I went where She went, heard what She heard. She threw in all the elements that are now slowly being stripped away, until I am raw and ready to create my own. She speaks to me less now, though I listen harder.

We travelled some way this morning, to a quiet place where George's voice was the only sound I recognised. When we arrived, *he* was in front of us, but when we went inside *he* switched and followed us round. *He* stays close, but is hesitant – I can sense *him* edging around.

"Everything's packed," *he* informed Her when we entered.

"So I see. And your aunt, you're sure she's happy for us to stay?" She sat down, and stroked my head. I hear things the other way up now, as if I've moved a little away from the sound.

"Yes. Well, I didn't tell her the exact situation. But she didn't ask too many questions either. She's getting old, I doubt she'll want to get too involved. I told her it was just until we found a place to rent – she said she might even know someone with an available flat. I'll have to see about a job though – it's hard to look for one from over here."

"But you said you have some savings, didn't you?"

"A small reserve, yes. And you?"

"I told you…whatever I've saved I've had to use on the bills and on the baby. I hope you're not going to rely on me because I don't have very much left at all and you said you were happy to take us on, both of us, without any qualms."

"Relax, I meant it. I was just enquiring, that's all. I'm not expecting anything from you other than my daughter." *His* voice moved closer. "I'm not taking this lightly either, I know we can't let *him* find us."

"Damn right we can't."

He always makes Her feel better, George. When we arrive, She is tense, apprehensive, and after we've been with *him* a while She calms down. Sometimes I feel I am communicating with George without Her knowledge, as if George and I are colluding to loosen Her up. In reality though, I am unwillingly complicit in any game She chooses to play. I feel sorry for George; She plays *him* for a fool because sometimes She says exactly the same things to *him* as She does to George and no one knows it but me.

I sleep more when we are with George. With *him* there is no danger, no sudden movements, gasps or cries. Just mumbles, rumblings and the occasional address. *His* actions are more like Hers, though their thoughts secretly conflict. She has peace on the outside but the same turmoil within, whipping me up in a frenzy of untruth. She concocted me somehow between *him* and George, and only She knows where I'll lie.

I awoke as She raised herself and said goodbye to George. I heard them touch, felt *him* press upon me as a parting gesture before She moved us away. But as we went to leave with a clack and the outside poured in She recoiled suddenly, and I knew within one word that *he* was there.

"Hello," *he* says, and the world falls still.

And here we are, the four of us, together for the first time. Swaddled in the games, the mistrust, the promises, the *expecting*. Their breathing trembles, Her beats speed up, but I – the most significant insignificance – am not afraid.

She moves backwards rapidly, as far away into the space as She can get.

"What are *you* doing here?" She asks, holding Her voice steady through the shallow breaths that squeeze and release me in fear.

"What are you doing here?" *He* echoes, each word getting louder as *he* approaches. "You must be George," *he* states, a little away from us.

"Get out," says George feebly in response, lacking conviction as always.

He laughs, but then hisses, "not without my wife."

"She's not going anywhere with you" determines George, but She is jerked away from George with a cry and *he* remains where *he* is. There is nothing George can do now, and we all know it. The scene will play out as *he* sees fit…or unfit.

"Sit there," *he* commands as we are flung down and I am stuck now, unable to turn away from any of them.

"Don't you touch her!" shouts George, rushing over, but a loud smack results in *him* moaning from a point lower down.

"Is this your little love nest?" *he* shouts, as more thuds resound and George groans with each one. "Is this what you've been planning all along?" Thud. "As if I didn't know? As if I would believe everything she tells me." Thud. "As if I even thought this baby would be mine." *His* voice booms, on and on, until suddenly there is no sound other than Her whimpers. George is nowhere to be heard.

I hear *him* rushing back towards us, pulling us upwards with all *his* strength. I am loathe to react, incapable of changing anything. I have done enough damage.

Then it hits me, a massive blow, an earthquake to the room that has become my endangered prison. My world shakes, my body crumbles in a space too small for it to fold. My mouth opens and shuts in shock, liquid ingested and then filtered out. My head is spinning, and I can no longer tell Her position in relation to my own. I hear nothing but the rush of blood – the first sound I ever heard. I have come full carnal circle and fall into the black.

Time passes. When it clears, I can hear Her whispering to

me. "Please baby, please, please be alright," She's saying, over and over again, and Her hands circle the chamber, pushing against me gently. I squirm against them a little, to let Her know I'm listening. And I'm alright, I think, we're both still here. I'm wiser now, I can hang on. I know when to react, and how. I'm stronger, and better, and I'm used to the sound of Her voice, including when She's sobbing pathetically like She is now. I don't know where *he* is, but even *he* can't surprise me any more.

But then, I feel a huge compression, like everything is closing in on me and I can't move. I'm totally squashed; not like being caressed or shoved because it lasts longer and I can't respond at all. I can hear Her though – She cries out in surprise and we drop, and then She's crying whilst I'm still being squeezed from all sides. Then it's over, back to normal…except…it happens again, another wave pushing onto me and the only thing I can do is try to wriggle downwards, the weight on me all filtering down into my neck. There's an opening, suddenly, as something close to my face falls away and then the liquid surrounding me rushes out, leaving me bare and naked. I'm going too, I think, I'm being thrown out, finally. And it strikes me – then I'll finally be under *their* control.

3

D.E. Rhylis

Your face smiles back at me from the photograph. It has pride of place here on the top shelf of the bookcase. The place where I insisted that it should be after we lost you. Lost you so suddenly, robbed of goodbyes.

Thank goodness that I sent you the photographs of the family living abroad. It had been against my better judgement as they were precious to me too and I was afraid that they would somehow get lost. I know that you saw them before you shut your eyes for the last time. They were tucked down the side of your favourite chair here and were found when we got here that night. Steven and his girlfriend, Ian and I.

Soft, silky fur. Warm and comforting. Calming my whole body as my hand slides down its length. Further rewarding me with a soft thump of a grateful tail as it moves to show love returned. Sandie is now curled up asleep on your chair. She used to sleep on your knee when she was a puppy, your constant companion. When you had gone, she wouldn't lie anywhere else to sleep and still sleeps there. Curled in her usual position. The chair has to go soon. It is worn but it's a link to you. There is a reluctance to let it go. We will get her a new basket. Soon.

A tear now falls onto the warm comforting bundle of fur but she does not stir, feeling safe and secure in these familiar surroundings. Not allowing myself to cry much at the time, having to stay strong for the rest of the family. Being more used to dealing with death, they had looked to me.

I had been the strong one, too, when you were alive, on

your return from the hospital stays. My brother wrapping you up in cottonwool and pulling the sofa up nearer to the fire. Followed by the usual phone call to say you weren't progressing.

I would arrive and ask why you were not dressed. The hard one everyone thought. I would help you dress and say that you could go and lie on the bed if you really felt unwell, and that while you were in nightclothes you would remain a patient and feeling ill. I had been trained well I thought back in those days. Now I wish I had wrapped you in cottonwool too. If you hadn't died so suddenly we would probably be homeless now. You knew that we were running into trouble after I became ill and was made redundant. You didn't know the extent of the debt that we were in at the time. All those threats and being scared to answer the telephone. People had said that I had a good career. Illness and redundancy have the same effect on anyone, no matter what they do. You had helped us out a lot during the last few months before you died and now I will never be able to pay it back. The tide turns so quickly.

You used to get cross with me during the time I worked abroad and I returned home to visit you. Always stopping off at the huge supermarket on my way to you to stock up on all sorts of goodies and arriving in a taxi amid all the carrier bags and cases. We would laugh. You would scold and I would laugh more. I always arrived by taxi.

"When are you going to learn to drive?" you would say.

I still can't drive, so afraid of failing. I didn't and still don't like to fail at anything. It had taken being ill myself to realise that all the hours spent working for someone else, the twenty-four-hour on call, the invasion of my private life and a set of clothes by the bedside ready to slip into should there be an emergency, were unimportant. It is the people that you love and that love you that really count.

You never stopped believing in me and that gave me the

strength to achieve my goals and realise my dreams when I was younger. I was good at what I did.

"You must stop this," you would say, "I don't need all this food. There is only me here you know."

Your eyes would light up though and amid the hugs of delight at my being here I would open the fridge and discard the food that was out-of-date. You forgot to do that more and more frequently towards the end and I would fill up the fridge and freezer with your favourite foods and treats. Later you would search both and have the same expression on your face as an excited child at Christmas.

"I will never be able to repay you for all this," you used to say.

"What's to repay?" I would answer. All the sacrifices that you had made over the years meant a lot to me.

I was returning from a business trip when it happened. The usual phone call to you was not made before I went away, but the note with a contact number and the photographs had been sent a couple of days earlier. You had been getting so forgetful. The telephone calls that came were frustrating and disturbing.

"Why don't you send photos anymore?"

"Look on your shelf Mum, the latest photos are there."

There would be a pause and a sound of a shuffling of feet as you went to look.

"Oh yes," you would reply.

"Well fancy that. When did you put them there then?"

"Hello! It's me. No one phones me anymore and no one visits. I could die here and no one would know."

"Look on your calendar Mum, I was there two weeks ago and Steven called in yesterday."

There would be the usual meetings with social services, home helps and someone to come and help you shower and dress each time you were discharged from hospital. Being so far away worried me and you wouldn't dream of moving. It was reassuring for a while just to know that people were popping in and out and that you were alright.

Then I would wait to see how long it would be before you dismissed them all. Not wanting them to invade your home, space and life. The only person you kept on was a lady from the care agency to do your shopping and a bit of cleaning. The phone calls then changed to. "Someone has stolen my brooch but I know who has it. It's her!"

Most of the things that you said were missing, we found tucked away in the most unusual places when we were sorting out your possessions. Each time we found an item that you had claimed to be stolen stirred memories of the phone calls made. There was no reasoning with you.

Living away meant a long car journey to get to visit. It took half a day if I came by train. Being on call a lot of the time meant that I sometimes had to beg to get someone to cover for me while I came. If I needed to answer a call to my mobile phone, you would get irritated by it. It was a new job that I couldn't afford to lose, though I knew that I wasn't really recovered enough to be doing it.

Steven popped in twice a week, though you had made it clear that you didn't like his new partner very much and I know that you had argued. You had both made your peace though before you went, which was a blessing for my brother or he would have been racked with guilt.

I had felt a turmoil of emotions after one of your phone calls to me, telling me that his partner had driven you to your appointments at the hospital and also to the solicitors. Part relief that someone was there to take you but also anger and part jealousy. A woman that I didn't know was taking my mum to her solicitors. Why? I had wondered.

"What do you need a solicitor for mum?" I had asked.

"I've changed my will again."

71

"Ok." I had laughed trying to think who was out of favour with you at that precise moment. "Well you know I don't want anything; I am happy here so why don't you just leave everything to Steven?"

"Because there are two of you and things have to be shared equally and I'm not daft."

"You're not alright."

In spite of this, it always seemed to be my brother that you loved the most. Now I realise that it was just because he came to you with all his problems and, although a giant of a man and he acted tough, he is really a softy. He relied on you a lot, mostly as a sounding board when things went wrong yet again for him. He did a lot of coming home for a while to sort himself out when he was younger. I suppose I held my feelings and life happenings closer to my heart. Hidden deep for no one to see until I was ready to either make a choice or had already done so. He may look like your father you had said, but you are more like him in the things that you do. Not being an avid fan of my father, these words went deep. Deeper than you ever realised.

Sitting on the floor in a cold hallway in a rented house after my acrimonious divorce and talking to you on the phone in my coat. I was rock bottom in mood but trying to sound cheerful and you said, "Your brother is in trouble again, his marriage is on the rocks. He is moving in with me for a while whilst he gets his head straight. Thank God I don't have to worry about you. You always fall on your feet. You always have. My advice to you though is to never-ever forget your roots. Your granddad was a miner and that's the stock we are from."

I remember looking around and thinking 'never forget my roots'? And it made me smile to think that you hadn't a clue how low I had got. But the determination inherited from you got me through.

I had disembarked from my plane that morning at the airport and even took time out for a cup of coffee. As I watched the planes taking off and landing, I allowed myself a little time out to reflect. Then there was the metro train ride and a bus journey home. A listed cottage now, I had come a long way from my days of sitting in a cold hallway in a rented house and was trying so hard to hang on to all that Ian and I had recently achieved. The red light on the phone was flashing for the messages to be read. Usually I would take off my coat, make myself a drink and then go and listen. There would just be your voice on it talking to me. If there were other messages, yours would wipe them off as the stories you told were so long, and I would then phone you.

Why I didn't do it on that day I don't know. Now I'm biting my lip as I look at the phone here in the lounge and dare to remember. Those moments that I had pushed so far back in my mind and refused to bring forward. I had picked up the phone at the same time as dropping my case upon the nearest rug. It wasn't your voice on the three messages that were there. The first was from your carer saying please get in touch, with a number to ring. The second was from the hospital Accident and Emergency department asking me to ring them. The third was from the coroner saying that he was sorry for your death, with another number to ring and that I needed to go to the hospital to identify your body.

One, two, three. Just like that you had been taken from me. The pain in my chest that had risen to my throat had ended with an outward piercing cry. Who was making that noise I had thought. "Noooooooooooooooooooo!" I am the calm one. Stay calm. Breath. With shaking hands I had phoned the carer's number. There was an answer machine. I left a message. I can't remember now what the message had been. Then the uncontrollable shaking began. Continuing on with my quest, a new number was keyed into the phone. The staff nurse that picked up the phone asked me to wait while she went to fetch the person in charge. Next, a man's voice had said, "Hello?" then there was silence.

"It's ok," I had heard myself say almost professionally. "I know my mum is dead – I have a message from the coroner."

"We tried, we really tried," the voice had continued. "The ambulance crew worked on her all the way to the hospital."

"Please," I had said, "Don't say anymore." Then I had found myself thanking him. Why? You would have hated it all. Your wishes had been that if anything happened to you, we were to let you go quietly, with dignity, but instead they would have put a tube down your throat and bounced up and down on your chest. Had they broken any ribs? Oh God. We had to go and identify the body he had told me. Identify the body. How often had I heard that? Unexpected death they called it. Although you had been ill for a long time, and we had really thought that you would live forever.

I told the nurse in charge that I would travel up but it wouldn't be until the evening as I had to call Ian in London, where he worked, and, if he brought me in the car, the journey home would take him three hours and then we had to travel on up to you. I had asked if my brother had been contacted. He hadn't. I told the staff nurse it wouldn't be a good idea for him to come alone as he wouldn't cope and would probably be so angry that he would hit out. I would speak to him and we would come together.

"Don't worry," I had said, "he will be calm by the time we get there."

I had then telephoned the coroner. No reply from that number either. Be calm I had told myself. Stop and think now. Still shaking and so cold despite wearing my coat, I had wandered through to the kitchen, put the kettle on and went to the toilet. Before I attempted anything else, I just needed to stop for a minute or two. Somehow the coffee had been made and I was holding it in one hand, a cigarette in the other, and leaning out of the stable door of the kitchen feeling sick. I had sipped my coffee then had been startled by the phone ringing. It was Ian.

You really loved this one, didn't you? You got on so well, always laughing. He loved you too you know. Never a mother-in-law joke or not wanting to visit you.

"You ok love? Good journey?" he had began.

"No! Mum is dead." Silence. What a shock it must have been for him to be told like that. I thought that I was so in control. I said I was going to throw a few things in a suitcase and get the next train up here.

"No," he had said, "by the time you get to the station, wait around for the next train and everything, I will be home. I'm leaving now. I need to be with you."

All I could think of at that time was you, alone in that hospital. My mum. Not just a body waiting to be identified. All those annoying phone calls. What I would give for one from you now. I look at the photo on the bookcase and smile. Joking with you and talking out loud.

"Hello this is Mum phoning from heaven. Its real nice here, you know, and I'm just having a cup of tea with your grandma. Granddad says, remember your roots."

My friend from the next village had come through the cottage door without being invited. She had taken one look and wrapped her arms around me. My husband must have telephoned her. I cried then – a lot. It was alright to cry in front of her. It took a while to stop. With the tears pouring down my cheeks, I had insisted that I was ok.

"You think you are but I'm telling you you're not. Now listen, you go put the kettle on for me and I will repack your case or you will have fifteen pairs of knickers and bugger all else."

Then she had sat and wrote a to-do list. Her own mum and

husband had passed away the year before. She talked as she wrote and I know I should have been listening to her, but I can't recall a word she said. Thank goodness for that list that she had tucked into my suitcase. Me, the organised one, later crossing things off a list like a zombie as my muddled mind wouldn't take things in properly.

I had then phoned work to let them know what had happened and that I wouldn't be taking the on-call that night. They had said to keep in touch.

"Hi love, are you on your own or do you have people with you?"

"Why? What's up sis? Are you ok?" my brother had asked.

I could hear crowds of people in the background. He was walking through town; it was his dinner hour.

"I'll wait until you're back at work love."

"No, you won't. Tell me now."

"It's Mum, I think she had a funny turn. She fell."

"Is she at home or at the hospital. I'll go to her now. How bad is she hurt?"

"Erm, there's no easy way to tell you this."

" Noooooooooo!" is what I heard before the telephone went dead. I had stood rigid next to the telephone and waited. What had I done? I hadn't handled that at all well. The waiting had seemed like an eternity and then the telephone had rung.

"Why didn't they phone me?" Steven's hurt voice had said.

"I put my number on her calendar and care notes and it's my number on her previous hospital records probably." I had replied. He had people around him now he was back at work. I overheard someone say let's take a look at that hand

"What's wrong with your hand?" I had asked.

"Its ok," he said, "I scratched it."

We made arrangements to meet, have a quick drink and then go to the hospital together.

I look further along the shelf. We were out to lunch in this

photo Mum. It was a special day for you. You were seventy.
No age these days. You were plucked from us too soon. I smile
again as I look more closely at the photo, you with your glass
of wine and very red face as you were never a big drinker, and
me with my cigarette under the table trying to hide it. Ian
looming large as life, making everyone happy and laughing.
We had arranged a wheelchair for the trip. You had made so
many excuses not to go. Having lost your confidence for a
couple of years before you left us. It took until dinner time
before we finally had you ready and then you complained that
you were hungry all the way there.

I am laughing now. You would say the most outrageous
things after your stroke. Didn't care a jot and I got used to the
surprised look on people's faces as you made comments about
their appearance and the like. Before that you never said
anything bad about a person. If we did you would think of
something nice about them and say, "yes but—."

You were the entertainer. You loved people and especially
children. It was a cruel blow when my brothers ex-wife didn't
bring the children to visit anymore. I had tried to make
amends for this by having my children and grandchildren to
stay and, as part of our time together, we would always come
up here. The children all enjoyed it as the house is so near to
the beach. Happy, cheerful times. All the games that have been
played in this room. Then there was the time just after your
stroke when Ian and I decided to let you win a game of
scrabble. It would boost your confidence we thought. Oh, how
hard it was to let you win. You lost your patience quickly at
that time and when it wasn't your go would constantly say,
"Whose go is it now?"

It should have been easy for us to lose really as we just
found it funny and couldn't concentrate anyway. Then came
the time when you won for real and we knew you were getting
better. You knew what we had been up to and told us that night

that we would get a run for our money. You won the pile of pennies.

Always smiling, people opened up to you. The secrets you must have known about family, friends and neighbours. Never once did one pass your lips and you took them with you to your place in heaven.

Informing Ali and Marie had been especially hard on me. More so for Marie, being abroad and so far from home. She wouldn't be able to get back for your funeral and I knew that would devastate her. She was also pregnant and emotional.

"Oh no!" she had said, "I need to be there for you; I will find the money. We will come home"

"No," I had insisted. "Your Nan wouldn't have wanted that. She knew what a struggle it was to get the money together to fly out there. She was so proud of you and wouldn't want you to change direction now."

Marie had been on her own with the children and I didn't put the phone down until she promised faithfully to phone her husband to go home to her for a while.

Ali had been a rock. She had asked if it was ok to come up here and stay with me for a while. She was the strong one, strong for me. She held it altogether for everyone until late on the second day when she disappeared into the bathroom and broke down, thinking that no one could hear her. We let her cry it out. She needed a release.

Everyone felt guilty, Mum. Everyone had something to feel guilty about. I hadn't phoned you. Ali and Marie hadn't visited for some time. Steven had said that he should have called in that morning and why did you both have to argue? He had only been here two days previously. You know, don't you? You know that we all loved you and still do. There is such a huge void in our lives that you once filled. No one can imagine the impact of the death of their mum until it happens to them.

I met Steven outside of this house and we came in first followed by my husband and my brothers' girlfriend. Nothing seemed out of place until we reached the bedroom. The first thing we saw was your chair on its side. Blood had been spilt on the carpet by the chair, over the radiator and also on the bed. The curtain was torn and half-hanging where you had maybe tried to save yourself while falling. I remember seeing the tubing and the empty oxygen mask packets left by the paramedics during the attempt to save your life. I mentioned nothing to Steven or Ian but just picked them up and put them in the bin. That was my cross to bear, so to speak. Too much knowledge on the subject is not a good thing when it comes to one of your own. Thank god I had found and disposed of them before Ali had arrived. Being in the same line of work, it would have affected her too.

I hadn't met Steven's girlfriend before that night. I was too upset for awkwardness though and had insisted that my brother bring her. He would need a shoulder to cry on when we weren't together. Surprisingly though he didn't shed a tear until many months afterwards. I think the comment I made was, "Look, it doesn't matter who you are with. No one would have been good enough for you. Just do what you feel is right."

He had told me about the argument between you both. You had also told me. I had stood with the telephone in my hand and listened to you both within a couple of hours of each other. Obviously you were both very upset by it all. It was tearing at your hearts. Did it matter who was right? You were right though, Mum. He has moved on now and lives with Molly, and they are real soulmates. I can't really find any reason for you not to have liked her.

I had glanced at the thick plaster dressing on Steven's left hand and then at him.

"Lamppost," he said.

"Right," I had answered.

Ian had been the practical one, making a pot of tea and insisting that we all had a drink before leaving for the hospital. I think back now and know what a wonderful man he really is. He must have been feeling as bad as us because he really did love you, but no one acknowledged his pain at the time.

Steven went to the cupboard here. He had poured himself a whisky from the bottle that you always kept for him. He offered to pour one for us too. We declined as he was the only one that enjoyed a whisky besides you, except his was neat and yours was so watered down. We got a telephone call from Ali; they had been held up in traffic. So it was decided that while we left for the hospital, Ian would stay here and wait for her, Chas and the children.

We were shown to the relative's room and asked to wait. It was a stark, bare room with just the necessities in it. A table, chairs, a few magazines and leaflets about funeral directors and had one partially open window.

"Why are we waiting?" Steven had asked me impatiently.

"We have to wait for either the coroner or police to go with us to identify Mum," I had gently said.

He had been pacing, up and down, he was a coil in the old-fashioned clock, ready to spring release at the sound of the alarm. The pulse in his temple was throbbing; he looked deflated and wild at the same time.

He would then stop and say, "I just want to see Mum."

"It will be ok. Soon," I had replied.

A nurse had brought in a tray with some china cups and saucers and a pot of tea. Ironically, I smiled at this, the best china from the Accident and Emergency department, reserved for mourning relatives. I had been that nurse.

Then there were voices through the open window.

"There they are," I heard Ali cry. Not long after, both she and her husband came through the door. More hugs.

Ian had stayed behind here with the children. In an attempt to take their minds off things, he had in fact taken both the children and the dog to the beach in the dark. The tide was out and he thought that it would be an adventure for them.

We were led down half-lit corridors and outside a room where two policemen stood. They stood straight, silent and expressionless. The nurse had asked us to sit down. We had sat on the seats outside the dreaded room, waiting and gearing ourselves up for the moment.

Steven had turned to me. "I can't do this." He was ashen now and visibly shaking.

"It's ok. I'll do it." I replied.

I took a deep breath. I almost knew what I was going to see. So often I had been the one in the nurse's place as she stood there now.

"There will be a plastic screen," she said. I looked at the policemen.

"I would like the screen taken away please."

They had looked at each other and turned, opened the door and went inside the room.

When they came out, I remember standing and following them, at least my head and shoulders did. They were hurting with a strange sensation of pain and numbness. I had no idea where my legs were.

"I will come too; you shouldn't be on your own," Ali had cried then.

"No. I'm fine."

Every part of me wanted it to be someone else and not you. No thought was spared for some other poor soul that it may have been instead. Just that a miracle may have happened and there had been a mix-up. There was no mix up. I tried not to look at the tube still attached to the corner of your mouth. Not that it made any difference now, but knowing what you had been put through was the thing that hurt me the most.

"Hello Mum," I said. "Well, the things you do just to get us to come and see you." Crazy thing to say. I turned to the policeman.

"Yes. This is our mum."

Not caring that I shouldn't have touched you until the police had informed the coroner, I kissed your cold cheek and whispered, "It's ok. We are here."

I went back to the others. I tried to warn them about the tube and that it really didn't look like you, with the zipped purple hospital shroud that was now covering your body and that, maybe, it would be better to wait until you were at the funeral directors

No way. So I returned then with Steven, who broke down but did not, could not cry. Ali then followed on; she was also used to dealing with death, but not like this. This was up close and personal. I had turned and walked out when I saw that Chas had his arms around her and I left them to say their private goodbyes. The day was now becoming a blur, having been up so early, the flight and all that had happened.

The funeral director chosen, we had left with broken, heavy hearts. The weather outside matched our mood. Dismal, damp and cold.

The blur had continued on the silent journey back here. I know that Steven drove and that maybe he shouldn't have. But there had been too much on our minds to think of that. Each deep in our own thoughts.

The children had been put to bed and sandwiches made for us when we got back. The chair was back in place and new sheets were on the bed. Steven went home, his partner had a daughter and they needed to be back. The two men slept in here in this room and Ali and I shared your bed. Ali held my hand and hot, salty silent tears had streamed down my face in the dark, unseen by anyone and only felt by me. Having drifted off to sleep for a while, the urge to cry, really cry had been overwhelming when I awoke. It was still the middle of the night and I pulled on the first thing that came to hand. It was your dressing gown. It smelt of you. I breathed it in. I couldn't get enough of your scent. Oh I wanted you back. I crept out into the garden. It was raining now, lashing at the windows and the wind howled. It didn't matter. It drowned the sound of my deep gut-wrenched sobs as I dared let go, really let go of some of the emotional swell inside me. You can't go now, you just can't. Not with a new great-grandchild on the way. He or she would never know you. It would be robbed of you. Come back. Please come back.

As I stood in the thrashing rainstorm, hardly aware of my own state, my own guilty feelings had wracked my whole being. I had moved your chair to the other side of the room when the bedroom had been re-fitted. I had thought that it may make you use your stroke side more too. If I hadn't have moved it, would you have still fallen?

A new day and the children were up. I had made them breakfast and went through the motions of something that resembled a morning routine. I had glanced out of the window here and was surprised to see Ellie at the bottom of the garden. She appeared to be talking to herself. I had gone to her.

"You ok love?"

"Yes Nan, I'm just telling Granan that I love her."

"She knows," I replied.

"Oh but Nan, I told her that I would write her a letter and… and," she broke into heart-wrenching sobs. "I didn't do it Nan."

"She knows. Write her one when you feel like it and we will be sure to get it to her somehow eh?"

Freddie was younger but deeper. We thought that he didn't quite understand what was going on, but a story he wrote at school proved us wrong a few weeks later. Poor child. Poor children. He was kicking a football about on the back lawn. Ali was just about to stop him when I held her hand. "Leave him be, we need some normality in our lives right now," I had said.

They were going home that night. We had decided that it was best for the children to be at school, if they could cope, but they had both already made up their minds that they were to come with their Mum and Dad to the funeral.

"Do you think that's a good idea love?" I had said. "Yes, Mum, I do. They have to learn about life and death."

There had been so much to do; Steven was coming and the tin had to be found and looked into. We would do it together. The tin. Every time I visited, you would mention the tin. If anything happens to me, you must know where the tin is, you would say, and I would brush it off, saying for goodness sakes, you will outlive me. It has instructions in there, you said. Well, didn't it just. Right down to the last minute of the funeral. Only you didn't tell us if you wanted to be buried or cremated. Oh dilemma.

We sat here on the sofa and searched through that tin. Nothing! The undertakers had phoned: could we take clothes for Mum. Steven, now here, had said that you were proud of your dress clothes that you wore to the ex-ATS meetings. I wasn't arguing. Whatever he thought best. We went into your wardrobes. It felt so strange laying the clothes out on your bed and he chose a necklace for you to wear too. You would have thought that we would have got it right, wouldn't you? I smiled at the photo once more. Two people, one ex-army and another still in a uniform. Well, we didn't, did we? Right top, wrong skirt. Bet anything you were laughing at us fumbling about, trying our best. I phoned the number four on your list from the tin. There was a will at your solicitors for us. I explained that we would be down later to collect it, but could they perhaps look and see if there was any mention of a burial or cremation. There was. Cremation. Steven wasn't happy.

"It was her wish love, not what we wanted," I had said.

Steven, Ian, Cassie and I went to the undertakers first to drop off the clothes. At least we now had something concrete to tell them. Cremation.

They were just wonderful people, Mum. We felt that you were really taken care of. The funeral couldn't be scheduled for another week as the Crematorium was booked solid. Steven only went once to see you there. He just couldn't cope with it all. He would ask if you were ok, though, as I did my daily visit to sit and hold your hand and talk to you. Ian also went once, but willingly took me to see you whenever I wanted to go, while he was here. Other times meant a taxi.

What a funny sight we must have been. There was a lady funeral director and she would make tea or coffee, and we would sit either side of your coffin and talk about all sorts of things. The coffin they left open – I had instructed them that it mustn't be closed until absolutely necessary, as you had been claustrophobic all your life.

Ian went back home and onto work. I stayed here and sorted some more things out.

There was never a cross word between Steven and I. Usually, we argued like cat and dog, but now were united in our grief. I made a scrapbook of photos and laid it in your coffin. It was of photos of all the family. The family that loved you and that you loved back. I made the lady at the funeral directors laugh. They had got your date-of-birth wrong on the metal inscription screwed to the side of the coffin. Only by a few days, but I had said if they didn't get it right, you would turn in your grave. We were both nearly hysterical with laughter when I realised what I had said, and I know that you would have laughed too if you could have.

Ian and Steven had taken on the role of informing people that may like to come to your funeral, and I wrote the announcement for the paper and one for the obituary column, called the vicar and we all sat with the stand-in minister in this room and made our plans, consulting the list from the tin as we went. At one point, I got very angry with him when he tried to talk us out of having a hymn that we wanted. How dare he? Whose funeral was it anyway?

Ali and Marie telephoned every day. Ian phoned often. Steven was in and out. It was hard talking to Marie, words of comfort aren't the same by telephone and I couldn't touch or feel her. I knew that she had taken the news hard and was grieving on her own with no immediate family around her.

I liked being here alone with my own thoughts when not arranging in-between. I think that everyone realised that I needed that time, everyone that is except the neighbours. They would come around in the day to check on me and to offer their condolences. Nice I thought, but leave me alone now.

Weird things seem to happen while you are in the state of grief. The clock that Steven had bought for you on the wall over the mantelpiece started doing its own thing. It struck whenever if felt like it. Mostly when Steven was on his way here. Steven took it away to his house and it behaved itself after that. I was sitting that night trying to sort out a tape that we had bought to play at your funeral; I was on the floor in front of your chair. I was a child again, you were brushing my hair. How many stories had you told me that way? Wedding plans, life plans. Some had happened. Some had not. The tape recorder had a tape inside it. I took it out. The title was 'me and my girl.' I laughed and cried at the same time. The morning that I peeped around the bedroom door on hearing Sandie on your bed, she hadn't been eating and wouldn't be tempted by anything anyone tried. There she was on your bed playing with a toy and looking in front of her, wagging her tail as if there was someone there that only she could see. A few minutes later, she was eating in here and there was a soft thudding noise from the bedroom. Your favourite perfume had fallen from the shelf onto the bed.

Weird things happened at both the girls' houses too for a

while. Who knows? I would like to think that you played a part in all of it.

The night before the funeral, Ali, Chas and the two children arrived. I was busy preparing what I could for the people that were to come back to the house afterwards. Elli disappeared into the garden almost straight away.

"She has a letter for Nan," Ali had said." Do you think that the funeral parlour would open for us? I know it's late but she wants to take it."

"They closed the coffin last night," I said.

"It doesn't matter. She needs to go; she has hardly slept."

I went with them both, Ian waited outside in the car and I waited outside the room where they had taken your coffin to. It was tastefully done. Ali and Ellie went through the door. Ellie clutched the letter. She came out without it.

We were all here then, the people that were closest to you. We talked and played games with the children. We drank our favourite tipple. It was just as you would have liked it. We talked of when we were children, about the good times. We poured you a sherry and left it on the shelf here. You were with us, we knew that.

Then it was on us. The day of the funeral. I had been up early laying out cloths on the tables and putting out what food I could that would keep out of the fridge.

People were deep in conversation when Freddie strolled in. "Wow Nanna, are we having a party?"

"Yes love, later," I had replied, smiling but trying not to laugh in front of him; everyone else was smiling too.

"Well, can I please bagsy that cake there?" he had continued.

"Only if you put a piece of paper on it with your name on," I had replied. He had run off then to find a pen.

I had stood at this window, watching for the funeral cars to arrive when the phone call came. The voice said, "Is Dad there please?"

It was Steven's estranged son. As I handed the phone to Steven, I heard the voice shout, "Is there room for one more in the funeral cars?"

"We will make room."

Steven was beaming then. "I am on my way up to you then."

We were all impressed with the funeral entourage, Mum. All American style with your car being led by a man with a baton until we were on the main road.

"Wow," Ali had said. "Nanna would have loved this; she would be giving everyone the royal wave." She then bit her lip as she realised what she had said and we both stifled our giggles.

When we got to the Church, well what a surprise. All your ex-ATS chums had gathered either side of the entrance in their dress uniform. We had no idea that this was going to happen. I thanked them all. They were there inside the church too with their banners held downwards in respect for you.

I touched your coffin for the last time and told the men to be careful with you. Ian, Steven and his son were part of the four pall-bearers. It had been Steven's wish. "Mum has carried me all of my life," he had said. "This time I will carry her."

Ian then had also offered to help. Chas was to be the third one but graciously stood aside for Jez. He had grown into a fine man now.

There was a sea of faces in the Church, some I recognised, some I didn't as we followed your coffin in. The service was lovely and I held all the emotion back. The vicar had suggested that it wasn't a good idea for me to read in the Church as I probably wouldn't be up to it. If the men are carrying her, then I will read for her. I had told him.

"Well when the time comes," he had said," I will look your way and if you are not up to it, just shake your head."

"If I go to pieces," I had said, "Church will not be the place."

I stood up and read a story about your life. It had been hard to write, trying not to miss anyone out and making it personal to them. I knew that I would be alright in the Church; it would be at the Crematorium afterwards with just very close family that would be hard for me. To see your coffin finally disappear, that would be the hardest part.

We had permission to leave my mobile phone on in the Church and I knew that Marie, so many miles away would be listening to part of the service. That was hard, I couldn't reach out and touch her, but knew it was what she wanted.

There is always that inappropriate moment at a wedding or a funeral and yours was no exception. I smile now. That man and wife that pounced as soon as we got outside the Church and were ready for the next step of the journey.

"This perhaps isn't the right moment to ask about the mobility scooter," they had said.

"No you're right, it's not." I had replied.

"Well then. Can we come and see you tomorrow?"

Keep walking, I had thought.

To say that a funeral procession was lovely is perhaps not normal. But yours really was, on the second lag of that journey. We took the coast road to the cemetery. It was a beautiful sunny autumn day, the colours of the leaves still on the trees glistened and the reflection from the sun on the sea gave an eerie silvery glow to the tainted windows of the car.

"Wow." Ali said.

I smiled, the last journey you took was certainly impressive. Perfect. You were at the head of the family where you had always been. Free now, free from pain. Flying, yes you were flying ahead. We had picked up speed along that coast road and everyone's spirits lifted.

The coffin moved towards the black curtain and almost out of sight. Then the finality hit me. I couldn't hold back any longer. Ellie was sobbing too and Ali sat between us softly, telling us to let you go now. Everything seemed to happen at once. The song that I had chosen as the last song was playing. I saw Chas pick up Ellie and carry her outside, someone had Freddie's hand and they were also moving towards the door.

Steven I saw mouth to his son, "I have to get out of here." They made a quick exit. He was struggling to keep it together and from that direction came Ian. One arm went around my shoulder and one around Ali's.

"I'm ok," I heard her say from a distance and she got up to find and comfort Ellie.

"We have to go now, love." Ian had said.

"No, I have to stay until the end of the record. I chose it for her!"

"Ok," he had said, holding me tight.

I don't remember the walk out of there. I do remember the funeral director saying she must have been one fine woman and actually shedding tears himself.

"She was."

We gathered in this room here afterwards. People meeting up again after years of being apart. So much news to catch up on. Steven and Jez went into the garden to talk privately. Freddie, with big round eyes, had his cake and was eating it. Ellie sat on your chair with Sandie on her knee. Smiling now as Sandie muzzled into her legs.

We were here until late that night. The crowd had dwindled down to the original eight now. I wondered if anyone else was feeling the enormous relief of the day being over that I was. I think so.

The family were asked if they wanted anything to remember you by. They all chose things that held dear memories for them. All of them wanted to know if the old stool that you used to whiz them around on as young children was still here. Sadly it wasn't. So Marie asked if she could have the two little figures that she and Ali had saved their pocket money up to buy you as children. Ali asked for your cup and saucer to put in her dresser.

Steven chose two sets of your earrings for his daughters and Jez surprised us the most by wanting your carpet sweeper that he had played with as a child here. You didn't have a lot, Mum, but all they really wanted was to keep the good memories of you alive.

The next morning was a fiasco. Ellie opened the door to the people that were interested in your mobility scooter and brought them in here. Freddy was shouting that there was a present for me. Four more people were shown in by Ellie to pay their respects. Behind then stood the funeral director, with Freddie dancing around wanting to know what the present was.

I look full on at the photograph now. You would have thought it was all so funny.

You had returned. This time as ashes in an urn that was concealed in the present box. I took the box from the funeral director and placed it here on the high shelf. Mainly out of Freddie's way. It would have been awful if he had opened the present and you had spilt onto the floor. You would be safe there until we could scatter your ashes properly where you wanted to be. The noise had been deafening. Ian saw my face change, pleading with him to please get all these people out of my mother's house. It seemed immediate that he was thanking everyone and ushering them all out.

Then Ali was packing to go home. I waved and smiled until they were out of sight, then turned and cried. I knew that you had done that too when I was the one that was leaving. All at once the house was quiet. Ian was making coffee. I sat here looking out of this window, calmer now. The white unmarked van parked outside and then a man with a 'for sale' sign walked across the garden and started knocking the signpost into the ground. There had been a mix up with the dates. I broke down completely then.

"It's our family home. It's where we all come."

"Oh love," Ian had said. "I wish I had the money to buy it for you."

"If it was a toss up between this and the cottage, where would you rather be?"

Strange how things turn out. I look at your photograph and the other additional family photographs on the shelves below it. Three new lives since yours ended. They won't get the chance to know you, but we will be sure to tell them stories of you. They will all have a scrapbook of photographs.

Steven said that he couldn't possibly live here, too many memories of marriage break-ups and other things, he said. My memories here are good ones. I see my two girls as babies playing on the carpet and running on the lawn with you when they were younger. I see you taking out orange juice and cakes. I see you meeting me from the taxis, laughing. A happy warm place.

It only took us a few weeks to sell our cottage to a couple that fell in love with it, as we once had. We paid off all our debts and paid Steven half of what the property was worth. He moved into his own small bungalow but sold it, losing money along the way though at present he is with his new partner some miles from here. We phone often and meet when we can. He is happy now. I can see it in his face and eyes. He still misses you terribly, we all do, but we want you to rest in peace. I am happy too. I have so much better health since the move here. Life moves on. I am the eldest of our family now.

We walk on the beach on most days when Ian is home with Sandie. We talk to you there. I talk to your photograph. You will always be within our hearts. You will always have pride of place here on the top shelf, with the additional family on the shelves beneath. I find such peace here. We are the stable couple that the rest of the family turn to. Family often come here to stay. Yes. They remember their roots. They all come home.

4

Mark Kotting

Time.

I've got an hour to make up my mind, less.

Who does time wait for?

I've got two piles of photos, they're growing, the good the bad. He'll be around in an hour, husband with his new glowing wife, to look at the happy, white, wedding shots. He's already rung.

Hope they're in focus. Was the first funny thing he said, ended it with, *Does my wife look like an angel?*

Heard her by his side. He didn't give me time to answer, the receiver went giggling and gurgling dead.

Angel, I haven't seen any of them in a while.

Decisions, decisions, look at the time, the clock.

When I take a photo, I get in close; hear the lot, the braggers the boasters, the ones walking the aisle because they've put their prick in a pretty frock, when maybe they should have left it resting in the dark.

I'm a photographer because of mum, simple as that. She carries a picture of her son, my brother, from room to room, even travels on buses with it, buried deep inside her coat. He died when he was young, I can't remember him and she can't forget him. That's what a picture can do. I thought carrying a photo from room to room was a normal thing to do, like carrying a cup of tea. It isn't. Photos hold power, cast a spell.

I capture the day's worth of dreams of the cloned ones,

bleating bah, bah sheep, with my dream catcher's net. People of no conversation, they'd never acquired the knack; they hang themselves up by hangers brought from the latest hip-hop, uber uber, design shop.

Uber, Uber. How many times could a man hear that in a night?

Another word making its clichéd way up onto the bleating sheep's tongue. There's a list of them, they come, they go, last one to get stuck was *gob-smacked.*

A room of dusted, puffed up blind, look at me fools. All they want from life is perfect teeth and to be strung with Chelsea pearls. Their problem? They all want to be someone else.

I've got their photos by my feet, by my side, stared at them in the moonless night. Spilt wine on some. I ain't doing this anymore. I pick up a photo, rip it with anger. Something inside has changed.

I've taken the money my entire professional, clicking life. Given up weekends. Perfected, a perfect fake wedding smile to go with the cutting of the cake.

Stood alone, unnoticed, taking that rainbow-winning wedding shot and its bollocks.

Followed one couple from wedding to grave, they liked my photos that much. The marriage didn't last that, he died of some cancer, I don't know which. It didn't matter. Dead's, dead. The wife wanted a parting shot; I took it, the box being lowered into the ground. She didn't seem bothered and nor was I. A farewell shot. Could have been cans being dragged behind the newlyweds car. It don't matter to me.

I'm chosen because I'm different, I take a candid shot. I'm unnoticeable, I don't talk, I get on with the job in hand. Catch the moments of the day; nothing goes past my lens and me.

Not anymore, how long can a man hold a fake smile?

There's a time when things end. I'm close. My hands are shaking, I grip the table and wait, it will pass, it usually does. But my dreams aren't sweet no more. Revenge.

Do I show them the photos they want to see? I've got them. Smiles, the flowing angel's dress the champagne popping corks.

Or the ones of an unloved son?

How many times does a six-year-old boy need to cry in a day? When does the wailing stop?

The first thing he said looking up at me and my lens was, *How old do you think I am?*

Sixteen, I replied.

No, stupid, six. I've lost a tooth, see?

He pointed, I looked, he had.

But the tooth fairy didn't come.

Oh, why not? As I said I don't usually like to get involved.

Sheryl knocked it out.

Knocked it out?

Sheryl was going to be the boy's new mother. Time was ticking down on this boy.

It's still under my pillow, the fairy wouldn't take it either.

I'm sorry to hear that. I said. He looked at me, said nothing for a while then said. *Want to play football?*

No, I replied. He smiled, bent, picked up a stone, threw it, walked away.

A wedding's not just for the bride and groom. They're all in there fighting, elbowing, might as well have it stapled on backs, *look at me.* There's jostling going on, pigs at the trough. Push and shove.

I've had a bride walk out crying in disgrace. There'd been a lull at the table, silence where noise should have been. She ended her sentence with *that's how I accidentally took crack.* She'd just married into old money. What had started as a marriage at two was, by all counts over by five, it happens. I know I was there. Taking the shots. There wasn't dancing that night. Me, standing in front of disco lights and a DJ wondering whether he was going to be paid.

The guests, galloped away into the night. The unhappy couple left in separate cars. And I found it hard to get my money from an embarrassed parent. I saw her two weeks later, in her Pimlico retreat.

Do you think I want the tarts photos? She said as she handed over the money.

No, quite agree. I replied. One's got to be polite.

I'm a dream catcher, says so on my card. Page 922 if you're interested, I come at a reasonable rate.

I capture the dream, the caramel skies, God's rays on a golden bride. Handle the envelope of dreams. I check my watch.

A picture for a wall or a mantle piece, I don't give a damn, which, I send the magical day back, remit done. Click, click.

I'm the photographer who makes modern man and wife believe they're stars for the day.

Do witches exist?

I'm strangling the latest bride and groom in my hand. Mr and Mrs Bates. Smiles, happy white teeth.

Weddings can be happy, cruel or kind. But who wants the cruel, not so nice wedding shots? Where do those go? I've got them in a box, that's where mine go.

The second thing, Sammy said, that was his name, was, *can you pick me up so I can fly?* I picked him up, flew for as long as I could hold him up there. *I like you,* he said as his feet touched down. *Can I be your friend?*

I pick up a print, Sammy crying on a haystack. He was alone in the sun as it shined on him, that's why I went there, caught my photographer's eye. Thought it would make a wedding day shot. The sun with its rays, that sort of thing, the son on the happy day. I can get poetic. But really I'm at the bottom of the artist heap.

I took shots as I walked down, I didn't realise Sam was crying and if I had, would I have taken the shot? You bet I would. He rubbed his eyes when I got up close, forced a smile, life had already taught him well.

I'm looking at the haystack shot now, him with his red, young, suffering eyes.

Sheryl doesn't like me.

I'll say again, I don't get involved with the guests, unprofessional. But here was a six-year-old crying on a haystack with not another adult around.

No? I said. *Course she does.*

But she doesn't I've the proof.

No she doesn't, she thinks I'm an awkward child. What does awkward mean?

I left him crying on a haystack as the sun shone down, that's what me, the coward done.

Sammy's father, what did he say to me? *Just make sure you don't get in the guests way. I don't like things in my way.* Said it like he'd won some Victorian Cross going over some bayoneted wall. But we weren't fighting. I was get instructions at Victoria, platform nine. He was late he didn't apologise.

Click. I got him, his back, his bald head, a clock showing his late time.

See I'm sorting Mr and Mrs Bate's pictures, the nice, the not so nice, with a decision to make. They'll be here within the hour; I look at my watch, yeah, within an hour.

There are two sides to everything, good and bad. In my case take the money or do what's right. I walk over to the other side of the room, give the bird some food. Place two chairs by a wall, put a roll of gaffer tape on top.

Another minute gone.

His new bride brushes up well, her flowing grace, out of white lace. Yes, give the crowd a wave; turn smile, show a bit of shoulder, not too much mind. Dreams, in her eyes, in her Cinderella shoes, her wedding cake dress. I'll capture you, you little fucking butterfly.

I've been capturing butterflies for years. I hadn't seen her evil bile yet.

Oh yes, give us another wave, and another, a picture as she comes down the glass stairs in grace. Attention, on her. Hadn't been like this since she'd slid from the womb, into her tender mother's hands. Yeah and this the angel shot. She sparkles like a diamond, moves like a dove. It's the witch's day.

As I took the angel shots, her new husband came up to me and said *Make sure you get it, you are getting it, right?* He hadn't needed to worry. His new wife showed more honey, showed me all the tricks she'd got, she wasn't a one trick pony, she'd been practising for this day all her life.

I look at another.

I've got ideas, now what am I going to do? Dark thoughts that are slowly growing.

What do women want out of men? What do men want out of women? And why do men and woman have child?

I stare at the ceiling. What have I got left on the clock? Forty-two minutes, with the little hand running around and around, ticking.

The bride's father's behind her in this one, couldn't smile for her, sure as hell wasn't going to smile for me. He hadn't smiled in years. He'd lost the knack. Catholic, I'd heard. Wasn't happy his baby was marrying a man with a child. A child out of wedlock at that.

Disgusting. Was a word I heard, hail a thousand Mary's to that. It was the old man's Catholics words that shocked me most, *it's a good job you're marrying money because Tim's a spineless cunt.* His daughter was up against a wall her throat was in her daddy's hands.

She couldn't protest or protect her new husband to be. I moved out of the room, I got my shots though, her and her dad with their fangs hanging out. Eyes turned up, taking counsel with the devil or the Lord or whomever else they might talk to.

And her father in this one, him with his sizzling anger in his Catholic eyes. He didn't want to be there. He was oozing that. Couldn't contain that in his over priced suit. He had his mind well and truly made up.

That's my trouble I don't have faith.

Is there any love left in this world? Or is it lost in the lace of the new dress, with a hand waiting to get underneath and poke and pull.

The wedding lasted two days, they're getting longer, and some go for weeks. Guests piped in, like dishes for a banquet.

Digital, makes it easy, click, erase or keep. Adobe's, where I play. Any idiot can do it. And if I give it up? What have I got? Nothing, I've always known that, all I've got is a clicking eye.

When I take a picture, you don't even realise you've been had. I've robbed you, mugged you, had you.

And look here, the mother, turning and swaying, chucked up later in a sink. I got it, me and my camera, her, her puke and the sink. Too much for the catholic mother was it? And when she wiped her mouth, I got a shot of that as well. Didn't see me my Nikon staring back. Tripped and fell, came down close to my polished wedding shoe, got some glare when I took that. I didn't ask her if she was all right? I didn't care. They came running to see the brides' mother splayed on the floor. Before she'd passed out she'd been spurting how well how daughter had done, *she's bringing money into the family, shame about the chid.* She said to one fat 55inch arsed lady, eating ice cream so as to keep it that way. *I thought that.* The woman replied, *terrible, ill mannered little brat.* She said as the ice cream went down.

Who do I hate most? Mr. or Mrs. Bates?

And in this picture, her whispering, sucking his ear.
And in this her out in the cut corn field, holding her new man's hand. The boy running wild behind. The first shot looked so good I took another and another. A new family, a tender loving hand. I carried on clicking, saw the gesture of the new bride's hand. It was behind her husbands' back I'm looking at it now, and it's still doing the same thing, shooeing the child away. As you would a dog. Sammy stopped, the couple walked, the gap in the cornfield grow bigger.
I kept clicking, they kept walking, the boy, he dropped to the ground.

It was a wedding for Man, Child and Beast, said so on the invitation, all were invited, child and dog, the card was the quality type, thick, bold, felt good in the hand. I took a picture of it as a reminder of the day. I haven't a real emotion left, lost them at wedding days. I've seen best men fighting, taking chunks out of each other, brides taking bites out of maids. I keep the nasty shots, in a cupboard in a box under lock and key.

And this lot of happy dancers, strutting showing arses, bulges from the zipped already married pants. I photo high, photo low, doesn't matter which, crutch or box. I'm on the look out, the prowl. Anything that gets my, oh, so, artistic eye. The parent's, the children, the bride, the groom. Or, the diamante dog with its eye hanging out, I don't care. *Click. Click.* I shout to the room, the room that I call home.

I'm sure it's killing me off, clinically I might already be dead. That's what I've got to do, make my stand. Plant my fucking flag, the flag of goodness and hope. Something, to hold onto in later life.

I lean back in my chair.

Sammy is in my hand playing with other children. Well I thought he was, but when I got over, they were giving him the loser sign. They make an L shape by their temples, makes them look like Spanish Bulls. They were all laughing, Sammy was crying.

Tell them to stop it, make them go away. He yelled. And what did I do? What did I do? Not a goddamn thing. I clicked away.

Am I a bad man? Would a jury have my hanging by a rope? I'm splattered with man, woman and filth.

I rip another up.

The clock, the clock, not so many minutes to go now.

Kids will always give you some shot, moments turning up, sure as night or day.

I didn't have to follow these kids around, I'd been given the same table to eat off, in the kitchen. Even the groom's son was in there. The little curly haired six year old hadn't made it to the big table, wasn't going to be sitting by his father's side.

Odd, son not next to dad. On the biggest night of his life.

Says something about a man, who'd do that. Wouldn't want his son to join him on a night like that.

Sam's new mother had been talking to a bridesmaid. I was taking the bride and bridesmaids shots, there's an order a protocol. The ones where friendship is displayed.

He's just not a very pleasant, the new wife said. *And I do try.*

I know you do, everyone can see that. She burped then went on. *I didn't think he was a nice child.* Her best friend replied. Then added. *Thought it the minute I saw him. He didn't even make an effort to dress up.*

Exactly. He wanted to ruin my biggest day. The bride added.

He's six I wanted to shout. *He's only six.* I was awakening.

And in this one, Sam, with an imprint of a hand on his face. Red stripes across his cheeks, put there an hour before the lunch by his new mother. I've got the shot.

I came around a quiet corner, there they were. A new mother, new son, no one else around.

She wasn't smiling.

You're ruining everything, you shit, why don't you just run off and cry. He didn't say a thing back. It was in his eyes, he wouldn't have dared. She raised her hand and slapped. Shouted.

What you need is a Norland Nanny, you bastard brat.

He didn't hang around, he ran off, did what he was told, went and cried on his own. Sat under an old oak tree as I zoomed in, took a long off shot.

I was surprised to see him sitting at the table, with all the other children, but where would he have gone? Still had the red mark of the witch. Put there when she thought no one was

103

looking. I was, I've got the shot. Here, now in my hand and I'm looking at it.

Buzz.

The front door buzzer goes, gets me every time. I look at the clock. They're early, in a hurry to get their shots. I can see the car, some expensive type, even got a driver up front. The son's staring out the window, sitting on a leather seat, he can't see me. But it's him.

Early. I say as I open the door.

So this is where you live then. Says it as if he's been looking for me. Adds. *Where are they then?* Rubbing his hands follows that up with. *Going to show?*

I'm going to show you something all right, rubbing my eye, you impatient bastard.

There's nothing about this man I like, nothing.

Hello. She then says following in behind her knight. His manners had already slipped, dropped.

She's had her day, in exchange for her life, women taking vows, giving up lives.

Are those ours? She says, all excited.

They're photos scattered all over the floor, by where I've been sitting and pondering.

We're so excited. Can't wait to see them, can we, Tim? She says blurting it out.

If I hadn't seen her innards, her insides, her bile, I would have said she looked radiant, relaxed. Happy with what she'd snared, happy with her image to the world. But I had seen, heard, watched, seen the evil, seeping, oozing out.

I'd listened to the registrar talking about the size of her loving, caring heart. He'd told the room *how special and warm hearted the bride and groom were.*

How's Sammy then? I ask, Sammy's on my mind and I want

to slow things up.

Why on earth would you remember his name? She says it as if it's an itch. An itch that won't go away.

Because I asked and I've been looking at photos of him.

Oh! Mrs Bates turns and looks at her Tim, her Mr Bates, her chunk of loving gold.

Your son told me.

Told you what? She says, annoyed not to have the photos in her hands.

His name.

He's not my son. Says it in a slow, uncaring way, the only way she can be.

Sorry your stepson, how silly of me.

I told him not to pester people.

Her Tim, her Mr Bates says. Says it like an order. An order that should be heard, obeyed and if not someone close will be swatted.

Someone, me, now, here at this moment, should shout do something.

Something.

Who do people like this fly so fucking high?

He wasn't pestering me, I just asked him his name. I've always found it polite to do so.

Jab.

Oh, so do you go around asking everyone's names?

Mr Tim says.

Jab.

Just the ones I'm interested in.

Oh, I see. Mrs Bates says coming to her hubby's side.

Can we have a look at the pictures, that is what we're paying you for. Why we're here in fact. She's sounding like him now. A good match, a match made in heaven.

I'll give you something to look at you bitch.

There on the floor over there, I say. Mr Bates starts moving.

105

I'll get them. I say laying down some aggression.

I bend, pick up the pile on the left, the ones they'd like to see, the album shots, the smiley shots the ones for the staircase wall. Straighten them, tap them, bring them together with order.

Didn't Sammy want to come up? He must have wanted to see the happy shots?

No of course he didn't, why would a silly little boy want to do that? He was hardly interested in the day, pauses, and adds, *you must have noticed that?* Mrs I haven't a heart says.

No, can't say I did.

You ain't so happy now. I can feel their uneasiness.

He isn't remotely interested. Mr Bates says. Mrs Bates takes his hand giving it a gentle squeeze.

Can we get on with this? We've a honeymoon to have.

Oh yes, going anywhere nice? I ask.

Yes, the Seychelles. Can't contain her glee when she says it. *Ever been?* She adds.

No, of course not. I say.

What I want is for Sammy to lift the handle, pull open the door and run. Run down the street yelling, yelling, please will someone help me grow, before his life goes up in fire.

Who's a pretty girl, who's a pretty girl then?

They both spin as if joined already from the same hip. It's Max, my Parrot, my company, my friend. My Max. Laid an egg two years ago. I thought about changing him to Maxine, but the egg's our secret.

Say hello Max, I say, while picking up the prints that won't be making it to the album they'd want to see or show. I drop them into a box.

Who's a pretty girl then?

He always says that. He couldn't be further from the truth

with this one.

The door's open, will it fly out? Mrs Bates says taking a step back, scratching her leg with one of her expensive looking shoes.

More to the point is it safe? I've heard that they can get rather nasty. Mr Bates says, going back in the same direction as his wife.

Jab.

He's ok, shouldn't bite, not unless he doesn't like you, and that shouldn't be a problem, should it? Come, please, sit down.

They're standing awkwardly in the middle of the room.

I point to a couple of seats, they're old, stylish in a way, sturdy bought from a market. The Bates look at them.

Drink? I ask.

No thank you. They take their seats, sitting ready for the punch and Judy show.

I'd like you to look through the photos, take your time. See what you think. If you want any blown up, more than one print, tell me and I'll put a cross and the number on the back, is that ok? These are just the viewing copies. The finished prints are of a much higher quality.

And when I've finished saying it I think rat a tat, tat.

Fine. She says. *We'll do that.*

I walk the album shots over to them.

Yours? Mr. Bates says, handing over the roll of gaffer tape from his chair.

They look at each other, smile, Mr Bates holds out his ringed, married fingered hand for the photos. I look at him, then her.

Don't you think Mrs Bates should see them first?

Jab.

Yes exactly, I would have passed them to her anyway. He's taken it like the boarding school boy I'm sure he was.

You know I would don't you darling? Mr Bates says looking into his wife's eyes, trying to cover his manners.

Of course you would, she replies.

They start to look, turning the photos in their hands, stopping, moving on. Her climbing out of the car, him by a good looking hinged gate.

One after another.

Showing them their beautiful day. Friends, flowers, presents and drinks. Sunny smiles, chink, chink.

Oh, that's a nice one, look Tim? She says.

Lovely. Her husband says, approvingly, patting her on the thigh. *And this one, look, oh god that's great.*

They're looking at a picture of a jar, full to the brim with love heart sweets.

Jab.

For all the love that was going round at the wedding, I say, and then add some sugar. *I don't think I've ever experienced such a lovely one.*

It was just perfect? She says, turning slightly, smiling, ever so proud of herself, adds. *Some of these really are very good. You should be very proud of yourself, shouldn't he Tim?*

They talk to me as if I'm a child. As if they've got the eye.

Well, they haven't, I just delivered it to them on a plate. Faces reflect in the glass, I'd angled it that way, little arty shots through the jar of hearts, for a beautiful wife and groom and their bull shit day.

That's a nice one, don't you think darling? How many of those do you think we should have? Perhaps they could be printed up as thankyou cards? What do you think?

I don't know. Mr Bates concentration is already on the wane, he's sounding impatient. It's a picture of a rainbow.

Just make up your mind. He says, checking his repulsive big watch.

Show some interest please, love, if only for me? She's

already having to talk to him as if she's on her knees.

May your love last. I say from behind their chairs.

What? Mr Bates says, raising a thick black eyebrow.

Your love, may it last forever and ever, sir. I say. May you have all the love you two can muster up.

Thank you. His wife says, looking into another shot, not looking back at me.

I pull a long piece of gaffer tape.

Rip.

Rip it off, and another and another, stick them to the back of Mr Bates chair. He turns, I smile, make an eye gesture to the pictures, point and he goes back to looking at his wedding, his wife, his new life.

Good boy. Decision time.

Rip.

You know what, fuck them, fuck them and all they stand for. I rip another piece of gaffer, hold it long and taunt, what am I? What am I? A fucking mad man if I do it.

I'm taping him up in a frenzy I didn't know I possessed. Wrapping the roll around and around like the lunatic I've become, his head, his mouth, I don't care where it sticks. He's getting ready for the post. She hasn't even looked across she's deep in her wedding day vanity shots, transfixed by herself.

I've worked with gaffer all my life, I'm quick at making a loop, pulling it tight, cutting it through with my teeth.

His eyes have been blinded, mouth gagged, he tries to stand. I kick the chair and down the mother goes, down, down to the floor. The floor on which he belongs.

I've got bulk on my side he's more of the gangly type. Then she looks, she's noticed now. I'm on his back pushing his head into the carpet, pulling his arms back, wrapping the silver tape around and around.

Hi, I yell. *Yee ha, riding the horse, here honey, riding it all the way down to the piggy bank, what do you say to that? Your turn now Mrs Righteous.*

I shout that bit. She's confused, she has every right to be. He's making this err sort of muffled sound. I think he's choking and I wish he'd stop.

Never mind him, he's tied up. I say. She drops the photos she's just cottoned on, the penny has finally dropped. She's got a situation going on here.

Hey careful with the photos, lady, don't just drop them like that.

What are you doing Timmy? She yells.

Max, I shout, *here boy.* Say it like a man would do to his faithful dog. Max, flies out of his cage, Mrs Bates doesn't like that, terror in her eyes, crosses her arms, covers her eyes. Makes it easy for me to tape her up.

Across her mouth I run my guitar sharp fingernail through so she can breathe, but I don't give her full use of her jaw, there'll be no silly yelling from her. Then do the same to him and before I know it, it's all done.

I'm standing over them Mr and Mrs Bates are on the floor.

Off Max! He's on Mr Bates' back, pecking away. He's always been a judge of character. I put my arm out, he flaps, gets on. I carry him back to his cage.

Good boy I say as I put him back in leaving the door open, one never knows when one might need a parrot.

I walk back to the loving couple, the chairs have fallen in the confusion and fuss, I bend and pick them up.

Mr and Mrs Bates, may I help you to your chairs? He doesn't seem to hear, so I have to huff and puff him up. Do the fucking same with her.

Mr and Mrs Bates may I pronounce you, man and wife and welcome you to my room. I say.

Seven minutes and they've been turned into silver

mummies.

I walk over to my workstation, god it's a mess, I wish I could be tidier, but I'm just not that type, never was. I pick up a scalpel walk the blade back turning it with finger and thumb, bend, lift the man's head, hold it, and cut him some hearing ear muffs. Making sure I don't damage his tender winning skin. Then do the same to his wife.

You've got this smell on you, darling, I can't quite make out. I say as I pull away.

She's pissed herself.

I go over to a shelf and pick up two brown paper bags, big enough for heads. One for him, one for her, draw a king and queen with big smiling faces, making slits for the eyes and mouth. So they can see out.

Here, I've got something for you. I say, walking back to the happy couple, I raise their heads, pull the tape from their eyes. Each of them makes a particular sound when I do it. His was AHHH, hers more URRRR.

Now, do I have your attention? I'm going to be giving you a hat, I'll put them on, all you have to do is breathe. Do I make myself clear? He even nods. I laugh. Her eyes are showing a mix of fear and hate.

And before I know it I've got a king and queen in brown paper bags.

I pull their feet tight, gaffer them to the leg of a chair.

Rub my eyes, shake my head, smile at my thoughts.

I walk to the window Sammy's sitting down there, waiting; he'd be waiting all his life, but not now, not now.

I leave the room, give the happy couple time to look at each other with their eyes. Her bag's better than his, I sort of rushed his, didn't get the crown quite right.

I go down in the lift, walk to Sammy sitting in the car. He

waves, he remembers, knows who I am, I'm glad about that, I'm taking a risk here, he waves, makes it seem worthwhile.

His Dad wants him to come up and choose a picture. I say to the hat wearing, gloved driver. He nods, opens his door, releases the boy.

Really, can I choose one? Sammy says all excited. *Am I really allowed?*

Yeah, you sure can. Choose as many as you like. I say, *follow the dream catcher.*

Dream catcher he repeats. *What's that?*

Never you mind.

And we leave the driver waiting by the car.

We take a few steps then I say. *So how have you been?*

Fine he says, but he doesn't look happy when he says it. He's got small feet for his body, I hope they're given time to grow. We walk some more, move to the lift. Then I notice his arms, they're full of red sore looking cuts and scratch marks. *How did you get those?* I say, *they look sore.*

He smiles, looks down as if noticing them for the first time. *These are worse,* he replies, lifting up his shirt as we come to a stop on my floor.

Bastards, I think.

How the hell did you get those? They look like a thousand pin pricks, like someone has gone over his back, putting a pin in, taking it out.

It's the bitch, I think.

I've got eczema and hay fever. Says it like it's a good thing to have. I knock on the door, turn to Sam and say, *You never know what they might be up to. Could be kissing.* He smiles up to me. I make the shush sound with my finger.

I open the door, the king and queen sit there, they couldn't have gone I'd done them up tight.

Is that daddy? Sam says pointing to the right bag. *You look funny Daddy, why are you hiding?*

I don't know, I say. *He said something about playing hide and seek with you.*

Hide and seek? Sammy pauses then says. They're smiling, *is daddy a king and Sheryl the queen?* Sam asks, turning to me. *Got it in one.* I shout.

Shall I go and hide, where shall I hide? He says in a young confused way.

No, remember we've got to choose some pictures first.

Can I choose daddy? You said I could, didn't you. Says it pleadingly, giving his father all the respect he doesn't deserve.

Who's a pretty girl then? Max says, not wanting to miss out. *You've got a parrot.* Sammy says. Noticing Max for the first time. Max is sitting on top of his cage.

I've always wanted a parrot, they talk, don't they? I look at him, then Max and say *They're very clever, did you know that?*

What cleverer than grown ups? Sammy says, working his mind.

Even cleverer than that. I say, smiling, there's a rustle from under one of the bags. I don't know which. Sammy doesn't notice, he's only got eyes for Max now.

Do they know their times tables? Sam says, then, *Can I touch him,* taking steps to the cage. *What's his name?*

Max, I say, *say hello Max.*

Who's a pretty boy then! Max squawks.

Go up to him slowly and hold your arm out and he should jump on.

Sammy puts out his arm, Max looks at him, waits, flickers an eye, gets on.

Look, he's on my arm, he likes me. Sammy says.

I think he does, I reply.

Look Daddy, Max likes me, can you bring me a parrot back from your honeymoon?

Mr Bates' eyes flicker from the darkness of the bag. I don't know if that's a yes or a no. Mrs Bates is shaking her head, so I guess it's a no from her. I walk over to the desk pick up the box with the alternative photos in.

So, shall we choose Sam? I say. Sammy only has eyes for Max. I pull out the first photo, it's a picture of a kid's shoe sticking out from under a bed.

I show the picture to Mr Bates. Hold it in front of his eyes, then in front of his loving wife's.

Recognise the shoe? I say, young Sam's there, *your unloved son* I whisper.

And this one? I'm whispering again. *I think it has you in it Sheryl, hope you don't mind me using your first name? Slapping Sam, remember? See her hand Mr Bates? Your wife's.* I'm still whispering. *See the imprint her hand left on his face, must have hit him quite hard.*

Sammy is still making friends with Max. I start to throw photos at her, one after the other.

So where exactly is your love Mrs Bates? Where's your big heart? I tap her where I think it is. She flinches, I'm sure she thought I was going for her breast. *You haven't got a drop? Did you know that about her Mr Bates, her lack of love? You seemed to have married a witch Mr Bates, did you realise that, or did she cast a spell on you, are you blinded Mr Bates?*

I know what a witch is Sam says suddenly joining the conversation.

Do you? I say, looking around at the little boy, *what's a witch Sam?* Pause, then add, is there one in the room? Sam lowers his head, I've put him on the spot. I shouldn't have done that.

That's unfair.

He doesn't want to but he does slowly raise a finger and points at the queen, Mrs Bates, Sheryl, his new mother. The witch has been found in the room.

The next picture I lift up shows Sheryl's screaming face,

inches away from a scared little boy, her veins are up. The picture captures her venom, poisoning Sam. He's got terror and confusion in his eyes.

Do you know what you do to witches, Sam?

No, he says.

You drown them. That way mummy will be witch free?

She's not my mummy. Sam says coldly.

Sheryl, how about you, you must want to be, free of the witch? I know Sammy wants you to be, don't you Sam?

Sam looks up, looks at his parent's heads in bags and slowly nods his own.

Will she be nice to me then? Sam asks, *if the witch goes away?*

Of course she will, won't you Mrs Bates?

The bag moves.

I think she nodded Sam.

I put the photos back out of harms way, I don't want to ruin them, they're my proof, my evidence, to get me out of this mess, Sam out of his.

Social services would like to have a look at these, her pulling his hair, her spitting in his face, unfit to be a mother of any kind.

I take Sam's hand and walk to the kitchen. Max is still on the boys arm.

He likes you, I can tell. He wouldn't do that for any old fart.

Sam looks at the bird on his arm, then up at me.

Do witches really drown?

I'm busy filling the bucket in the sink.

Course they do, that's why they fly on broomsticks so as not to get wet. When have you ever seen a wet witch?

Never, Sam replies.

See.

The water pours into the bucket. I turn the tap, pull the bucket out, it scrapes as it comes.

Come on, I say turning from the sink, *Come on lets go get that witch.*

Yeah, lets go. Sam shrieks.

When we enter the queen's shaking and so is her king.

See, the witch is getting scared. It's like washing hair, pour the water over and watch the witch disappear. Sheryl's trembling as I approach.

Will it leave on a broomstick? Will it fly? His eyes are half covered and he's holding onto my leg. Will I see it? Will it get me?

That's a good question Sam, I really don't know. Shall we wait and see?

I'm scared. He says.

No, don't be scared Sam. I'll look after you now... I say. *Now watch this!*

And I pour the bucket, the bags sucked in, hard breathing, spat out. She's gasping now, really gasping. Terror and fear with every drop, she's fitting on the chair.

See, it's trying to wriggle out Sam.

The bag's sucked in, spat out, sucked in spat out. I didn't pour it all, sometimes enough is enough.

I can't see it, where's the witch, where's the witch? The boy yells, grasping jean and skin. *It can't get out.*

It will, it will, just wait. I say. Won't it Sheryl, you won't be cruel anymore, once that witch has gone!

And the bag gets sucked in, spat out, sucked in spat out.

It's not leaving, I don't like this, the boy yells. *I can't see the witch.* And he starts to cry. *You don't have to do this to daddy, do you?*

No, I think we can leave the king alone.

Buzz.

The front door buzzer goes, gets me every time. I lift my eyes, turn my head, know exactly who it will be. I put the gaffer tape down on a chair and walk to the door.

Mr and Mrs Bates stand arm in arm, the happy man and wife.

We're not late are we? Mr Bates asks, stretching out a hand, which I take.

No, I look at my watch. Ten minutes early. Please do come in.

I say with a smile. No Sam? I ask.

No he didn't want to come, Mrs Bates replies.

Gaffer tape, two empty chairs, brown bags on floor. Their feet enter the room. I've a decision to make.

Do you know what my mum used to say to me, near as damn it all the time?

No, Mr Bates says, looking at me, *why would I know that?*

Dreamer, you're nothing but a dreamer. I say, *she might be right.*

That's Supertramp. His wife, Mrs Bates says and starts to sing.

5

E.C. Seaman

Every Thursday afternoon, I die again and go to heaven. That's what it feels like, here in this room while she massages my back; all the pain melts away, and for an hour or so, one short hour in a long week, I feel almost at ease with myself.

Her hands look too small to work such magic, but they are square and strong; very capable. I have always preferred women to maintain their nails a little longer, more feminine-looking, but her hands are the ones that do the job. When I first came to the clinic, I was treated by a physiotherapist, middle-aged, brisk and efficient. She used a kind of pain relieving gel on my back – it felt cold and chemical on my skin and she had to wear thin rubber gloves like a surgeon so the drugs didn't absorb into her body. Then she'd make me bend and stretch in all sorts of contortions, send me away with sheets of exercises to repeat diligently at home. After six weeks of these twice-weekly sessions, the doctor told me I'd progressed as far as they could hope for and would be put into a maintenance programme of deep tissue massages once a week.

When I saw Hana waiting for me here in the massage suite that first afternoon, I wondered whether there was any point in letting her continue. The physio worked in a bright, clinical room, lined with anatomical textbooks and a dangling articulated spine of yellowed chunky plastic, as though she'd ripped the backbone from a particularly recalcitrant patient, *pour encourager les autres*. Hana's massage room was rather disturbingly boudoir, with low lighting, softly piping music and gold-framed prints of a serenely smiling Buddha. It didn't seem an environment where any kind of medically-approved healing process could take place. I was especially sceptical when she told me she would be using aromatherapy oils.

"What scents do you like?" she said, a tiny frown creasing her forehead.

I had never really thought about it.

"I like black coffee on a cold morning, crispy bacon and the smell of cut grass," I said crossly.

"Oh," she laughed, "but I cannot rub you with bacon," and then she suddenly looked very serious, "It is awfully important that the oils we use have the right therapeutic effect."

"Something fresh then," I said, "to wake me up a bit." I didn't give a damn really, my back hurt so badly that afternoon, I just wanted to cut to the chase, to her hands smoothing out the bumps knotted into my spine from hunching over a computer all week.

"Then Bergamot, I suggest," she said, "which is a member of the citrus family, and also Pine, which is very cleansing."

I must have looked askance at that for she said quickly,

"Not for the cleansing of the body you understand, but the cleansing of the mind."

She nodded thoughtfully. "The blend I will use, some of the oils are included for their warming beneficent effects," she said primly, and then added with an enchanting little smile, "and some because they smell oh, so very nice."

I think I may have quivered visibly when she said that.

If I were a younger man, less careful... When she went out afterwards to let me re-dress, I rubbed a towel all over myself to mop up every hint of oil so that it didn't stain my clothes. I didn't want Danielle to pick up the scent of the massage and question me. Later, at home, when I unpacked my bag, I took out the towel and was hit by the scent of it, the scent of Hana. I closed my eyes and pressed my face into the soft fabric, drawing up that spicy warmth, like hot sunshine through a forest canopy. Instead of putting the towel out for laundering, I thrust it to the back of the wardrobe, knowing that with that perfume, I could conjure her up in a moment.

When I need to distract myself from what Hana is doing, I let the scent pick me up and take me away. I think about the high forests that rose steeply behind my Mother's house. When I was a teenager, I used to escape for hours, breathing in that cool crisp mountain air, walking until my legs ached and I could fall each evening into a deep and dreamless sleep. I once saw an adder lying on the path, curled neatly like a coil of rope, fat and languid in the sun. It scudded off into the sparse undergrowth when I approached, a surprising turn of speed from such a squat creature. I liked to climb up above the tree line, ramble through the wind-stunted gorse and bright lilac heather and low bushes of bilberries. Plucked carefully from their hiding places, they would burst in my mouth with a deep purple sweet-sour tartness, almost perfumed in their intensity. Such wild country.

Despite these attempts to distract myself, I do get aroused. Of course I do. Lie any man on his belly with all that glorious pressure bearing down on his cock and have a beautiful woman run her hands up and down his body – he'd have to be dead not to get an erection. But I can control it. I'm not an animal. If walking in long-felled pine forests doesn't distract me, then I re-run old cricket matches, or even think about work. Sixty seconds absorbed in the intricacies of line code or overseas transactions – well that could deflate anything. Hana always leaves me for five minutes at the end of our sessions, drapes warm towels across my back and lets me rest. After a few months, I suddenly wondered if she does that not so much for her therapeutic reasons, but to let the blood flow back to my brain – maybe she actually knows how aroused I get. I'm not going to think those thoughts. They might lead me to do something stupid, and this isn't that kind of place, Hana isn't that kind of girl. Can you imagine? There are places I could go, I suppose, if that was what I wanted. But that's not it at all.

I wonder how much we really know about each other. For a long time, I thought her name was spelled Hannah, British style, though I could tell from her accent that she was foreign. I didn't ask for ages, didn't want her to think I was too interested. I thought she might be Scandinavian, but she didn't look quite icy-fair enough for that. She is Polish, it transpires. I joked with her, rather nervously,

"I suppose you'll be off home then, now our economy has collapsed."

She looked at me reprovingly, "It is not all about the money, you understand."

She can't know much more about me than my name, and what does that tell her? John; like a tart's client, or police slang for a dead body. Such a very dull, common name. There have been very few interesting Johns in the world, not many men who've managed to rise above the limitations of such a very lacklustre start. My dear Mother may as well have tattooed "I have no imagination" on my forehead. I like the way Hana says it though – she softens the 'J' into something closer to a 'y' and lifts the 'o', so that in her mouth, my name alters gently, exotically, into 'Yan'. I can see him, this Yan; he would be a fighter, a lover, a dashing hero. He'd never wear grey.

I do. I always dress soberly, reassuringly, in shades from pale slate to dark charcoal grey, except for a selection of turquoise shirts to match my eyes. That's my one vanity, I think. Danielle once said I have piercing eyes, when she was upset with me about something. I feel I would have been good at interrogation, at the real hands-on spy stuff. But it's not like that anymore, if it ever was. You could call me an office-based agent, I suppose. I spend my days looking at lines of data, movements of figures, tracing tiny ripples and criminal footprints across the world's economies.

The job complicates things. Or maybe it's not the difficulties of the job, but of being the sort of person who would do this job in the first place. I'm not good at parties, not a natural at small talk. Danielle forces me out of myself, likes us to 'socialise' as she calls it, even dragged me to a dinner party with her colleagues. I did try, for her sake.

"I'm an analyst," I said to the woman on my left, in response to her polite question. Her face lit up delightedly,

"Oh you're a psychiatrist? Which school do you follow? Jungian, Freudian or CBT?"

"I'm a financial analyst," I said and her face fell again. Women love talking about themselves, it's their favourite topic of conversation. I suppose she hoped she'd get free therapy if she chatted me up. I'm not exactly a financial analyst either, it's just what I say; something so dull and incomprehensible to most people that they change the subject and tell me about their own fascinating careers in waste management instead. But that's what I am paid for, to be closemouthed, to be discreet. I can't let on what I really analyse; it's a matter of national security. James bloody stupid Bond wouldn't last 10 minutes in the real world. Great blabber-mouthed idiot; telling everybody his name and rank and then poncing around in a dinner jacket; about as camouflaged as a penguin in the Sahara. I don't ever tell women what I do, even if it would help me get them into bed more easily. Even Danielle has only the haziest idea what I do all day.

God, my erection is so hard it feels as if I could balance on it. If this keeps happening, I will have to stop coming, so to speak. Maybe I could ask Hana for a facial or something instead, just so that I could keep seeing her. Though that might cause me even more difficulties. After several months of coming here, I got careless, left some receipts lying around after emptying my pockets. Danielle pounced on them.

"Honestly John, I can't believe you spend so much money every week on a massage."

I could tell that she thought it was in some way dubious, even though this is a proper clinic. She put those little invisible quotation marks around the word 'massage', the way women do when they are trying to distance themselves from something, to show their disapproval.

"I'll rub your back myself for that kind of money," she said, only half-joking.

"It's a sports massage," I said quickly, "more like a type of physiotherapy really."

Thank God I can make it seem respectable.

"Besides, it's on BUPA," I added, "It isn't actually costing me anything."

She raised her carefully pencilled eyebrows, but seemed satisfied by the innate propriety of therapy paid for by private health insurance. BUPA certainly wouldn't be paying for any funny business.

Sometimes I try and analyse what goes on, here in this room. A kind of enchantment, I think. Hana is certainly beautiful, in that unpreening way of women who have no idea how gorgeous they are. I have never seen her stop and look at herself in the mirror that hangs in the corner of the room; most women can't pass any reflective surface without stopping for a sly prink and a pout. Or perhaps she is so used to being naturally lovely that she has forgotten and simply takes it for granted. She has tiny little hands and her feet in flat black shoes look like a child wearing plimsolls ready for PE. Sometimes when it's warmer she wears those flip-flop sandals and when I lie with my face through the padded hole in the massage table, I can see her toenails gleaming beneath me like pink shells on a beach.

She looks very natural, not made-up. I like that in a woman. Well, I like it in Hana, anyway. I loathe it when Danielle slumps around my flat on Sunday mornings, all whey-faced and pink-eyed, her mascara rubbed off in fat black clumps on my pillows, her lipstick smeared on my coffee cups. Hana always looks fresh and delicately rosy cheeked, never painted. She used to wear her hair in a ponytail, and once when she was leaning right over me it fell forward and slithered against my neck. I flinched, didn't know what it was. She apologised, stopped and tied it back. I watched her pinning up all that fabulous long hair, like a length of black silk, longed to say to her, "No, that felt great, just a bit unusual," but since then her hair has always been pulled back and plaited tightly, so it can't ever swing loose again.

To get Danielle off the sofa and out of my flat at the weekends, we go to a café, eat breakfast there. She likes to people-watch; it keeps her from getting restless and chattering to me; she can fork up cream cake and watch the world go by while I read the newspaper and drink coffee as black as my thoughts.

She's always guessing about the people passing by, making up stories.

"I'm interested," she says, "Don't you look at people and wonder where they are going, what they are doing?"

"I don't look at other people at all," I say.

I have recently realised that this long-cultivated detachment may actually be hampering me at work. People who joined after me have risen higher because they have that easy knack with people, even though my skill with data, with patterns, is unchallenged.

"John here is our financial expert," my Departmental Manager said, laying a heavy hand on my shoulder as he showed the latest Minister around. I felt patronised, as though he was condescending to me in some way, although we both knew he could never understand what I do in a million years.

"One of the backroom boys," the Minister smiled blandly, already searching the room for the next photo opportunity. I never thought of myself like that, always thought I was on the front line of the war against terror, at the bleeding edge of technology. I suppose what I do could be considered dull, by some people. But then Bond doesn't get BUPA.

*****

His every muscle is so very sharply defined beneath the skin; it is as if he is made out of knotted string and strong sticks. I think that you could use him for teaching anatomy classes, as a mannequin for showing the major muscle groups. I am not saying that he is a perfect specimen. I do not think, for example, that he would be able to model; he's far too pale, too skinny. But the way his back triangles down from very broad shoulders to narrow hips, well, he is certainly possessing a kind of male beauty.

I must know John's body more intimately than his girlfriend – does she ever look at him this closely, or does she no longer really see him, observe every freckle and mark, every scar and wrinkle? I wonder if he even knows he has stretchmarks across the base of his spine, those silvery threads as if a snail has crept along the surface of his skin, crossing and branching like streams across the plateau of his back, spreading out from his slim hips. When I massage him, I feel the bones clicking beneath the skin, moving like well-oiled engine parts beneath my hands. Yes, he is quite perfectly constructed.

He is much younger than I thought; it was the almost white, silvery-blondness of his hair that made it hard for me to judge him. I looked at his records you see, I checked up on him. I do not trust easily, and I find that some people take this the wrong way. Especially men. But I am determined that people will fool me only once.

"Oh, Hana, but your English is so good," they say, a little disappointed when they realise I comprehend them, as if I would really have cast myself adrift over here without being able to speak, to understand what was happening to me. That would be much too scary. Even so, at first, I was quite overcome by the strangeness of it all. The voices around me, all speaking in a different tongue, the many accents and tones of that language, they sounded like roaring waves crashing over and around me.

When I arrived here, the employment agency sent me for a position at an establishment that was in need of masseurs – The Kensington Clinic. A very nice name I thought; it sounded like what the English would call 'posh'. Well, if that was posh, then I am the Queen. I am not stupid; I could see what sort of place it was when I went there the very first day. It looked very clinical, all white tiles and shiny floors, very clean, but I noticed that everything was wipe-cleanable, disinfectable. Not very pleasant, if you think about it. If you are doing your massage properly in a therapeutic way, you shouldn't be needing to hose down the walls afterwards.

There was a bouncer on the door but they did not call him a bouncer, they called him Gerald. And all the cubicles had the little spy holes in the doors so that Monique, the supervisor, could check-up on the girls. I wondered if they had, you know, the hidden cameras. They seem to be crazy for them here in this country so it would not have surprised me at all if they had cameras to look at the clients and take dirty pictures. I was thinking they could make a lot of extra money that way.

The uniform for all the girls at that place was like a comic sexy nurse, a tight white gown with pop-fastenings down the front, very low cut. Monique looked me up and down, frowned at my flat shoes and suggested I might want to wear higher heels, and possibly a more enhancing brassiere. An employer should not be so very interested in the way you look, should they? That was not an encouraging sign. Oh, they were ridiculous outfits, designed not for comfortable movement, but instead for easy access. It wasn't hard to tell which girls were doing what they called 'extras'.

"Now Hana, my girls often like to use a different name at work," said Monique, "For security purposes, you understand. I thought you could be Veronika," she added.

"There is no V in Polish," I told her, "it does not work on my tongue."

She gave me a funny look, snapped, "OK, you can be Zsa Zsa then. Is that exotic enough for you?"

I did not stay long. I was not going to participate in the way they wanted me to. It is not what I was trained for; I shall say no more than that. I think that some girls there actually liked the power and the big tips, but only for their attractive clients or the ones who looked rich. I waited for my first week's pay, for I was not going to leave without what they owed me. When that woman handed me the envelope of money, it felt very light. I opened it and counted out the notes in front of her. She sneered a little, but I was not yet accustomed to the British notes and wanted to be sure I had enough.

"There is in fact some money missing," I told her, after

counting through twice.

Monique sniffed, "Well, we deduct the price of your uniform and name badge," she said, "We can hardly reuse them on another girl can we?"

I made sure I took the uniform with me when I left. I use it now for when I am cleaning my flat. I dropped that name badge with the silly Hungarian name in the trash. Then I went back to the agency and told them exactly what I thought of their so-called 'Kensington Clinic'.

And so, I came here instead. This is a good place, a real clinic approved by the doctors for therapeutic treatments. Here I can do what I trained for, what I love. People come in bent and worn and tired, with aches ground deep into their bones, their muscles all tight with strain and fatigue and sadness. Then after an hour with me they walk out of this room with a spring in their step and a dreamy smile on their faces, a new look in their eyes, as if to say that for a little while at least, they can cope with anything. I rub them with the scented oils, creating a blend to lift and inspire them, warming it first in my hands if I like them, though sometimes I am putting it on cold if they have been rude or disrespectful to me.

I look down at John, stretched out on my table in total relaxation. I have never dripped cold oil onto his back. I love the silky sheen of his well-nourished skin, healthy and glowing with the friction of my rubbing, gleaming in the low lights. My hands merge warm and gentle with his flesh, feeling as if I am becoming part of him. My clients very often fall asleep, but what they do not know is the trance state the massage can bring on in me. If they do not chatter and fidget, but let me get into a steady rhythm, then the scents of the oils and the soft music and the warmth of the room can take me into a state beyond myself, quite calm and powerful.

The sleepy clients apologise, embarrassed, as if they think

they are the only ones who do this. I should some day tell them that I prefer the silent ones to the people who try and make conversations. I do not like to talk too much myself, so I do not like a continual stream of chattering.

"Shut up!" I want to say, "I am not a counsellor, I am not what you call a shrink. I don't need to know this stuff about you, I do not care." I cannot let myself care.

I am not always unfriendly like this, and am not really lonely, you understand. I have even had one boyfriend since I came to this country, though I do not think that he understood me. It was all about appearances, showing me off. He always wanted to *miec sex* with me, but never wanted to talk. I tried to acquaint him with my life back home, but he would laugh at me. I once told him how on *Smingus Dyngus* last year I was soaked with water by the town boys.

"Smingus Dyngus? What the hell is that? It sounds dead stupid."

"It is our Easter Monday," I said, "a kind of celebration, where the family throw water on anyone who is caught sleeping late in bed, and then boys throw it at the girls in the street. It is a sign of popularity. Fathers get annoyed if their daughters are not drenched." Of course I did not have a Dad to be proud of how many boys threw water at me. Being wet through is supposed to mean you will marry in a year. I told him of this and he laughed,

"Well, I s'pose if you haven't got proper TV, you have to make your own entertainment somehow."

I do know he admired me, for he would gaze at me, with that certain look in his eyes.

"As rare as black diamonds," he said, picking up my hair and letting it spill over his hands, "as dark as your heart." Wrong I thought, there is nothing dark about me, I make very sure of that. I am always being sunny and smiling a little, for I do not like to be thought of as miserable. So maybe that was some kind of English joke. I don't know. I think he was kind of a jerk, a *swinia*. It is always hard to tell with men, and harder even still when you do not even think in the same language.

I do get some strange looks when I am speaking Polish on my phone, or when I am talking to people in the street. Some of the folk here, they can be very unfriendly. They are hissing at me in the supermarket when I stop to look at the foods in the Polish section. Imagine that – the shops are so keen to help us poor Polish spend our wages that they stock shelves upon shelves of our foods. It is all wrong though; stuff that tourists would buy, or people longing to remember their childhood, nothing you could use to make everyday meals. There are sweets and tinned pickles and the little gingerbread cookies that we only ever used to eat at Christmastime, but they can never recreate the food my mother used to make. Besides I mostly like the English food, there is a whole street in the supermarket just for breakfast cereals of every kind. How can you not love a country with so many choices?

They do not all love us. I hear the old ladies making their remarks; loud enough so I can hear, but not so much that they can't pretend that I have misheard their private conversation. I sometimes wonder if they think we have no feelings.

"They're taking over," one woman muttered, "All these bloody Polish and suchlike."

"They kill the swans, you know," her friend said, "They go to the park at night and catch the fish, then they kill the ducks and the wild birds so they can eat them. That's all part of their culture, over there." She looked across at me darkly.

Now that is all so wrong. I do not know any Poles who eat swan – the very thought. And anyway, why would anyone go to all that trouble when everyone can buy £3 chickens from the Tesco? These women are so very silly.

The men don't seem to disapprove as much – they have a kind of longing in their eyes, looking for foreign meat. There is a hierarchy though, I find. If I were blonde, they could happily think I'm Swedish, because you see, North European is classy, Mediterranean is sexy, but we are merely slutty Bolshevik peasants. Even here, in this nice place, there have been moments. That is something I like about my manager, Kathie. Once she had hired me, on my first day, she said she wanted to have a little talk.

"Massage is very much misunderstood, and I am aware that you will probably be the most vulnerable of all my therapists."

I couldn't pretend that I didn't know what she was referring to, though I didn't feel it was the correct time to share my experiences at the Kensington Clinic.

"I want you to stop and leave the room if you ever feel uncomfortable," she said sternly, "I don't expect you to take any nonsense. Massage is a therapeutic profession to rank alongside physio or chiropractics, not a way of getting a cheap thrill."

I thought she was a very sensible woman for that, though actually her rates here are not particularly cheap.

It was not so very long before I encountered a cheap thrill client. I unpeeled the towel from around this young man's waist a little, to reach his lower back muscles and found he was not wearing any under things. I said this to him, in surprise, and he said,

"I don't wear them love, don't like to have my old man constricted, nowarrimean?" No, I didn't know what he meant, so he rolled over and waggled his *czlonek* at me like he was pointing a little *pistolet*. Kathie said next time any man does that I am to hand him a pair of baggy disposable paper underpants and tell him I am leaving the room until he puts them on.

"They generally don't try that one again," she added grimly.

I have to keep my nails short, though the continual immersion in massage oils and beauty creams makes them so strong and well-nourished that I could grow them into inches-long talons if I wished to. Sometimes, when I have a really annoying client, one who hasn't showered, or who insists on taking his shorts off, I wish I had let these nails grow and could then dig them in so hard that I'd draw blood, leave ten scarring crescents across their flesh. Explain that to your wife, I would say savagely. Mind you, I am also thinking there are some men who would feel that pain an extra treat.

City boys, they are the worst. The more they are spending, the more truly horrible they are. Oh, they think they can buy anything, anyone. Like that man with no underthings, flaunting his nakedness.

"But I'm paying for you," he said, and he grabbed my hand, moved it down to his crotch. He probably thought his weeny little thing could lift him off the table, like a one-limbed press up. To me it looked flaccid and wrinkled and a dull purplish colour like an overripe *sliwka*.

"Plum is very fashionable this autumn," I wanted to tell him, though for sure he would take that the wrong way.

Mostly it is ladies of course who come for the massage. They are usually okay. There is one older lady I do not like at all. She has the oil poured onto her straight from the bottle in an icy-cold flood. She was telling me about a Spa she had visited in New York, where male masseurs rub the ladies, a place where they ask – do you want everything?

There was an avidity in her eyes when she looked at me.

"I suppose you girls know all about it, don't you?" She said, licking her lips. I didn't know I had to be warned about the women. She thinks there are really special pressure points – so you can make an orgasm without penetration, without rubbing. Oh it is so crazy – don't you think someone would have made money by selling that secret by now?

Women's parts are less defined; it is less easy to arouse them, though sometimes I wonder how much my ladies do enjoy themselves. It is a very delicate balance after all. So, you are invading their personal space and for some that is painful, not therapeutic at all. I have found that there are even some ladies who come for their first massage without knowing what it really means, not understanding they will have to take their clothes off.

"It hadn't occurred to me," one girl said, red-faced, "I mean that I'd have to be naked."

She was in fact wearing a pair of quite large panties that covered her plump *posladki*, but I could see that she still felt self-conscious, the way she was cupping her breasts in her hands.

She calmed a little, eventually, let me massage her into relaxation. Her chest was soft and slippery, and I was feeling the little buds of her breasts beneath my hands, the firmness and gentleness of her all together. Quite different from the men, rather beautiful. Is this what I am like, I thought, is this how I feel?

*****

Danielle moved out last week. She said I was never there.

"I don't just mean physically," she said, "though it's taken me a week to find a big enough space in your diary to even have this conversation with you."

She said it with a kind of grim humour and for a few moments then I did have a pang of regret, remembering that her easy laughter was one of the reasons I let her move in with me.

"I don't need this, John," she said. "I'm not exactly a minger but you make me feel like one."

"No," I said, "you are really quite beautiful." But I said it with detachment because I was thinking, yes, but you are blonde, not dark, and I can see your roots.

"I deserve better than this John. There's a reason why someone gets to your age without being married. You're emotionally unavailable, a toxic bachelor."

Maybe I am happy being a bachelor, I thought, not everyone has to pair off two-by-two like animals going into the ark. I once heard a joke about marriage that sums it all up for me – why do men predecease their wives? Because they want to. Something about being in a relationship changes women, and surely marriage would only make that worse. Once a woman starts to relax into a relationship, she stops wearing sexy scanties and starts dressing for comfort. The first time you find your girlfriend curled up on your sofa in fleece pajamas and fluffy pink bedsocks you know it's the beginning of the end. But why should you relax, settle for second best? I didn't change; I continued being exactly the man I always was, I still spent my money, took her to expensive restaurants, so why did she feel able to stop doing the things that I enjoyed? Looking gorgeous was her part of the bargain. I don't get it. When she stopped making an effort, perhaps I should have started taking her to Burger King instead.

"You don't want a girlfriend, an equal, a *partner*," she said angrily, "you just want an escort."

She started to disapprove of everything, all the things that make me who I am. She wanted to me to change. Even my flat, so carefully created, so stylish, became a source of dissatisfaction. The huge picture windows have no curtains, but I like them that way, open to the view across the river, the lights twinkling across the city. There is no noise from the wind or the streets so far below unless I open the sliding doors to the terrace. She wouldn't sit out there, said it was too cold and blowy, too high and exposed. And she wouldn't ever make love in that room, although I pointed out that it would practically take the Hubble telescope to overlook us there.

She even hated the huge flat-screen TV mounted on one wall.

"A home cinema system," she sniffed, when I had it installed, "so vulgar."

I loved it, the way the ambi-lighting wrapped me in a sensory daze, rendering me unable to pay attention to anything else while it was on. I suppose that's what annoyed her, my total immersion. Now she's gone, I can see how it dominates the room. I put on a DVD last night and had to switch it off after half an hour. I felt dizzy and my head reeled and I had the unwelcome sensation that there was someone else there in the shadows with me.

"All these boys' toys," she used to say, "these funky gadgets. Who are they for, who do they impress? You never have friends round, don't really have any friends, so who gets to see them?"

I know they are there, I thought, I can tot up the amount spent on hi-tech hardware in that flat and know that it comes to about twice the average annual salary. Everything perfect, everything shiny, all mine. I created that space meticulously, but I spend no time in it. I realised this week how empty it is since she left. At what point did minimal cross over into empty? And when did peaceful become silent?

It's quiet here in Hana's room, but never silent. I have become used to the faint music she plays in the background, to the soft rustle of her dark-green uniform, the delicate swooshing of her oiled hands as they move across my skin. I wonder what she thinks as she is rubbing me, where her thoughts wander, whether she has her mind on her job or is creating mental shopping lists. I've never seen her outside of this room. Maybe I wouldn't recognise her if I saw her in jeans and a t-shirt, with her hair swinging free. It is hard to imagine her life, shopping, cooking, talking to friends. What does she do when she isn't here? Maybe the clinic wraps her in cotton wool, tucks her away in a cupboard at the end of the day. That's why she always looks so fresh, so perfect.

I watch her shadow moving across the cream-painted walls like an echo of the strange foreign animated films I remember seeing as a child. Her shape is dream-like when silhouetted; her usually graceful movements seem oddly jerky. For one moment the shadow of her hands looms jagged against the wall and I realise again how little I know this woman for whom I literally lay myself bare every week. It's so hard to tell who's friend now, who's foe. I instinctively feel I could trust her with any secret, but I couldn't even ask her out, could I? A man in my position consorting with a masseuse? It would become an office joke, if it ever became known, maybe even a disciplinary affair, if she was an illegal. The kind of thing that ends careers. Now if I really were James Bond, she'd be a honeytrap, a SMERSH agent and soon we'd be at it like knives, rolling over the massage table while she clutched me tight with her firm, well-oiled thighs.

Arghh. Don't think like that, John. I stare at the carpet, trying to distract myself, gazing intently at its small tough loops. I start counting, can see at least six shades of blue and some grey and purples and even something pinkish mixed in there. Strange, don't you think, that someone sat down and designed this carpet with so many intricate colours that blend to create an overall impression of, well, blue? It must be an odd job, being a carpet designer; perhaps they call themselves 'flooring colourists' when women ask them what they do. That's better, I feel calmer. My mind sometimes drifts into strange places, banal avenues when I am being massaged. Though that is better than the times when my mind turns in on itself, when I start to examine my life.

Some people might think my profession unusual, it has occurred to me. But you end up with the job that suits you. I naturally gravitated towards the secrecy, the sense of knowing things that would curdle the blood of the average man on the street. There is a degree of power. It would be so easy to check up on Hana, to trace her. So tempting. I could call in some favours, run a few checks, uncover her immigration status, her parentage, her education. I could dig as deep as I like, find out her friends, her lovers. I could discover whether I should really trust her.

It wouldn't even be an abuse of my position, not really. Even our old Director General didn't take the official secrets act that seriously – first she published her memoirs, then it was novels. Honestly, what a joke. Everyone knows if you tell a woman anything then it's not a secret anymore. I can only hope that she was just a figurehead and never entrusted with how this place really works, what's actually going on out there.

"Token," the lads called her, a sign of the times, nothing more. They joked that they never kept her in the loop, had all their really important meetings in the men's rooms so she'd have to bug the toilets to find out what they were up to.

Women are so unpredictable. I Interflora-ed my Mother for her birthday last week, a few clicks of the mouse to send her a bouquet in creams and pinks that wouldn't clash too badly with her chintzy Edinburgh sitting room. She eventually phoned last night, expecting to speak to Danielle, so I had to tell her that we'd parted. It was all quite amicable, I informed her.

"I've just not met the right woman." I said breezily.

"What utter nonsense," Mother said, unusually tart. "It's not about the women, there's nothing wrong with them. It's about timing. No-one will ever be right until you are ready."

I don't understand why Mother got so upset; I always thought she didn't like Danielle very much.

No-one at work needs to know that Danielle and I have broken up. They only met her a couple of times after all, when it was advisable that I take an escort along to a function. Sometimes it looks suspicious for a man to appear on his own, yet what guarantee is there that his partner will be compatible with his work, especially with what I do? It has always seemed so incongruous having office parties – as Danielle always commented, we could hardly go down to the pub and talk shop, could we? She laughed, rather snidely I thought, but well, she had it exactly right.

It's easier to live like this. When Danielle left, she was very calm, very cold. That's how I knew she really meant it. It was almost a relief. I still dream of her, for my subconscious seems unable to accept that the status quo has changed. Funny, because I rarely dreamed of her when she lived here; her absence obviously means more to me than her presence. The flat will not have changed at all since I left this morning. No magazines tumbled on the sofa, no cosmetics strewn across the dressing table, no strange food in the fridge, no spits of toothpaste in my bathroom sink or smears of mascara on my towels. All the things that used to enrage me when Danielle was there, the crumples, the mess, the clutter of feminine impedimenta. All gone, all smoothed away, everything tidy and just how I like it. I wonder if there will ever be room in my life for another person.

The kitchen will still be spotlessly gleaming with stainless steel, even the work surfaces sleek and grey and shiny. There's a four-slice toaster though I rarely eat breakfast, and the Gaggio squats redundantly now, for it seems a waste to fire it up for one solitary espresso every morning. I am back to using the kettle, its sleek bullet shape so unexpected that sometimes I have to look around the kitchen and remind myself how to boil water. I have a lady who 'does' every week, though I don't see her for months at a time. She lets herself in and lets herself out, the emptied bins and folded laundry and polished floors my only proof of her visits. I leave her an envelope full of tenners in the kitchen and it is gone when I get back, even her fingerprints neatly wiped away behind her.

"I feel you're clearing the decks ready for another relationship," Danielle accused as I helped her carry her boxes to the car. "Is there some other poor girl in your sights?"

I shrugged. "I have nobody in mind."

That was a lie, I now realise, for Hana is always on my mind, though at the time I believed I was telling the truth.

I have never touched her. Not once. I have no idea what her skin feels like, what her hair smells like, how it would be to hold her. I do think about her though, fantasise I suppose you would call it. It is always her calm impassive face I start with, then her hands, kneading and pummelling then gently massaging, stroking. I think about the oil, warm and flowing along my newly released, suddenly lithe spine, as though stiff leather has been kneaded into supple skin by her hands. Then the oil becomes water, warm water and we are standing together in a shower and she is soaping me, working up a creamy lather with those strong hands and the blasts of water are falling hot and hard on our heads. I want to come here every day, block-book her to massage me exclusively, I don't want her touching anyone else. Oh God, that way madness lies.

I can't explain my feelings for Hana. Who would I tell? It would all get so very misinterpreted. I once mentioned that I had massages for my back to one of the lads at work.

"Do you have a Jackanory?" he said with a leer.

"What's that?" I said impatiently, wondering what he was on about.

"You know; a massage with a happy ending."

Hearing that from him made me feel a bit sick.

My hour is nearly up. I want to stall Hana in some way, but I can tell by her rhythm that it is nearly over, that soon she will be taking the warmed towels from the rail, moving quietly from the room, letting me come round. And then I will be cast out again, away from this comfort and into the blaring, blasting brightness of the city. It's like when you go to the cinema during the daytime and then are wrenched from those visions, thrust back into the real world.

Sometimes I worry that I am becoming invisible. That as I get older my skin will become as colourless as my hair, my eyes will fade to grey and eventually I will slip into the shadows, finally disappear altogether. I hate change, always need everything mapped out and planned, leaving no room for spontaneity, for danger. That was the last insult Danielle threw at me before she left, tossing it back over her shoulder like a grenade.

"You're probably borderline autistic you know," she said pityingly, "everything has to be exactly the same, day after day, so safe, so sterile. Even your wardrobe is colour coded, which considering you rarely wear anything other than blue and grey, is pretty sad." I must have looked surprised, though I said nothing.

"You should take a real risk once in a while," she continued, "throw away your comfort-blanket, reach out and really touch someone."

Maybe I could ask Hana. I could take that chance; for once in my life abandon the calculated moves. Danielle would be proud of me. Actually she would be bloody furious if I finally took a risk, made a bold gesture, and it wasn't for her. But if Hana said no, I wouldn't be able to come here anymore and surely it's better to have her for one hour a week than never at all? And yet, and yet...

*****

He's lonely I think. If John had a girlfriend or a wife who really loved him, he wouldn't need to come here. Any woman could do what I do, learn how to massage, take the time to rub his back until his muscles relax and unknot. I don't think he unwinds easily; he is too wary, all taut like a spring. Very handsome, he is, though his eyes are hard like aquamarines under water and his lips carved in a way that gives his mouth a secretive look. There is something ungenerous about him – it is not a face that smiles easily.

He must be rich though, I have seen the label in his coat when he hangs it up; one hundred percent cashmere. He always tucks his scarf into it carefully as if he is afraid a chill will touch him. He looks cold like permafrost with that silvery hair and those icy eyes as if he spends too much time in darkened rooms. He needs a blast of warmth, some sun, maybe a long holiday. I do not mind the cold at all. The houses here are all so hot and sealed tight that it is a relief to step out into the air and feel the wind on your face. It is never really cold here anyway, it does not snow from year-to-year and when it does, everything grinds to a halt in piles of dirty gritty slush.

It is not like home, in so many ways, though it has taken me a year over here to realise that there was nothing actually wrong with the town in which I grew up. No, it was not bad, simply different. My Mama encouraged me when she heard of her friends' children who were going abroad, finding jobs and nice places to live. It wasn't even that she wanted me to be sending the money home, for she must have known I wouldn't leave her until it was all over. She simply wanted something better for me. She didn't need to tell me, I could see how little we had, how it was different from the places I read about, the glamour I devoured in pictures and films. The world was out there and available for the taking, I could not pretend any longer that the little we had was all that there was.

She was terrified that I would fall for a Polish boy, become trapped the way she had.

"Men are all the same," she used to say, "only after one thing. Even the ones that seem to respect you, well, you know what they say; men put a woman on a pedestal so they can peer up her skirt."

She is right, I find. There is always something else they want isn't there? They are blinded by appearances, wanting an ornament for their arms and never looking at the real you. My boyfriend here had no idea of what I was like, the real Hana. And these English men, they say one thing and mean another – it is all in the tone of voice. I am not yet getting the hang of it.

I am gradually becoming what they call *half na pol,* or half-and-half as the English would say. We London *Polski* are developing our own little rituals, our own dialect even. *Ponglish* they call it, mixing the languages, taking their words and giving them our own accent, our own twists and meanings. It is a way of making this place ours, making it more like home. Some things here I will never get used to, such as their liking for milk in their tea, like babies. Ugh. And also their horrible sausages like fat pink fingers, with no spice and no flavour. And then instead of one tap that mixes the water nicely, their sinks have two taps, one hot and one icy, so your hands they either boil or freeze. I do not understand this. It is a good job I have my fingers in the oils and creams all day or they would be worn red raw by this, I am thinking. This is why they have ugly hands, why they are all needing false nails.

I knew though that this clinic would be a good place, a lucky place for me, when I saw the colour of the front door. The door and the uniforms and furnishings and towels are all of a rich green. That beautiful dark green like the pine forests of Lubuskie, where I used to walk with my Mama, sometimes gathering mushrooms for her famous Hunter's stew. Every woman had her own recipe, her own variations on the theme, but they never tasted as good as the ones she would make. Though actually, she was not all that much of a cook. Oh, I do not know why today I am thinking so much of home. Maybe I am starting to feel sad, for I see the drops of oil falling like pine resin, and close my eyes for a few moments as if they could trap my thoughts like amber.

Last year on All Souls' Day, I could see the candles gleaming in the graveyard, fluttering in the night breezes. You can see them for miles around in the darkness, like tiny golden stars, very beautiful. As a child I found them eerie, thinking of each candle being lit for a loved one who had died. But that evening I found the sight reassuring, knowing that there was one out there for my Mama. That was the last night I spent at home. I didn't wait even the month or so until Christmas, for I knew I would find it more painful there without her than to go somewhere far away, somewhere new, with no memories.

John is very far away today, very tense. It is like rubbing a bundle of twigs, so wiry and tall as he is. But still that is better than the doughy ones, where I lose my hands in the rolls, and don't ever feel I am reaching the muscles under all that flab. I have studied anatomy – I know all about soft tissue release and muscle energy techniques, but really, some of these people defeat me. I cannot distinguish one single muscle in the whole of their big fat bodies.

"You give of yourself too much," Kathie said. "You are a very open-handed person. Maybe we need to psychically cleanse your massage suite, to ensure you do not take on any bad vibes."

I do like her so, even when she talks like this. I think maybe she is interested in me, a little.

"This room so calming," she said, "that's the lovely atmosphere you create, Hana."

"I like it to be so. A tranquil space," I reply, "It is more therapeutic that way."

So I let her use a smudge stick to purify the room. It is simply a little bunch of herbs set alight, giving off a smell like burning paper. But she insisted, after that man with his little *czlonek*, to chase away all his negative energies. I thought that was quite sweet of her.

"People like that can be so polluting," she tutted. I think she would like to ban men altogether, but so many of the medical referrals here are men.

Over coffee the other day, she talked to me about her plans for the future. She would like to set up something she calls a retreat, where people come for holidays. She could be charging a lot more. "We'd get a very good class of client," she said hopefully, "not so many of these medical referrals."

I do not know about that – I like to work with those who are really ill, who really need my help and I can see them really improve.

"I'd like to start offering a four handed massage," she said, "two therapists working on the body at the same time, it's the latest thing."

That sounds a little odd to me. I like to work alone. It would be hard to pick up that flow, get into my trance with someone else there to distract me. It would not be so pleasurable. I do not think some other masseurs even like people at all; they simply see them as flesh to be kneaded like so much dough for dumplings, not individuals to be analysed and helped. I thought about that older lady and her pressure points and the city boy with no underpants.

"Four handed massage sounds peculiar," I said, "maybe a different name would be better."

"Hmm," said Kathie, "that is not a bad idea, Hana." She looked at me thoughtfully.

"How about a Sports Muscle Rub?" I said, "It could be very invigorating for the men, they worry about the treatments being all pink and girlie."

"Genius," said Kathie delightedly, "I knew you were the right person to join me in this, you understand people so well."

I do not really understand at all, especially men. They are so very silly. My Mama struggled without my father, but she survived. She always said that no man at all was better than a bad one, that she didn't really need a man. I wonder whether there were friendships I knew nothing about, whether she was shielding me or whether she really did spend the whole of her life without the company of men. No man in her bed, no-one to wake up to. She was worn out, old before she needed to be, with no creams and make-up to help her to be the beautiful woman I know she must have been. She was always wrapped in blacks and dark browns like an old lady, her hand shielding her tired eyes, strained from the translation work she took to make extra money.

I worked hard at school and at college because I wanted to leave it all behind, didn't ever want a life like hers. It has taken me a long time to realise that wishing this was not disrespectful to my mother. I was simply being honest. Communism was like a bad joke, especially to those people who were so very damaged by it.

"It will never happen again," she used to say, then would mutter fretfully, "No, there may be something even worse." She was always looking over her shoulder, always scraping together enough to get by on. I am sure that permanent low level of stress contributed to her too early death.

When we learned about the effects of stress in my Diploma course, something broke inside me and I cried and cried and could not stop, great gulpy sobs and one of the girls had to give me tissues. I could not explain to them what my mother's life had been like, but I was sure then what had caused her to die. She always used to be hoarding things. Little pathetic things that might be useful, pieces of string, rolled and tied neatly, paper bags folded smooth, candle stubs. Things that here would be thrown out into the trash. Then sometimes when she had been shopping, she would produce little luxuries for us. It shames me now to remember how even then I was moving beyond what she could provide for me. The littleness of what she could offer embarrassed me, but beneath my shame, I knew there was so much love, and that made me cruel. Oh how very much I loved her, how much I would give to have her here with me, enjoying these everyday things that they all take for granted.

I have a huge sense of homesickness, or rather childhood-sickness. I don't want to be back there now, how it would be with Mama gone, but I sometimes crave the safe place of my childhood. There was a drabness, a concreteness to much of the town, but the countryside around it was so very beautiful. I suppose I could go back and visit my cousins, my aunts. But there seems little point. I have nothing to go back for but memories, and they do me little credit. My life is here now, here in this room, my safe place.

And my flat of course. It is very small, but it is mine and I am paying for it all myself. I save my money for further training, for my home, for safety. I hoard my money as she hoarded her tins of meat and potatoes. Maybe I will finally let myself grow roots, but aerial roots like the orchids Kathie grows in her office, stretching out, always reaching up, not confined. I couldn't give up my space. No-one is allowed there. This room, yes, they can come to, undress, bare their bodies and unburden their minds, but my home is my own.

John shifts beneath my hands, as if I have been pressing too hard, as if my anger is spreading through my hands into him. My wrists ache. Sometimes I want to say to my clients, 'Hey, my back hurts as well, why do you not rub me for a change?'

I would love to see their faces if I did that. Kathie, I think she would laugh. Recently she sent me on a special new course, designed to alleviate the strains we put ourselves under. I had not realised until then how much she cared.

"You need to save yourself," she said, "for a long and healthy career." It is true that sometimes I go home with cramp in my arms and stiff fingers, aching legs and sore feet.

"Maximum effect with minimum effort – that should be your mantra."

I think she is right, for when I get in my trance, that is how I feel. I do not even need to think, but can perform like a perfect smiling robot.

The other week I heard a song playing in the foyer here –

the radio was out of tune, so the words were faint, but I could hear them well enough and they stayed with me all day. "*Everybody needs somebody,*" it went, a jaunty melody. It made me a little sad though. They say that we are all the same, under the skin, and I know that is mostly true. I have seen so much skin, many colours and wrinkles and rolls of flesh. And yet the people are very similar, for all that. There is a yearning for contact. That is why they come here, for the power of touch, for the feeling of my fingers on their body, making them feel loved, wanted. There is a need in John. He thinks I don't notice, or hopes I don't. He won't ever do anything about it; you can tell the ones who will, the ones who will never utter a word. It is a shame.

"Same time next week then?" He asks me, trying to keep the hope from his voice.

"You will have to check and see if there is an available appointment," I say. Cool as spring water. It is our formula, a safety thing. I know it will be free, for I ask Kathie to block it out every week for him. But he mustn't know that. I would say yes though, maybe, if he liked. If he ever asks.

6

Guy Mankowski

This is the room where I got to know the body of strangers. I don't know how many Visitors have been in here. At times I wonder if it's hundreds or merely a few tens. When there are too many to mentally hold I think of them as units. Units of intimacy.

It doesn't seem important how I got to know this room, or how it became an extension of my body. Perhaps what happened was a consequence of having been alone for too long. If some of what follows seems strange, I believe the solitary nature of my work can at least partly explain it.

I always believed that a person's home is an extension of their body. I first developed this belief as a little boy when my father, for reasons still only clearest to him, swept me in his arms without notice and took me away to somewhere we couldn't be recognised. I had never experienced the sensation of being torn before, but somewhere inside me I realised that this feeling would become familiar. When this happened so many times that the feeling it brought was no longer a surprise, I resolved to do three things about it. Firstly, I would to find a home in words. Secondly, when I could, I would find a home in people. Thirdly, I would one day find a home in certain rooms. I decided that when this happened the home would embody me.

It only makes sense then that the room that I embody as an adult is like a limb to me. Therefore, the people who have occupied this room are in some way a part of me, as they are a part of my body. What troubled me at first was the thought that I did not know everyone who is in there. The Key Players had been explained by Anna, and after a fairly short while I got to know them and allowed them to exist in here with me. As a consequence The Key Players are rarely a threat, as I have had time to familiarise myself with their presence. It is The Visitors who cause me the most trouble.

Anna and I discussed this early on in our relationship. We decided that it was normal for a couple to entertain a certain number of Visitors. It would not stop us being a couple. It would merely make us more socially minded. We devised The Formula for how many people we should entertain. When the numbers eventually started to become too much of a struggle for me, Anna took over that business on my behalf. When I had to think of them, I depersonalised them as a series of situational occurrences. Each one was tied to a very specific event. By not allowing them the colour of a personality by tying them to one scene, I stripped them of their power to threaten me.

The first Visitor chosen by me was hesitant and distant. Tiffany was a dark-haired student in her late-twenties who was working at the college. She had a steady unflinching gaze, although her dress suggested a certain absent-mindedness, almost as if her mind was occupied with something of extreme importance. She saw my advertisement for a lodger and came around to visit that very afternoon. This straight away suggested that Tiffany did not have many ties, and this was fine by me.

Tiffany appeared at my door with a brown leather satchel over her right shoulder. She was wearing no makeup, but there was something lunar and iridescent about her clean face. When I opened the door she was looking straight at me, confidently, as though she knew the precise moment that she would be revealed. Her face broke into a tight smile. It was not an unattractive face, with fairly soft features and large brown eyes, but it was a serious face. On the rare occasions that she smiled she looked nearly beautiful, but she had a mole on her left cheek that was pretty much a blemish. In a black leather jacket with jeans covering her heeled boots, at first glance she just looked like another postgraduate student, lost in the earnest thrust of words.

"Hello," she whispered, "I've come to see the room?"

I opened my arms.

"In that case, I must let you in to show it to you."

Curling a lock over her ear and pulling the satchel closer to her chest, she stepped inside. It was at this moment, as she stepped inside that I first noticed the lights changing. I remember glancing over her shoulder as we made small talk and it registering with me. She explained how she was working on a thesis, something about feminist writers in South Africa. Her type of work was close enough to mine that I knew she would fit in.

As she composed herself in the bathroom after seeing the flat, I stood and waited in the living room. The room was bare and night had fallen while we were talking, seemingly without either of us realising. My flat was one storey above the pavement, and a small road was visible beneath my windowsill. In the day you could see the city from there, but at night an ochre sheen rose from the row of streetlights. In my youth I had imagined that it covered the city with a romantic, almost filmic sheen. With experience I learnt to be wary of such thoughts. As I noticed its shift to something darker, for a second I imagined that the crumbling wall opposite my window had been hit by a bomb, and that my flat was somehow still standing among the surrounding rubble. A black car slid slowly past, hesitating outside my door, and then switched its lights off. I watched as it slowly eased down the hill.

I remember standing closer to the window at what seemed

like an important moment when Tiffany came back in. She said that she thought she could be happy living here. It was only later that I realised she had little choice but to say so.

For a second we both stood underneath the bare lightbulb that was hanging from my living room ceiling. I saw her eyes pass over the ochre light that had moved onto my dark blue shirt.

I said I was happy for her to be a Visitor, but there had to be boundaries. I said that if it is my home, and therefore an extension of my body, then there must be boundaries. She agreed that this was understandable.

Certain things were placed in her room so that I felt the room was still mine. This little infringement seemed reasonable, even Anna agreed. At first it was merely a lampshade, and a broken fridge (which I said would soon work) and a gilt-edged mirror that I had owned longer than I like to remember, which was adorned with cherubs. Tiffany was quite mild and she agreed that this was okay. I sensed that she wanted to ask why those three objects had to stay in her room while she was there, but she did not ask and so I did not answer. Had she asked, I would have said that the room belonged to a brother of mine who had died, and I wanted to keep some features of the room as they were when he was alive. I need hardly tell you that that would have been a lie.

Life started well with Tiffany. She had a great deal of books, and when I passed her room late at night I often noticed that the light was on. I must admit that occasionally I listened in close enough to hear the sound of pages turning. Sometimes quite a few pages were turned in one sitting, so I took from this that she was studying late into the night.

The problems started when a different sound emanated from the room. I have not yet mentioned that I am a translator, work that has made me a great deal of money and more success than I had planned for. At that time I was working on translating a brilliant paper by a young French scientist called Gerard Lefèvre. Most of my life had been spent alone among the voluptuous comfort of words. There have been few people in my life whom I have shared an understanding with. As a child I spent a great deal of time in my father's library, which in fitting with the nature of his work contained mostly books concerning strange approaches to science. Spending little time with other children I developed my worldview through the depersonalised language of his texts. I used this analytical framework to deal with the world as I grew up, and in the relationships I engaged in.

This formative time alone in my father's library made me view the world as an experiment. I learned novel ways to incorporate pleasure into this paradigm during my student years, where I found cold pleasure in certain interactions with some of the elder women on my course. My time at university was spent alone learning languages, and in allowing myself occasional sexual contact. Having immersed myself in foreign words at an early age, I developed something of an awkward turn of phrase in English, which I apologise for. Once I felt that I had mastered the necessary languages, I took to translating key works of literature that captured my imagination. My perfectionism caused me to be in fairly great demand. On a few occasions my work even gained coverage in national newspapers and this led to requests for interviews so that the public could know more about me. I always turned such requests down. Unfortunately, this fuelled speculation about who I was, which had the effect of leading to me be in even greater demand. In the public eye I was discussed as a reclusive but excellent translator. I still felt, however, that my greatest work was to come. I merely worked hard, a single characteristic that separated me from my fellow man. As a consequence of this interest I came to isolate myself, in order to be able to maintain my standard, the standard that was my lifeblood.

I usually came home at nine o' clock, when Anna was out working. On this return, as I was passing Tiffany's room, I heard another set of footsteps behind hers. Her footsteps seemed to be moving in tandem with another. Clomp, clomp. One step and then, a half-heartbeat later, another. Clomp, clomp. The steps grew louder... and faded. And then they ceased, with one big clomp. The light stayed on, burning brightly. A shuffle. The light went out. And then a new rhythm began, swish swish swish. Swish swish swish. Faster and faster and then fading. And then wump, wump, wump. It was then that Anna returned after work and the troubles began in earnest.

It was clear that I no longer had control of the room. A new stranger had entered it without me seeing, and had obviously spent the night with Tiffany. Therefore, a new part of my house, and therefore my body, had forced itself into reckoning. Although this was not a problem in itself, I was unnerved by having been unable to plan for it. I felt that Tiffany had made an aggressive move. She had staked a claim to my territory. I decided that there were two ways to deal with this situation – either to meet the man and to familiarise myself with this new limb, or to seduce Tiffany.

Seducing Tiffany was a slow process. I had to start slowly and had to appear to be an individual whose personality was almost diametrically opposed to mine. From experience I knew that I could not be myself if I hoped to seduce a woman like her. If being myself had caused me to fail completely at this in the past, then if I wanted to be successful at seduction I had to assume a personality that was a complete contrast to my own. I therefore presented myself as a man who is interested in other people. As man who is interested in the trials and tribulations of his fellow man. As a man who has an altruistic tendency to others. This extended to an interest in the academic work of others. Having broken into Tiffany's room during the day and read her work (not all of it, there was some in yellow folders that I didn't feel certain I could open without leaving a trace), I began to understand where her passions lay.

It only took three or four afternoons in the library (this was no trouble, it was very near to my place of work) to find out about feminist writers in South Africa. I spent my life among words; they were like elaborate buffers for the edges the world presented to me. Therefore, to absorb words on an unfamiliar subject was a process I was comfortable with and I found the new words to be a soothing challenge. They presented paradigms for representing the world that were in contradiction to my own, and in assuming their shape for my purposes I found a certain dry pleasure. I also drew comfort from knowing how secure my own representations of the world were. Merely assuming another viewpoint, as if to indulge another, filled me with a heady confidence in my own beliefs and methods.

On certain evenings I ascertained that Tiffany's mind was in the state of flux in which the attention isn't drawn to some necessary chore. This was when I started to ask teasing questions about her work, which I slowly built like a web around her. She became complicit in a debate that hinged on the very passions that had made her choose this work. It wasn't long before I could anticipate Tiffany's responses to a certain question and provoke her into a debate. I knew what conclusion she wanted me to reach, and I stalled from making that conclusion until she had earned it. When she had, I gave the impression that I had been convinced by the power of her eloquence. This was so she would start to associate me with a feeling of satisfaction. A feeling that I shared her worldview. That my academic mind could be overcome by hers, and that consequently I made her feel more powerful for it. When we met in the hallway, or when Anna was at work, this led her to feel warm in my presence. It was only a step or two, or a functional sentence, before the seduction was complete. If I don't explain how I seduced her, it is only because these details were only too important later.

It made sense that the seduction took place in her bedroom. I had realigned myself with the objects I had placed in there. The objects were again useful, as they were reminders of my stake in the room (after all, surely only useful objects can ever be beautiful).

After I had seduced Tiffany I felt that the objects were again charged with my presence. If her Visitor came back, he would now be nothing more than a guest, as I had made it my room, as we had been together in there in a manner that he could not supersede. The objects had witnessed it, and they would look condescendingly on him if those acts were repeated. The Visitor did not have superiority over me, because I had laid the objects there to witness him myself. From now on I possessed her, and therefore the consequences of her actions were also my possession, because the objects I had placed were, if you like, guardians of my superiority.

Once that had taken place, no more was said on the matter. Tiffany occasionally expressed some concern that I no longer wished to make love to her, but assuming the persona of man who is opposite to me, I had answers that kept her in my flat. Now I had her under my control, I did not want her to leave. I knew that if she did she would only be replaced by someone else who might lay claim to my body.

The problems escalated when the man returned. Tiffany had tried her best to hide this from me, but I knew the shuffle of her pages, the swish of the sheets, and the wump of her mattress only too well. It was a comfort to know that the lampshade and the fridge were there, maintaining my superiority in the room. What sparked difficulty was finding a filofax of his during a routine check of her room. In itself, of course, this wasn't a problem. I had three objects in there to his one, but it was probably fair to take this as an aggressive act towards me, an attempt to liberate Anna. My first thought was to check that it was his possession, but deep down I knew that it had to be. As suspected, on the first page, in bold, black lettering carved into the page, were the words 'Paul Reid'.

A wave of emotion rose up inside me that I couldn't quell. At first I felt a powerful anger that crashed through me like a wave, instilling in me an almost euphoric hatred towards the man. I felt a strange venom course through my limbs, filling them with a potent and strange, swinging pleasure. My first thought was of violence, but soon the ecstasy started to fade from my blood. My analytical, cold and dispassionate mind started to leave such feelings behind. I realised I could find a way to overcome any designs this man may have.

The first stage involved finding a way to observe Paul Reid and Tiffany in their most intimate moments. This would be essential in order to deliver the second stage of my plan. Soon my mind started to torment me at work. I had to overcome this extra Visitor, while he was full of body and still had the potential to cause me mental harm. I began to think of more and more ingenious ways to carry out the first stage of my plan. What constants were there in the room? The fridge, the lampshade, and the gilt-edged mirror on the wall. By chance, the room adjacent to Tiffany's was a study, which was only accessible through a hallway.

I drew surreptitious advice from a detective I had worked with in the past who had helped me track down a rare manuscript. With his advice, I was able to buy, for relatively little cost, a camera small enough to fit into the gouged out eyes of one of the cherubs on the mirror. From this I was able to observe the goings on in the room in acute detail. It was only one afternoon's work to remove a panel in the fridge and replace it with a recording device and then to feed a small microphone (purchased from the same company) to the exterior of its casing so that I would have an audio soundtrack to accompany my images.

I worked on the principle that only by calculating the exact amount of pain a person can inflict upon you can you measure its retribution accordingly.

It is important to mention that I observed the events in her room for no personal thrill of my own. In fact, in the proceedings that follow, I was surprised that my observations caused me no pleasure in any sense. This was a functional act by a reasonable man to regain control over his house, and therefore his own body.

It was four days later when Paul Reid returned. Him and Tiffany talked quietly in the kitchen for between ten and fifteen minutes when a 'tish, tish' sound signalled that they were making a drink. When they retired to the room, I drew the blinds. That ochre light was still moving into the room. It didn't blast in or make efforts to intrude, but it formed a semi-circle on the white floorboards immediately beneath the window. The night had now fallen and Anna was not due back for at least two hours. I looked outside to see if the same car was slowing down in the road beneath the window. When I saw that it wasn't I was unsure whether I felt relief or panic. If something is watching you, in a peculiar way it is a relief to know that it has persisted with its intentions. If it suddenly stops then it is likely to be an indicator that events are to change, that there is no longer a need to observe you. With the fragility of the moment, perhaps I even wanted to be observed. Later on I heard a cars engine sigh by that window and then build in motion as it sped away, and I felt satisfied.

It suddenly struck me that I was about to witness something unique. Two people alone in a room navigate their interactions almost purely on guesswork. There is no textbook, or agreed tome as to how a man should react when he is meeting a woman following an intimate encounter, when they have not yet formed an exclusive relationship. There is the unspoken promise that, all things are equal, the interactions will lead to such a pairing, but although this conclusion is reasonable (and in retrospect even defensible), it is unreasonable to explicitly state it as the reason for returning until the relations between the two people are deemed inevitable. In similar situations that I had encountered, I had been surprised at how difficult it was to measure the minutiae of such actions. When was it appropriate to sit close? When was it appropriate to make her laugh? And when was a suitable time to advance on this weakness you had exploited?

I had walked through these motions in seducing Anna, and I had been successful. I realised that I was in a special position being able to watch another man try to reach the same conclusion with the same person. All variables other than me were excluded. It was the perfect experiment. From observing this encounter, I could gain an unusual insight into how the actions of our bodies cause consequence. I could learn what actions of mine, repeated with another woman would be successful or unsuccessful, without having to risk the rejection myself. I also gained a certain satisfaction from suspecting that I had made these steps before Paul Reid.

Through the scope of the camera I could see that Paul Reid was leaning on the edge of the desk, sipping a drink. Tiffany was tracing her fingers along a bookshelf, and I could hear through the microphone that she was laughing, although I could not make out her words. This lack of information did not cause me to be concerned in redressing the balance I was seeking to make my retribution complete. From watching their behaviour, I conceded that when I had been alone with Tiffany she had not laughed as frequently as she was with him, and she had not used her face as much when she did. I had driven the occasion towards a functional goal, whereas Paul

Reid seemed to be almost revelling in the enjoyment of the process.

She took out a book and passed it to him, and he moved to the end of the bed to receive it. Now he was leafing through it, turning the pages backwards and forwards while she stood over him, one hand or her hips, curling the lock of hair behind her ears. This was the same motion she had performed with me before I had enquired about a book in her room. She was now laughing yet again, and as she did she stepped back. She pointed at the book and he looked up, held her gaze squarely and then returned a glance that lasted a second longer than was merely platonic. He dropped the book, opened his hands and cocked his head to one side. With the tips of his fingers he motioned for her to come nearer. She did, under the guise that she was reaching for the book. With a sudden and strong movement, he pulled her onto his lap.

I had performed this motion differently, and was surprised that the deviousness of his approach had worked. I understood that a kind of 'open deviousness' in these situations alone was not undesirable. Tiffany was an intelligent woman who would have known that she was putting herself in a situation that could allow this to occur. When I had been in her room, I had been studying a paper on her desk and she had stood beside me to show me the lines on the page that I had feigned interest in. When her hand had reached over me, I had seen this as a sign that she was willingly invading my personal space, and in a second (to make her action seem instinctive and natural) I had placed my hand on top of hers and looked squarely into her eyes. Paul Reid and I had this motion, as a precursor to a kiss, in common. I had then kissed her squarely on the lips, whereas Paul Reid had opted to start with a kiss on the neck. I learnt from this. I realised that, in so doing, Paul Reid had allowed her the time and physical reaction to want to be kissed on the lips, whereas I had created a situation where it was likely, but not necessarily wanted. I suspected that, as a consequence, Tiffany felt she wanted to kiss Paul Reid more than me. I accepted this as a mistake that would have to be taken into account.

In that second two things happened which were telling. Tiffany reached for the book at the right of his waist, as if she was sitting on his lap to have an excuse to reach it. I caught a sudden smile. When his head raised (and presumably the volume of his voice relative to hers), she pulled in the smile so that it did not seem as wide. His hand started to stroke her hair, and smiling she twisted her head away from his. Paul Reid responded with an almost comic reaction, which seemed well-balanced. He took her head in both hands and looked into her face, his expression earnest to the point of being funny. She laughed, a wide, mirthful laugh, and twisted her head away from him. In that second he kissed her quickly on the neck. I thought I saw her shiver and smile. This was different to how I had first kissed her, when I had done so directly, grabbing the back of her head, forcing her to kiss me firmly to extract any pleasure from it. Paul Reid kissed further down her neck, the muscles of which were now protruding under the harsh bleached light. He had again given her further time to want him to kiss her, whereas I had seen such a pause as risky in allowing her time to reconsider her position and withdraw. I had traded surety of success (a lack of confidence) for an act that would guarantee her more pleasure and therefore, in the long-term, lead to a deeper connection. I again learnt from my mistake.

She was now lying flat on the bed, in a slightly awkward position that was only offset by the firm smile on her face. Her position looked slightly limp, but at the same time unnatural, and I saw the back of his head as he moved his legs around so that he was straddling her feet. He appeared to be holding the tips of her fingers and making her laugh, whereas I had pushed her hard onto the bed and ground my body against her in a way that almost forced a physical response that would make her visually complicit in agreeing to have sex.

Although either approach met with the same result (that we left our saliva in her mouth), they were still almost opposite methods. How could opposite methods of seduction lead to the same result? I realised that they did not, it was the approach that precisely defined the reaction, and this was what affected me most in what happened next. His inclusive, tender approach would lead to an increased intimacy that mine had forsaken. Pulling her hands nearer to him, seemingly with the 'open deviousness' that he wanted to hear her better, he suddenly started again to kiss her neck and the smile returned to her face, a smile which he could not see, in contrast to the serious expression on her face when I had glimpsed at her during this act. She seemed to be enjoying him more than me.

Her body squirmed and flushed as he kissed her neck, down to the nape of her shirt, which revealed a chevron of pale flesh. He unbuttoned the top of her trousers and she lifted her trunk, allowing him a second or two to peel them off (and with a small giggle that implied they both wanted the same thing) and her white knickers. This was a similar arrangement to mine, without the laughter.

The movements of his elbows suggested he was unbuttoning her shirt and, as his mouth moved down to her waist, her breasts surged forward, dressed in a more elaborate lingerie than they had been for me. In giving her more time to realise the inevitable seduction he had allowed her to plan for it more effectively. And in them both acknowledging this preparation he had in turn made her see the importance of him to her.

Instead of caressing the underside of her breasts while kissing her firmly, he was gently kissing certain features of her body (I ascertained from the way he lingered at her torso that he was kissing the mole above her pubic hair as though it was some sort of medal). Her body was twisting, in a manner that I had not had the time to afford her. Her shirt fell from her chest, and with one hand she unclasped her bra and allowed it to loop over one elbow.

Suddenly I heard through the wall a cry of delight as his mouth made contact with her vagina. Her vagina had been only partially moist when I had moved my fingers over its exterior but judging from her reaction to his mouth she had been expectant of it in a way that increased her pleasure and intimacy when it did occur. My tongue had only briefly passed over the outside of her vagina (to ensure her readiness) but I watched as her slightly large white thighs trembled as his head gyrated into her waist. Her fingers clambered over the back of his head and pushed his tongue further inside her. When I had performed oral sex on her, her hands had remained limp and only partially open at the sides of her head. They had barely quivered. When my tongue had moved over her clitoris it had been with a firmness that was in stark contrast to his gentle lapping, and although my approach had initially caused her to shriek more loudly, his was causing a crescendo of pleasure that made it appear she might orgasm for real.

I had allowed her the courtesy of a fake orgasm at this point, pretending to ignore the lack of any kind of physical response. He seemed to almost have no interest in the physical consequences of his actions. Paul Reid seemed single-minded in his determination to increase her pleasure. Her fingers were now moving through his hair in an exaggerated manner to exacerbate his desire to pleasure her. Her ululations against him increased, her body writhing harder against his mouth. Her hair whipped over her face, settling in a half-open fan over her nose and against her lips, rising and falling as she blew in pleasure. The frequency of her trembling increased until her body hung for a second, suspended in a fairly short orgasm, and then her thighs relaxed.

He moved up her body to kiss her, but in a second she had slipped her head down against his side, untying his belt and letting his erect penis move out. He stood perfectly still to allow this to happen, and to make sure there was no interruption. My brief oral contact had led to me unbuckling my trousers and then, on the second attempt, pushing my erect penis into her vagina, increasing in force. With one glance up at his face, and a lopsided smile, she licked her lips and pressed the tip of her tongue to the top of his penis. Her tongue was wetter than it had been beneath me as she salivated over the swollen red muscle, which looked almost furious with anger. Looking up at him with doe-eyed commitment, her lips trembled down the sun-starved white flesh of his penis, dribbling in small bubbles in a way that the corner of her lips had done as she had kissed me. His white bottom lifted from the covers as he pumped into her mouth, her sticky open lips smeared with lipstick that spread to her cheeks as he masturbated into her nose and cheeks, ejaculating in a white messy stream on her face. I was being superseded.

At this point, I felt I had gathered enough information for me to secure my retribution, and I left the lovers to their privacy. As my head leant away from the image on the screen I felt exhausted. I had observed such minute details of their interactions that I almost felt I had undertaken some form of physical exertion. In spite of myself, I felt some connection with Paul Reid – the same invasive connection a man feels when introduced to the ex-boyfriend of a lover. A situation that demands that you feign politeness, even friendliness, although festering under the surface is a vile raft of intoxicating questions. In such a situation, our evolution compels us to assert our authority over the other man. We have to balance an outwardly friendly appearance (to placate the partner present), but at the same time manage to acquire enough information to convince ourselves of some kind of shallow and pathetic superiority. We scavenge for scraps to make ourselves justified in our efforts; we convince ourselves that we are superior in looks, intelligence, dress, ambition. In such situations, it is possible that when left alone the two men will even engage well due to the unspoken agreement of some shared prey. Yet, given the opportunity to exercise violence on one another in a socially acceptable manner, the men will be barbaric. They would exercise cruelty through channels slick with the slime that evolution's impossible demands leave on us. Impossible demands to assert our authority covered only with a veil of societies' requirements for rational behaviour. Violence would be cathartic, not only as a physical manifestation of superiority, but also as a method of establishing who was The Key Player in that environment.

At that moment, I felt a tremor arise in me at the thought that I might not be The Key Player in the house anymore. I quelled this fear with the same ferocity with which I approached my work. With the same quiet assurance that allowed me to conduct my life calmly, through knowing that I had something over my fellow man. From what I had gathered in Tiffany's room, Paul Reid occupied a teaching position at the university. From this I took solace in the exclusiveness of my abilities, in knowing that what I had to offer was more unique than him.

A man can know his place in the world by knowing how easily he can be replaced, and I knew I was less replaceable than him. The key sources of comfort to me were in earning more than him, in commanding more respect than him, and in knowing that in a contest for her affections I had more power. He was younger than me, but not so young that my experience would be a disadvantage. Physical strength and appearance barely featured in my thoughts. If my movement was more precise than him, the pauses in my speech more evocative, the structure of my face better under a stark strip-light, then that accentuated my advantage. This man was nothing more than an appendix to the text I had written on her. He was there as a consequence of my decision. On a base level, I simply felt better at knowing that I had slept with her first as well.

As I turned to the window, I asked myself if these protective feelings that festered in a man were really necessary. Feelings that were hidden with various degrees of success, but which were doubtless present in every man. I knew that the most cunning of men would profess to not even having these feelings, as it would offer them an advantage. Would the most honest and virtuous man therefore wear these feelings on his sleeve? Was it noblest to be savage in expressing these interests? If a woman invests in a man, she needs to be sure that the man will not invest in another woman to her detriment. A man, on the other hand, wishes to know that his investment is to be protected, that he will not be investing in another man's offspring. These are emotions that have been developed over millions of years in hostile conditions, where violence was the only medium, and there has not been time enough to remove them from our instincts. Society has moved faster than evolution, in requiring the man and woman to feign apathy towards how exclusive their relationship is, if only to be viewed as modern and forward-thinking. But evolution, progressing faster than society, has taken choice from the equation. The instincts of violence are still there, and a person can either sublimate them by finding a way to construct a feeling of exclusivity with a partner, or find a non-violent way to ensure that the partner is worth the investment. Without this feeling of exclusivity (often found in shades and points of principle), surely we are simply cast adrift among the countless ghosts of previous lovers?

In the face of repeated evidence that the partner is not worth the investment or is too high a risk, the woman, or man, will no longer find value in the relationship. It was then that I realised Paul Reid was in my power. Paul Reid did not know what had happened between Tiffany and me before his arrival. I had the knowledge which suggested that she may not be an investment. But, similarly, Tiffany had the same power over Anna and I.

You may think it odd that I took such an interest in the relationship between Paul Reid and Tiffany. But we cannot measure our affect on a lover without knowing the intimacy they have indulged in before us. Without this knowledge, we cannot know where the bar needs to be set to create a unique intimacy in the future. Without measuring our relative effect on another person we are therefore unable to measure our own worth.

I knew exactly what intimacy had preceded me, and consequently exactly how to supersede Paul Reid. In superseding Paul Reid I would be able to keep control over The Visitors, and ensure that they would not become a more potent threat as Key Players.

I suddenly felt a wave of fear pass over me at the thought of the ghosts I was contending with. How can a man leave his mark on the world if he is completely replaceable and transient? How can a man even remain in this world if in some way he is not made to feel unique? Surely, without a way to feel at least a trace of superiority, he will be cast adrift, with no point of self-reference? If he cannot leave his permanent mark anywhere, what does he have to draw certainty from? Without a guiding light, even a sense of worth in the universe, what use can a man be to anyone?

I fell backwards. The ochre light on the floor grew stronger; it almost seemed to be warming and swelling beneath me. I could hear the wump, wump, wump of other bodies moving in the room, of people who had been here before me driving themselves, smashing themselves closer to one another. I could smell the stench of their bodies like raw meat, building and mingling and slipping over one another as they rose to some selfish crescendo. Knifing through that smell, more insidious and poisonous than any, I could smell the fluids of their bodies, secreted like snails, staining each other irreversibly, soiling pure flesh. I could hear the reckless, bold movement of a man and woman, of the soft cry of a woman welcoming a man into her. This roar filled my ears, a roar of disgrace at their actions and of how paltry my efforts to follow in their footsteps would always be. The roar of superior muscles, clenched deeper and more invasively than mine, of kisses wetter and fuller than my own. Of movements that changed bodies and the mental responses and the expectations of their lovers forever.

The Key Players were laughing at me. I could hear their horrible, sickly laughter echoing inside my head, and I knew there was no way to get it out but to tear it open. I staggered forward, over to the windowsill, and the swinging, dark movement in my brain tried to clutch onto a way to drain this sensation off me. I clawed for the opening of the window trying to let in a shaft of something else, to suck some air in and to feel some semblance of nature to bring me back, but the thought that it was nature that had caused this made me twist in agony at my inability to escape it.

I felt the laughter rise inside me, in my own throat. Suddenly I felt as if a knife was charging through my chest, buckling down from my neck. It seemed to plunge straight into the pit of my stomach and tear it open. I was completely abandoned, couldn't even hold onto a concept. I was swimming in a void of mental tricks to see me through the next minutes that were tentative enough on their hold on reality. I could see sinews of other bodies, covered in black hair. White and yellow flesh twisting in saggy dragging shapes. I could smell the moisture of open glands as it filled my nostrils, making them smoulder. In that moment, as I swung back against the side of the window, I saw the car pass outside. I was sure that I saw it, and as I tried to focus I made out its shape, slightly blurred around the edges as it slowed down. It seemed as if it saw my silhouette in the starkly lit room above it, before accelerating and sliding fast into the distance.

I tried to take a deep breath but the air buckled in my throat and I choked, coughing it out. I steadied myself, brought my feet back on the floor, pulled myself up with my arms. Breathed in, breathed out. Let the thoughts calm, kept them still with great effort. The car had visited again. I was still worth being watched. I still had a role to play. The feeling started to fade. I stepped forward and breathed in deeply, a deep breath that almost induced tremors in my body from the comfort it gave. I was back on my feet.

I knew that this sudden overwhelming sensation had been a sharp reminder of what I was fighting for. It was the threat of The Visitors and The Key Players taking over my mind that I was fighting against, and I had to work harder than ever not to let them succeed.

I had always known this sensation was somewhere in me, ready to burst out. I had occasionally felt it twitch at the back of my mind, but it had never engulfed me with such strength before. From then on, things started to unfurl. Perhaps because this feeling had taken me so by surprise and had been so overpowering, I felt driven by a need to act quickly to halt its return. Perhaps I neglected to use my ability to analyse, the ability that had previously been my one strength.

My attempt to seduce Tiffany again, in order to supersede Paul Reid, was a failure. I did not plan as I had planned before. I did not wait for the right opportunity; I made the mistake of using my heart and not my head. My heart had always failed me in the past, with its egotistical lunges, and my head had always had to make up for its failures. But now my head was consumed with this fear or, more precisely, the fear that this fear might return. I am almost too embarrassed to recount my failed attempt to seduce Tiffany, but always remember it as an attempt to regain control over my mind, to reclaim my home and my body, and nothing more.

I spent a couple of days planning my seduction. The first time I had spent at least two weeks but these fears were now on my heels and they were ready to overwhelm me at any point – and so I had to act fast. I had to also feel that I was acting fast, and that a solution would be in place soon so that I could return to normal. Over those next few days I started to cut corners in my research. I went with what I knew. That pretending to be fascinated by some aspect of Tiffany's work would again give me access to her. While she was out I read through her recent essays and formulated some new lines of enquiry. Perhaps because I was compelled to act fast, I didn't leave her papers in exactly the way they had been.

It was one evening in the kitchen, while Anna was still at work, when I raised an interest in Tiffany's work again. She was chopping carrots on the cutting board, with an urgency in her movements that in retrospect suggested anger with me. My first line was greeted with what was almost a sigh. When I raised a question about her work, she wanted to know "where this was going?" She said, outright, "The last time you were interested in my writing, your sudden fascination disappeared as soon as you'd slept with me. It's back again now, is it? Now you can see that I won't fall in love with you?"

"It was always there," I insisted, gently stroking her arm, the arm that ended with a knife. "It was just that I felt bad. I felt guilty for Anna and I felt that I was putting you in a difficult situation. My fascination with you has not receded at all."

There was silence for a while, while she continued to shred the vegetables with a ruthless precision that seemed to imply some pain in her that I hadn't predicted. Perhaps I hadn't thought too much about her feelings over this, and now I had to think very fast about them if I was to avoid being beaten. I moved closer and held her elbow. The chopping stopped, the evening felt suspended in mid-air. She looked up, her hair hanging slightly lank as she stared straight at the wall.

"I know what you're doing," she said, with a slight aftertaste of hatred in her words. "I know exactly what you are doing, and exactly what you have done."

"No, you don't," I retorted, grabbing her elbow and pulling her round precisely as Paul Reid had done. "You don't know the first thing that's in my head," I shouted, before I even had a second to think about what I was to reveal.

"You may well be surprised," she sneered (so much less attractive now as she began to chop again, ruthlessly), "that I know all about men like you." She pointed the tip of the knife at me.

"Don't forget," I warned, looking straight up at her. "This is my house."

"Yes, I know all about your house. Your possessions. You like to think of me as another of your possessions, don't you?" Her voice was almost shaking now.

"I would never think like that."

"Well, how else do you explain it?"

"Explain what?"

"Explain your sudden powerful, yearning interest in me, which blinks off like a light as soon as you have slept with me. You may be master of your work, but you are not master of everything in this domain."

This slight wounded me in a manner that surprised me. I grabbed both of her elbows and pushed her round, and she didn't look surprised.

"Tiffany. How can you be so wrong?" I pushed, furrowing my brown in false concern.

"You want the women in this house to be at your beck and call. At your command. Because you are the great translator. Because you think you are so attractive." She spat the words, as if they were more my own than hers, draining them of any pleasure. "Well, you have weaknesses other men don't have, and you are more unattractive for them. You only want me here so you can make me your own, when you want to."

"That isn't true, I –"

"Prove it."

"What?" I took a step back.

"Prove that you don't just have me here to control me. To use me when you want. Prove that I am still here because of a genuine fascination, that that is what all... all this is about."

"What? You are being absurd. I didn't use you, what are you –"

"If you can't even prove it, or even pretend to want to try and prove it, then there is even less to you than I already thought. I wonder what Anna would do if she knew that there was even less to you than *she* realised?"

A furious anger was rising in me. The best alternative seemed to be to throw Tiffany out of the house, her and her new lover. To take on new Visitors that I would be able to manipulate in a way she seemed determined to resist. But something about this idea stopped me, perhaps something in her genuine hurt. I was cut by the accusation that she knew what I was up to, and I was concerned at what kind of power she may have over me if I threw her out. I also wanted to beat this Paul Reid and seduce her in a way he never could; however distant a possibility that seemed right now. I wanted to erase his ghost from these rooms, from being anything that could be a threat to me. I realised that the only way I could do this would be to humour her, or at least pretend to.

"Prove it then," she said again. "Prove that your interest in me is as wonderful as you say it is, that you don't just want to use me as you use others."

"How?"

I moved closer, stroking her arm again. For the first time her muscles relaxed.

"Let Paul live here with me."

Something rose in my throat.

"What?"

"Only for a week or two. After that he is probably going away, on business. And perhaps that will convince me that you are real."

"No way. I'm not –"

"Remember. Remember what I know about us. Remember what Anna does not know. I can move out of here at any time, and my passing comments can be anything. Absolutely anything. Remember that."

"There's no need for that. I don't mind if he stays. But not for long."

She smiled, and cocked her head to one side. I felt how fast my heart was pulsing in my body, echoing through my head. Then she turned her body and held the knife against me. My heartbeat rose. The tip of the knife was pressed between my neck bones, at the opening of my shirt. I felt the tip part the cotton, and push against my flesh, squirming to cut it at any second.

"It won't. Be. For long," she whispered, pouting slightly at me at the end of each word.

I spent the evening alone in my room. At the start of the night I spread out the papers for the Lefèvre translation but soon realised that the work required a dedication that my mind couldn't allow at that moment. I spent at least on hour looking at the blank page. To its right, emblazoned in neat, sloping handwriting was the original text, twitching with innovation.

But my mind could not leave Tiffany alone. In relationships it seems that plans as elaborate as cathedrals are constructed only for the briefest wars to destroy their underlying faith. I had slaved over Tiffany as I had slaved over my translations, but I was unable to translate her language into the simplest sentences. My designs on her were merely the start of an attempt to deal with the apparitions that plagued me, and yet now I was further back from dealing with the poltergeists than ever. I felt like I was teetering on being swept away again merely at the thought of Paul Reid moving in. The whole plan had been to manage her intimacies and to slowly become familiar with The Visitors that occupied these rooms. At least a familiar evil would not be able to surprise me. Now a Visitor was coming in who was becoming more powerful than all my most intricate designs.

At times of turmoil I could never help but return to comforting thoughts of Anna. Deep in my mind, were the knot of feelings I had for her that had caused all of this to happen. My emotions for her were what had caused definitions of The Visitors and The Key Players to even come into existence. They were the reason I'd had to manage Tiffany and her lover, and the reason I had been engulfed in that feeling that had almost poisoned me.

Anna would be home at any moment, and as I waited for her I thought of the way it had first felt to touch her dark blonde hair, which had grown black as we had drawn closer. I thought of the first time we'd met, her as a student of mine, and how a discussion had led to a drink and a walk along the river. I thought of what passed between our bodies as we spoke directly into each other's faces without any self-consciousness, realising that we were creating a maze that we would inhabit together. Wasn't that any relationship? An attempt to construct a maze for you to both lose yourselves in? An attempt to create a web of sanctuary full of reference points you could draw comfort from by mere allusion?

I remembered the channels that had been created between us and how, in realising its presence, we had been drawn closer into that first crushing kiss. Blazing into my mind in vivid, potent colours, kaleidoscopic with emotion, I remembered how this had led us to pour our bodies out to each other on that first evening, to smash our limbs together. I remembered afterwards the realisation that we had left a tangible atmosphere in the room that even other people would recognise. That as lovers we had created a mist that we would dwell inside as long as we were together. That in those opening days and weeks she had talked so confidently of what I would become, of the abilities I had. That she had spoken of them not as if they were hopes or conjecture but as if the fantasies I had imagined for myself were a reality somewhere behind the scenes, waiting to be found.

In Anna's presence I embodied all of the attributes I had dreamt I could have. That rush of recognition, recognition of what I could become, had turned to longing whenever she left. In the times that we smashed our bodies back together I had wanted to embody her flesh absolutely, to move inside her in a way that would make us inseparable. The way she opened herself to me absolutely in the moments that we had alone together became so addictive. The longing soon took a darker turn as I realised that when I kissed her I was wanting to change her mouth so that another man's lips could never fit with it again. I started to dream of sculpting her body so that it could only ever fit with mine. After that I thought of how I had laboured to protect that wonderful mist, to keep that unquantifiable space sacred for us. I thought of how I had bargained for it when circumstances had changed, agreed to make allowances, and how Anna had so cleverly agreed what was sacred and untouchable between us and what we had to leave for the world.

I was still dwelling in the comfort of that imagined mist when Anna returned. She shut the door quietly and moved into the room, her back turning to me as she placed her handbag and keys on the side.

"Hello Anna," I said.

She turned and held her palm to her cleavage, as if shocked. "You made me jump," she whispered. Straight away, the curve of her lips as she spoke, the movement of her hair as her head turned made this mist wrap around me, this singular emotion rise up. I stood up and put my arms around her body, which felt slightly weak. I kissed her cheek. "How is the piece coming on?" she asked, her eyes looking just past me.

"Fine," I whispered. "I've missed you."

"I've missed you. Of course," she said steadily into my face. She opened her cigarette case and, after a shaking flash of fingers, she started calmly inhaling the cascade of smoke. "Can I see?"

I pushed the sheaf of papers towards her, as ever giving the impression of slight anger that she hadn't greeted me more warmly. The cigarette in one hand, her eyes passed over the words in flickers. "This is very good," she said. "Well? Come here then."

I sat on the edge of the table and she pouted, wrapping her hands around my head. Her fingers reached through my hair, and she kissed me delicately on the lips. "You are so talented," she whispered, among the smoke as she picked up a half-filled glass of whisky. As if a thought had suddenly occurred to her as she stood up and moved over to the laptop. A cold chill rushed through me as I realised that covering the screen to Tiffany's room was just one sheet of paper and, with a quick glance over her shoulder, I realised that the screen was still on, projecting through the white sheet, making it translucent and green with its glow. After the argument with Tiffany I had turned it back on, something I usually never did anywhere around the time Anna could come home. But on this occasion I had, just once, to study Tiffany's reactions to our argument and I had somehow forgotten to turn it off.

Now Anna's body was moving, her hand was moving so close to unsettling the papers that at once I snatched it and placed it hard on my hip. "You know, I think you smell sexy when you smoke," I croaked.

With one finger she peeled some skin from her lip, her thigh creeping closer to unsettling the page. I felt the same charge I always felt being close to her body as I placed one hand on her thigh, just a few inches above the hemline of her skirt. Suddenly I kissed her lips deeply, prising them open and she moaned slightly, kissing me back. I searched desperately for that opened feeling she used to give when I kissed her and I found traces of it, buried somewhere in her mouth when suddenly her lips withdrew.

"What's this?"

"What's what?' My answer was too quick. It was only a second until she had swept the page away and there was the screen of the camera, its unflinching portrayal of Tiffany's empty room bathed in a cheap green light looking up at us.

She stood up, her stiletto's snapping onto the floorboards. "What the hell is this?" She looked at me, her eyebrows creased in anger. I had a horrible feeling that the look would never leave her face again. "What. Are. You doing?" she hissed.

I looked outside. I realised no car had stopped outside tonight.

"My mind has stayed yours," I replied.

There was a pause as the implications of these words sank in. Her head turned to one side.

"We're not getting into this again." She looked straight at me, her lips curled slightly. "Have you been watching Tiffany getting dressed? Am I just not enough?"

There was a pause, and her voice came back. Louder this time, in a way that sent a chill through me. "Am I too old?"

"Anna, I've done nothing wrong. We agreed that our minds would be kept for each other, only wanting each other, and I haven't broken that. I haven't broken the pact."

"And your body? Under my roof?"

"It's my roof," I shouted, snapping to my feet.

"Under *your* roof then?" She flung the words out, more an accusation than a question. "And what exactly have *you* been doing with *your* body under *your* roof?"

There was an endless pause.

"It was only ever to keep The Visitors away."

She waited. "Not this again. Don't you dare bring this up again. I never even *knew* if that conversation was real. You can't be serious."

"If I ever slept with Tiffany it was only so that I could deal with The Visitors in this house. With the people who have been intimate in *my* rooms." I tore at my hair. "It was only *ever* so that I could deal with what has happened under this roof."

"We agreed," she said hoarsely, stabbing the cigarette at me. "We agreed that what happened with our bodies was inevitable. That infidelity with our bodies was okay. But that our minds. That our minds would only ever be kept for each other. You've used your mind. You've planted a camera, you've seduced her, you've kept all this behind my back. None of this was agreed. If there was any pact, you have broken it. You've *completely* destroyed it."

I felt the ghosts ready to charge back over me. I suddenly had a terrible fear that some violent impulse was about to overwhelm me. I wanted that mist back; I wanted its comfort to enshroud me so badly. I wanted Anna's brow to uncrease and kiss me in a way that told me that her body was open for me, that welcomed me into her soul again. I didn't want to have to control; I wanted to love, purely and simply, and for there to be no Visitors – nothing but us.

The dizziness was rising now, so strong that I felt it would push me over.

"Anna, please. I have had to deal with your Key Players. I have had to deal with your Visitors."

"Never in this house. If you have ever been haunted by ghosts those ghosts have never lived in this house; it's only ever happened outside. I would never allow it!" She screamed the last sentence, suddenly slamming down the glass tumbler, sending thick shards of glass into the air. I knew, with the awful feeling of a man losing something that he loves, something that he will ruminate over for endless hours to come, that I was watching my life as a man watches a car crash. With no control. Completely separated from any possibility of affecting how events could unfold.

"I have had to deal with The Key Players and I have managed it, I have buried them. I only had The Visitors to deal with, and I was *so* close," I answered.

"The Key Players, as you always call them, are my *clients*. They are how I make my money and how I keep the clothes on my back while you spend years over a few sentences for some academic to read. Those clients are the money that keeps this roof over my head. And if I am ever too tired to make love to you like I do to them, then perhaps that is because I know I have to keep the money coming in to fuel your obsession."

"You could have got a job."

"Not to raise the money we need to keep this luxury; it would never do that. Either you'd have to change or I'd have to do that. And I am hardly a common whore; it is a couple of very rich Key Players, not even very often, who keep this roof over our heads. You *know* that."

"But you're mine. I can be completely poverty stricken and be happy as long as I *just* have your body to myself. You *always* agreed that my body would be prioritised over other men's and there's no way that has happened. That was what The Formula was for, to work out what we needed from other people and what we needed to save for each other."

"I *want* this life. I always said I wanted this life, and it has to be earned. That is part of the reason I loved you, and I did it for you and for us. This life has to be bought, it doesn't come free, and it takes sacrifices." She paused for breath, her once beautiful face smouldering in the flames of recriminations held inside for so long. "You agreed that you would change with me, that we would change together, but if you can't understand why your body is not a priority to me all of the time, then you have *not* changed," she shouted.

"Certain things can change. But we agreed that certain things would be mine..."

"Not this again. Not this strange act that you seem to think ties us together. Is that what all this is about? This one thing that you know another man could never get from me? The one thing that it is unlikely another woman would ever do for you?" She stopped, turned the side of her head. "This is where this *obsession* stems from, isn't it? This lust to somehow control everyone who enters my life? Because you know only I would do that *thing* for you, that thing that somehow makes me yours. That you can't afford to lose. Because you'll *never* get it again."

"It's just a way of making myself feel that I can't be replaced."

"It's pathetic."

"No. You're just focusing on this to find ways out, Anna, when *all* of this stems from you. You being unable to make your lover feel unique. You and your other men, who we could remove *so* easily."

There was an endless pause as the words hung in the air. In a way that only a lover can, I saw familiar arguments formulate behind her eyes.

"Even if I did give them up. And there were no more Key Players. And we both somehow found a way to have no more Visitors in our lives; you would never be able to live with the ghosts of my previous lovers. Of men who have loved me before you were even in my life. That is what makes *you* different. It is them that fester in this room and plague you, just as much as anything in the present."

"It isn't. It is the constant reminder of them by the acts that you do every day that makes them a threat. And, anyway, you won't stop what you're doing. So we can *never* know, can we?"

The next sentence came from her so slowly; it was as if every word was directly aimed at my heart.

"I only ever loved you for your mind. And now your mind is no longer mine, you are no use to me," she said.

I breathed in.

"You are nothing to me," she screamed, and then raised the broken tumbler in the air, its jagged edges the last image that I can recall.

Those events now seem to now exist behind a film. I know that they happened to me, but they seem intangible, unreachable. One of the fallouts of what Anna then did to me is that I find it difficult to sequence events and to logically work out the best actions to be undertaken. I'm not unaware of the irony as it seems that my inability to logically make sense of relationships was what caused this to happen in the first place. My way of looking at the world was a consequence of trying to deal with Anna's job, to deal with those ghosts that could not leave me alone, and yet my strategy was so flawed that it caused me to end up here.

Why did I need to think of Visitors, and Key Players, and

Formulas? Why could I not accept that someone cannot be my own? It's also ironic that Anna loved me for my mind, but my mind is so damaged now that I could not even write this myself. It had to be dictated to one of the few people that I trust in the hospital where I live. By one of the people who now complete all of the daily tasks that I used to complete myself, tasks that I used to take for granted.

When I now struggle to make sense of the world, I know I have time to reflect on what happened and to make sense of it. In the past I was guilty of not being sensual about the way I related to the world. I was guilty of analysing my private life to the point that I made it violent and dangerous. Here, left alone to turn over the past and to recreate it, knowing that my thoughts cannot affect how I conduct my life, I can dwell inside realms of my mind that are more sensuous and perfect than the real world could ever offer. You may think that living here, having little interaction with the real world, I am ignorant about real life. That left to dwell upon the endless and often beautiful possibilities of my mind, I live in a state of ignorance. But to be free from the constraints of the real world, to be able to dwell in these realms and to have the agony of choice removed, I finally have the potential to be happy.

7

A.J. Kirby

The buzzer groans in complaint; like me, it never really seems happy when someone comes to the gated entrance of our flats and rings up for us to let them through. Because we're flat number one, we do get far more visitors than we're supposed to. We get postmen, suspicious-looking characters dropping off rainforest-buckling packages of takeaway menus, little moustachioed gasmen here to read the meter. We get local kids pressing the buzzer for a prank as they wait for a bus on the main road and we sometimes get wide-boys from the brewery asking that we can move our wheels in order that they can get their lorry in front of the bar downstairs and drop off their expensive beer so it can be watered-down properly.

Perhaps this dripping water-torture of the city's miscellaneous have-nots that arrive at our gate all share one thing; perhaps they believe that Flat 1 is the home of the caretaker or something. Perhaps they believe that I have nothing better to do than continuously traipse across our polished-wood floor so that I can offer them my assistance.

Some of them ask me where they can find the bus-stop which will take them to Newton Mills. I tell them that it's a bus that they are looking for; bus-stops don't actually go anywhere. Some of them ask me what time it is; I tell them that it's time that they should 'do one.' And yet, despite my best efforts, they still flock back to press the buzzer for Flat 1. The way that they all stare so expectantly into the pinhole video camera in the door access system convinces me that they truly believe that I am some kind of free information service, like the flat's own resident Wikipedia.

City-living, the estate agents called it. I know better now; living-hell, I call it. We'd have been better off living in the suburbs. At least you get a bit of privacy there.

The buzzer groans again. It's a low, insistent sound; it can reach right into your dreams and pluck you out of bed with Keira Knightley. It could be a wonder in the world of science; they could use that sound to wake up even the most deeply-slumbering coma patients.

'Can you get that?' I yell. Considering that we live in a flat which has, at best four rooms – I'd get the Trades Descriptions people in on that supposed 'box-room' if I had more time on my hands; I don't know of any box that would fit in there apart from a match-box – we do spend a lot of time randomly shouting through the walls at each other, hoping that we'll hear what the other has to say above our creaking cappuccino machine or the mood music that she puts on the Bang and Olufsen.

No answer. I stand there in front of the cinema-screen sized mirror above the fireplace, hair-sculpting mousse congealing on my fingers and consider whether it is worth another shout. She's got selective hearing, my missus; she'd bloody-well hear me if I whispered something about her alarm-bell obsessive collection of candles on the decorative display shelf (or mantelpiece as I call it).

'Rachel?' I scream. 'The buzzer's gone. Will you answer it?'

The buzzer doesn't bother her like it does me. She can escape from it during the day when she trots off to work. I, on the other hand, weave my wonderful webs on the internet from the comfort of my own home, meaning that I get all the straggling commuters in the morning, the local drunks in the afternoon, and the merry pranksters on their way home from school. I suppose I've grown to hate the thing. I've even switched it off so as to preserve my peace of mind, but missed supermarket food-order deliveries and random visits from friends which I blissfully ignored put paid for. Rachel wanted it put back on again.

Another buzz. Finally, she steps into the room and I realise why she hasn't heard my increasingly frantic calls for assistance. She has been in the shower. She's still got one towel wrapped around her sleek, dark flowing locks and another covering most of her supple body. I know that this is simply her uniform for crossing from the bathroom to the bedroom. It's badly designed, Flat 1; in order to get from one to the other, you have to pass in front of the huge windows in the living area. Perhaps the architect has one of the flats in the new block, which overlooks this one, and he quite fancied copping a look at my bird.

'Rach, will you get the buzzer on the way through?' I ask again, making busy with the sculpting mousse.

'I can't,' she says, sneaking past me on tip-toes as though I won't see her. I know what she's trying to do. She read that article in *Women on Top* about drip-drying being better for her body than towel-drying and she's mad-keen to get into the bedroom where she can stand around nude and let nature take its course. And fair play to her; she *does* always make these superhuman efforts to look her best. She's one of those girls that you see around town that are almost too beautiful for people to pester. Her features are sharp, and she gives off the impression that she's sharp with her tongue, too. But that won't help the situation with the buzzer.

'Are you expecting someone?' I ask, this time the annoyance creeping into my voice.

'Mark! You know what's happening this weekend; are you being deliberately brick-headed?'

I stare at her for a moment and weigh up my options. I have absolutely no clue what she is talking about. But to allow her to see any slack-jawed incomprehension on my part would be to invite all hell to break loose. I *could* just go and answer the buzzer, of course, but I've always had that dangerous stubborn streak inside me. If she is so concerned about what we've got planned for this weekend then why is she not dressed and ready to go? Why has she not leaped out of the shower, answered the buzzer and allowed me to style my hair in peace?

She sighs and flounces off into the bedroom. The heavy fire door slams behind her. I'm sure that she didn't mean to do it, but it is convenient the way that the door does that. Hands still sticky with almost dry mousse, I start to walk over to the video entry system. As if to compound my bad mood, Mr. Snootles chooses to start doing that thing where he trails in and out of my legs, virtually tripping me up with every step. Rachel claims that he does this when he's hungry, or just to be companiable, but deep down, I know that he does it because he wants me to have a nasty fall and bash my head against the hard wood floor. Then he can have his darling Rachel all to his slippery grey self.

Mr. Snootles is like Cato in the *Pink Panther* series; always springing impromptu attacks on me as though checking that I'm on the ball. If I'm late for an appointment, you can guarantee that the sneaky bastard will be there, balancing on top of a door, waiting to attack my newly coiffured hair before I go out. If I'm handling boiling water, he'll choose that exact moment to wrap his tail around my legs. Rachel never sees any of this. All she ever sees is the way that he curls up on her lap in the evening, that great self-satisfied grin on his chops, while I try to make myself comfortable on the piece of furniture that I refuse to call a pouffe.

'Get out of the way, Sy,' I snarl at him. Although he's unspokenly Rachel's cat, I was the one that named him, fed him, looked after him at first. Because of his big chops, I named him after Sy Snootles, the lead singer of the band in *Star Wars*. I thought it was a pretty cool name, as it happens. Rachel thought that *Mr.* Snootles was better. I thought it made him sound like Little Lord Fauntleroy; spoiled. Which he was, of course, being the supposed cure-all that was intended to bring us closer together again. I blamed *Women on Top* for that bloody stupid idea.

Mr. Snootles finally snootles off once I reach the video entry system. I swear that his tail is swishing madly at the air like a light-sabre; he's furious that he's not managed to kill me yet despite his best efforts.

'Yeah?' I say pressing the button to speak. All I can see on the small video screen is a close-up of a face. The face is so close that I can't even tell whether it is a woman's or a man's face. Sometimes you can tell that the no-marks that buzz-on for us have absolutely no clue about technology. They don't realise that by standing so close to the camera, they'll knacker up the image.

'Hi Marky,' says a breezy, sing-song Jar Jar Binks voice. It sounds like someone's taking the piss. I still don't know who it is, but it sounds as though it is one of Rachel's interminable university friends. They are the only ones left that still dare to call me 'Marky.'

'Step back from the camera,' I snap. 'I can't see you.'

Slowly, out of the blur, I start to define features on a chubby face. I see a little button nose and a tiny mouth, which is blowing snotty bubbles. I see a little woollen hat propped jauntily on his little head. I see the young face of Jack Richards, the four-month old son of Rachel's oldest friend, Samantha. Evidently Samantha thinks that I'll be somehow charmed by this pretence that a kid that can't even walk or talk or even clean up his own arse has taken it upon himself to climb four feet up a concrete wall and press the buzzer to my flat. I'm unaccountably angry with Samantha, and also with

Jack, too. But then, thinking about it, maybe this boiling rage *is* accountable; I've just remembered Rachel's big plans for this weekend. It hits me like a train.

We're looking after Jack. Two whole shit-covered, baby-talking, booze-free days while Samantha goes off to some goddam health retreat to get over the fact that Jack's dad scarpered as soon as he realised what he'd let himself in for. Sighing, I press the big button with a key on it and allow the thing that I understand least in the outside world into my inner sanctum. I must be crackers; if only I'd ignored the damn buzzer.

I go back to the mirror and try to rescue my hair. It's as though some Person from Porlock has interrupted my work of art in mid-creative-flow, and there's simply no coming back from the mess that flaps wildly back at me in the mirror. The problem with this style of 'intentionally messy' hair that's all the rage at the moment, is that it's only one small step for mankind away from actual bird's-nest. My hair needs to be slapped-down, waxed-up and chemically-treated before I'd dream of setting foot out of the door.

Talking of doors; where's Samantha and Cute Little Jack (as he has apparently been re-Christened)? I buzzed them through the gate about five minutes ago and still no sign of them. With a pang of something, which might have been guilt, I suddenly remember that Samantha now has to walk around with a veritable army-barracks of supplies these days. She'll probably have been struggling with her pram and her NHS-crippling bagful of nappies. *I'll* probably be in trouble with Rachel for not helping.

Action stations; I run to the door, somehow managing to avoid the attentions of Mr. Snootles. Just as I open it, I see the tired-looking face of Samantha. She's sweating what with the effort it's taken to get into the goddam lift. Cute Little Jack is wailing and smells like the bin store down in the basement. I try not to meet the eye of my neighbour who has opened the door opposite and is snarling in contempt at me. Perhaps he thinks that CLJ is my offspring from some ill-advised one night stand way back in the mists of time. Perhaps he fears that CLJ is going to be dumped on me for the rest of my life, thus ruining all of his afternoon sleeping bouts with such awful displays. In a way, you could see why he'd get that impression. For my meetings with Samantha have *always* had an air of unresolved awkwardness about them. Although she's never been a Rachel in the looks department – and certainly not now, when she looks so matronly – there's always been something about her. She's the kind of girl that always falls too deeply for men; she's always got this moonish, spellbound look to her – like Natalie Portman in the new *Star Wars* films – that convinces you that you could do pretty much anything you want to her and she'd just take it and perhaps murmur a polite thank you. There's something about her that makes you simultaneously shake some life into her and give her a shoulder to cry on; a recipe for disaster at the end of parties when everyone's had too much to drink.

'Hi Samantha,' I say, pecking her on the cheek and ushering her into the flat. I make sure that I grab the bag of nappies before Rachel gets a chance to see me not helping. 'How are you?' I ask, just to be polite. I already know the answer. It's written into her face; it's carved into the prominent frown-lines on her forehead and effortlessly shines through the rushed make-up job.

'I'm worn out, Mark,' she sighs. For a moment, I fear that she is about to cry, but her lip quivers and that's it. I'm safe for now.

Or maybe not. When asking a friend of a friend how they are, there is an unspoken agreement that you don't really care. All you are doing is making polite conversation. Bring a baby into the equation and all that changes. Evidently, Samantha feels that my enquiry deserves a frank and full confession of all of her medical difficulties since she's popped out the little bundle of fun. It's the kind of thing that I would have been shocked by before I started reading *Women on Top* on the bog while I was dropping my own kids off at the pool.

'I can't seem to lose the weight that I put on. My ankles are always swollen. I'm a walking pharmacy. My nipples are sore and bleed in the mornings. I keep getting sick and I'm worried about it being passed on to Jack.'

I stare out of the window. There's a bloke on the third floor – roughly at the same height as our flat – that works-out basically twenty-four seven. He's a beast for his weights. Only problem is, in all the time I've been living here, I haven't seen his body develop in at all the way it should be doing. He's going about it all wrong; still looks kinda like a Gamorrean Guard. Sometimes, when I do my own weights, I do it in front of the windows. I kinda hope that he'll see me and take some tips on board.

Suddenly, I realise that Samantha is staring at me expectantly as though she's waiting for me to respond to some question; probably whether I think she looks fat. Come to think of it, she is a bit more blurry round the edges. She's wearing baggy clothes and what looks like a man's coat as though she doesn't want people to notice the few extra pounds on her hips or some new curves she's developed.

'Rachel'll be out in a minute,' I say, for want of anything better to emerge from my ransacked mind. Already, this unfortunate twosome have taken over our beautiful front room. They've turned minimalist elegance into jumble sale disarray with their collection of bags, toys, nappies and clothes. 'Would you like a drink while you're waiting?'

'I'd kill for a glass of wine,' she admits, 'but I'm driving.'

I smile affectionately. Falsely. Wine hadn't been on offer. When had I presented this fallen woman and her terrible man's coat with a wine list? When had I invited her to sample some of Italy's finest and most expensive blends (a Wine Club Special Delivery for a fine customer) so that she could waste them by getting CLJ's snot in the cut-crystal glass?

'Tea then?' I ask, gingerly.

She nods, resigned-like, as though calmly submitting to her lot in life. I feel like advising her that wine was the thing that got her in this whole damn mess in the first place, but obviously I don't. The last thing I need is a screaming match and this woman looks close to the edge. Not only does she have big dark saddlebags under her eyes, but her old spots have come up. Her once-fine auburn hair now looks greasy and I swear has traces of CLJ's sick mixed-up in there somewhere. Her skin is deathly pale, apart from on her face, where she's over-compensated and in this light, she looks a little orange.

Come to think of it, maybe a nice glass of Pinot Grigot would have been a good idea. It would at least do something to break through the awful silences and the deep, unspoken things. Neither of us wants to be here. As I make the brews, I listen to her baby-talking with him. The lad will grow up not-all-there if she continues in this fashion.

'Mummy-Wummy's going away for a couple of days, Jacky-Wacky. She's going to leave you with good-old Auntie Wachel. We like Auntie Wachel, don't we, Jacky-Wacky?'

For a moment, I sense a chance of victory to be snatched from the gaping Sarlacc Pit of defeat; Rachel chooses that exact moment to come back out from the bedroom. I suddenly have this euphoric vision of my darling girlfriend telling this pathetic woman to leave. Rachel *isn't* the kind of person that you can easily call 'old' or 'Auntie'. In fact, she's the kind of woman that looks as though she is so well-proportioned, so perfect, that things like family and the ageing process are not part of her world. But, cursed fate, this is a new Rachel now, and it has been ever since the arrival of CLJ. Instead of knocking Samantha's cheeky head off – 'who you calling old?' – she trots in, hair still not properly dry, and collects the baby from her friend's lap.

'Hewwo, Cute Little Jacky-Wacky,' she sing-songs. And suddenly I feel as though I've entered some alternate dimension. This is not the flat that I know or the Darth Vader girlfriend that I know. It is not even the Samantha I know. Even Sy Snootles looks wrong, hovering back there by the bathroom door. But he's right, the moggy; he's right to be wary of these intruders and the changes that they'll bring. Maybe this could be the thing that bonds us; a mutual antipathy to CLJ.

Unfortunately, Rachel catches me looking at Snootles. 'And don't worry about the cat,' she says to Samantha.

'They do carry diseases... not great for a little one...'

'We're taking him to the cattery for the weekend, aren't we Mark?'

I wonder if Snootles knows his fate? I wonder if he's as forgetful as me? I still can't remember this supposed conversation where Rachel and I *agreed* that we'd disrupt our whole weekend just so Samantha could have a bit of me-time. One thing I am sure about is who will be paying for the cattery, and who'll be the one forced to try to coerce him into that carry-case that he so hates.

'I'll take him now if you like,' suggests Samantha. 'That way, you can both get to know Jacky-Wacky right from the start.'

She smiles then, as though she knows that far from helping, she is in fact storing up the problems for us later, when he's collected, all gift-wrapped and ready to attack from the cattery on Sunday.

'That'll be lovely,' coos Rachel. 'Are you sure you wouldn't mind?

Honestly, the way Rachel is talking, it is as though Samantha, not her, is the one bestowing favours. When the kettle finally boils, Samantha and Rachel are already embroiled in a deep conversation about feeding times and changing nappies.

Half-heartedly, I dig out the cat-carrier and wouldn't you just know it, as soon as Mr. Snootles spots it, he scarpers onto the top of one of the cupboards. I proceed to climb on the damn pouffe and try to follow him up there. Only CLJ shows the slightest bit of interest in my toils, emitting a loud belch as though by way of commentary. I shoot him an angry look and try to lever myself upwards, using the fridge door handle as a foothold. Mr. Snootles hisses in warning from somewhere higher up.

As I'm hanging by three fingers of one hand – the other is holding the cat-carrier – Mr. Snootles moves closer to the edge. I see that look of delight pass his evil eyes as he realises my predicament. And then he starts to lick my fingers; his rough tongue dances between them, tickling and probing. I know that I'm going to fall.

'Rachel!' I yell. 'Will you help...'

Too late; my fingers lose their grip. The fridge door handle makes a loud cracking noise under the weight of my foot. I feel myself falling backwards. Suddenly, everything's in slow-motion. I anticipate the pain that I'll feel as my unprotected back hits the floor. I know that it will be far worse than the pain I felt when I got into that scuffle with Samantha's ex. I know that I won't be able to hide these injuries from Rachel. I look up at the top of the cupboard through wide-eyes. I'm worried that the last thing I'll ever see will be that shit-eating grin on Mr. Snootles' chops. And the last thing I'll hear will be his goddam *purring*. The little bastard is in ecstasy that he's done this to me.

And then, with a superhuman effort, I reach out my arm

again and manage to grab onto the collar around his neck. If I die, I'm thinking, then at least I'll be able to take him with me. I feel the weight of him; he's actually quite a big cat these days. Maybe it's the lack of exercise; he can't exactly *go* anywhere what with us being in the city centre, and so he's house-bound just like me. His agility has never been allowed to develop properly. Like me, he falls awkwardly. Like me, he lets out this pained cry as he does so.

I land on the pouffe less disastrously than I'd expected. For a moment, I worry that I've been paralysed. Where is the back-cracking sacking pain I'd anticipated? Soon though, I do start to feel pain. Mr. Snootles is scratching and biting at my white-knuckled hand, which is still gripping his collar far too tightly.

'Let go of him, Mark,' growls Rachel, who has come quickly now that she's seen that her darling might be hurt. She slaps my hand off him and quickly and efficiently deposits him into the cat-carrier. He allows her to do this as meekly as a lamb.

'Are you okay, Mr. Snootles?' she asks, through the bars of his cage. He meows pathetically.

'What about me?' I yell. 'How about asking if I'm okay?'

Rachel and Samantha are both staring at me now as though I've committed some terrible crime. Rachel shakes her head dismissively; Samantha looks up at the sky, doing a great impression of exasperation.

'I'd better go,' she says. 'Before anything else happens.'

Rachel nods. I watch from the pouffe as the two dazzlingly self-righteous women wander back to the sofa area and to CLJ. I watch them with barely disguised contempt as they coo over him some more. Samantha is actually crying now, as though it's not just two days she's away for, but some longer, undefined period of time. Perhaps she fears she'll drown in the Jacuzzi at the health retreat. Or maybe she's scared that the masseur will be too rough with her and end up battering her to death. Or, scarier than all of that, perhaps she'll get so used to the good life that she won't want to come back to a world of duty and responsibility.

Samantha has left the building and she seems to have taken Rachel's confidence with her. Both of us now are kneeling behind the sofa, arms tucked under our chins, staring over into the cot at CLJ, waiting for him to *do* something but secretly hoping that he won't. We watch him gently kicking with his legs and blowing saliva bubbles from his slack mouth. In a way, the whole thing reminds me of a nature documentary about a rare species which has just been discovered in the depths of the rainforest jungle. This creature is so alien to us that we can *only* watch and wonder. It's like that sometimes with Mr. Snootles too; I wonder how something so small can be sentient and feeling. My eyes keep searching CLJ's all-in-one blue suit looking for the power button.

'Are you okay?' breathes Rachel. For a moment, I believe that she is talking to CLJ and don't respond. I should have known better; *are you okay* is the thing Rachel and I always ask each other. And I don't mean in a sweet, begging for reassurance kinda way or even that she's concerned about my earlier fall, I mean that we use the phrase as filler for the awkward silences. It's like lettuce in sandwiches. It doesn't mean anything. Just like when I asked Samantha how she was feeling; neither of us expect anything other than a grunted assent in response to *are you okay*.

She reaches over and touches my wrist. Before I realise what I'm doing, I flinch away from her. We've grown so far apart now that we're more like flatmates. Or like ships that pass in the night, to use that old pub-saying. I suppose I spend too much time in front of my laptop screen. I suppose I should make time for her when she gets home from work. But it's not my fault that she goes to bed so goddam early every night, is it? It's not my fault that she has to get up early too, while I lounge around in the night-smelly sheets waiting for her to leave so that I can catch a few more z's before I need to get up and start on my own work again.

It's a relationship of convenience; only through living together can we afford to live in a place like this and drive the nice wheels and assuage Mr. Snootles' seemingly unquenchable thirst for milk. Only then can we have the Bang and Olufsen system on the walls and the ridiculously expensive cappuccino machine that neither of us really knows how to use.

I look at her, leaning over the top of the sofa with her long dark hair now curling because she's not dried it properly. It's usually sleek and shiny, like in the adverts on the television, but now it looks like that of a normal, everyday bus-stop woman. I hardly recognise her. I realise with a lurching feeling in my stomach that this is because she has this hopeful look in her eyes. It's like for the first time in god knows when, she needs me here. Perhaps we're both having the same realisation at the same time.

'What should we do with him?' I ask, with renewed effort.

'We could take him to the park?' says Rachel. I don't know if she's asking or telling, what with the way that *most* of the things she says are concluded with this god-awful inflection at the end. In some television programme that I watched once hosted by Stephen Fry, he claimed that this was because of kids growing up raised by the television; most of the kids our age were immersed in soaps like *Home and Away* and *Neighbours* from an early age, and gradually started to talk like the young Aussies and the Yanks. I wonder if in a few years time, we'll all be talking like our text messages; kids seem to get them earlier and earlier nowadays. I wonder when CLJ will get his first mobile phone.

'The park?' she repeats. This time I know that it is unquestionably a question; it has that begging tone to it that she uses when she tries to get me to go out and do something. The two words are also full of the knowledge that an affirmative response from me is deemed to be in the 'highly unlikely' category.

'Looks like it might rain,' I say, with practiced decisiveness. 'We'll have to take the whole kit and caboodle; umbrellas, the pram, a change of clothes, a flask of hot tea. We can't have Jacky-Wacky getting wet or cold...'

Rachel gives me a fluttery little smile. For a second I think that she's bought my excuse, but not for long. When I look back over at her, her face has settled into that sulky expression she uses when she hasn't got her own way. She likes being out and about; she likes putting the fear of god into people with her frosty glare. She likes daring builders on construction sites to wolf-whistle at her. She likes it when men have to give her that surreptitious double-take look before they shuffle away, back to their bus-stop women and their humdrum bus-stop lives.

I hate being out and about. I hate the air of menace that exudes from the men that see her on my arm and automatically want to prove themselves against me. I hate the way that people become so jealous. They are all like children; they think that if they can't have a woman like that, then nobody should be able to. Samantha's ex-boyfriend is out there somewhere too, and after my last run-in with him, I can't walk down the street without seeing shadows by the wheelie bins and angry eyes burning out from the darkest ginnels and passageways. Flat 1 is my safe-house, just like it is for Mr. Snootles.

In here, we're kings of all we survey. And we've got everything we need. We've got the internet, the television, the games console, the well-stocked wine rack, the takeaway menus, the luxury shower, the cappuccino machine, the rowing machine, the weights, the pouffe, the decorative display shelf, the collector's-item *Star Wars* figures, the Alan Majchrowicz print, the subtle lighting, the wooden floors, the exposed brick-work, the king-sized bed... Oh, and CLJ. I forgot about him for a moment, but a ripe smell emanating from his nether regions soon reminds me of his presence.

Rachel wrinkles her nose but doesn't gag like I'd thought she would. When I first met her, she took about three showers a day and washed the sheets on an almost nightly basis. She had, she claimed, a very sensitive sense of smell. This meant that my Camel cigarettes were out; unless I wanted to go outside to smoke. It also meant that for the first few months I was seeing her, I never dared go for a shit in my own house lest it offend her nostrils. There were times when I could hardly move I was that desperate, but I developed a kind of obsession about it. I thought my natural bodily smells would be the thing that would drive her away. Even now, I make sure that I shower before she comes home from work.

But now look at her. CLJ has just soiled himself right in the middle of our majestically stylish front room like one of the old drunks that pass out in the bin store and she's barely even noticed. In fact, come to think of it, she's sporting this indulgent smile on her face like CLJ's social faux-pas is already forgiven.

'Has Jacky-Wacky done a shit?' I ask.

Rachel narrows her eyes and whispers: 'Not in front of the baby you don't, mister.'

'What you worried about?' I ask. 'It's not like he'll understand what I'm saying...'

Rachel elbows me out of the way and moves round the sofa. She picks up the little bundle of fun and dangles him over her shoulder, sniffing at his bottom.

'Pass me the changing mat from out of that bag,' she orders.

Meekly I submit to her will, just as Mr. Snootles had done.

The 'bag' is a euphemism; the carrying-case that Samantha has so kindly landed on us is actually the size of a small lorry. Even so, I can hardly unzip it such is the vast, over-flowing amount of crap that's been packed.

'Anyone would think Jacky-Wacky's moving in,' I mutter, discarding tiny socks, rattles, dummies and books on my search for the elusive changing mat. 'I didn't bring this amount of stuff when we moved here.'

'That was because in those days, you used to have a life outside the flat,' snarls Rachel. I hadn't noticed her getting angry, but evidently *something* that I've done – even if it was something entirely unconsciously done – has set her off. Perhaps she's still irritable about my perceived assault on her cat, or perhaps it is just my general uselessness and my seeming inability to find the largest single object in the goddam body-bag.

Finally, I find it. It's made of that terrible cheap material that sings when you run your fingernails against it; the sound goes through me. It must be easier to clean or something. Or does Samantha shop in the bargain bins now that CLJ's come along? I throw it over to Rachel and zip up the bag again.

In seconds, Rachel whips his blue all-in-one suit off him and starts unfastening his nappy. She moves with an easy speed, which makes it look as though she's done this sort of thing before, even though I'm pretty sure she hasn't. She isn't put off by the smell, or by the kicking from his little legs. She isn't even put off her stride when the nappy comes loose and a fountain of baby-shit sprays out onto our magnolia wall. I once spilled a bit of blackcurrant juice on that wall and she didn't speak to me for a week. Even Mr. Snootles got the cold shoulder after pissing on the rug, but here, she doesn't even seem bothered. I am literally open-mouthed, such is my shock at seeing her so willing to throw herself in at the runny, yellowy-brown deep-end. Even CLJ seems a little over-awed. He's not even making those cooing sounds or blowing snot bubbles out of his nose.

'Your turn next time,' she says ominously as she sellotapes the new nappy shut and hands the changing mat back to me. 'And will you get a cloth for the wall?'

CLJ has been crying non-stop for about an hour. It feels like longer; my ears are ringing and we've already had our polite neighbour knocking-on to complain on two separate occasions. The weirdo from the flat above keeps stamping on the floor too, making sure that his own grievances are heard. Jack's been crying for so long now that his face has begun to take on a purple hue and I fear that he might have deafened himself.

Rachel and I have tried everything; we've offered him warm milk, checked his nappy, rocked him in the cot, held him in our arms, sung to him and stroked his back. Rachel's tried to read him a story from one of the books in the body-bag and I've tried pulling faces at him. Nothing has worked. No, not even Rachel's CD of whale-song that she bought when she went through her relaxation-techniques phase.

'I'm going to call Sam,' says Rachel, rifling through her handbag to find her mobile phone.

'Probably a good idea,' I muse. 'She'll be able to get back here in about an hour and a half and...'

'We're not asking her to come back,' says Rachel, who now has the phone in her hand and is rifling through the address book. 'I just need a bit of advice... I need some help here and you're not doing a good job of it.'

Before I can even attempt to answer her latest jibe, Rachel has the phone up by her ear and a finger on her lips. She cocks her head and tries to listen to the ringing over the sound of CLJ's increasingly desperate yells.

'Come on, come on,' says Rachel, sounding worried.

I move onto the sofa next to her, starting to feel a little concerned myself now.

'She's not answering,' says Rachel, clicking off the phone.

'Don't worry,' I say, trying to sound as relaxed as possible. 'She's probably in some treatment room or whatever they have in these places. Maybe she's having her nails done. Just call her back and leave a message.'

Rachel actually smiles. She looks pleased that I'm here and able to play the voice of reason. For once, she does exactly what I say. She calls back and waits for the answerphone message to kick-in.

'Hi Sam,' she says, her voice sounding strange and put-on somehow. This is her phone-voice, the voice she reserves for use with her friends; the one that makes her sound less composed than she usually is. 'This is Rachel. I'm calling because... well, there's nothing to worry about, but Jack just keeps on crying and crying and won't stop. There's nothing seriously wrong, but I was just wondering if you had any suggestions... uh... thanks, Sam. Just don't worry okay?'

She clicks off the phone once again and starts to put it back into her handbag.

'Wait!' I shout. Suddenly, CLJ has stopped crying all on his own. He is now staring at Rachel's gold-covered phone with great interest. Rachel sees this too now and without a moment's hesitation, hands over her most treasured possession to a four-month old child. CLJ tries to grasp the phone in his tiny fat fingers. His eyes are wide-open with delight, his crying jag now long-forgotten. He *loves* the phone; loves the weight of it, the fact that it feels expensive.

'He'll be in telesales when he's a bit older,' I say, my relief at the flat's renewed silence putting me into a buoyant mood. Rachel gives me this look that tells me that she's about as sick of my lame jokes as I am of her refusal to ever answer the buzzer.

BRRRRZZZZZZ. BRRRRZZZZZZ.

The noise cuts into my sleep like the constant prod of a sharp knife into my chest. I yank the cushion over my head and try to settle back down into the dreamy caresses of Keeley Hawes, the actress of choice recently. I don't feel guilty about this fling with Keeley. Indeed, if it ever came down to it and I had to explain my actions to Keira, I could always call upon the fact that through squinted eyes, Keeley and Keira look pretty similar. Hell, even their names sound similar...

BRRRRZZZZZZ. BRRRRZZZZZZ.

Use the force, Mark; use the force... Nope; no good. Sleep won't come back to me now, whatever I do. Thoughts are already starting to dance round my head, and these thoughts don't tread lightly; they wear goddam Doc Marten boots, apparently. And whoever's wearing them likes po-going around, crushing my early morning optimism into the chalk-dust floor.

BRRRRZZZZZZ. BRRRRZZZZZZ.

There's nothing for it now but to get up. I crane open my tired eyes and for a moment, don't recognise my surroundings. Then I remember: halfway through CLJ's midnight caterwauling last night, I'd simply stormed out of the bedroom and dragged an old blanket out of the cupboard in order that I could sleep on our too-small couch. But even the front room looks different in the cold light of day; CLJ's jumble sale of crap is still littered over every surface and there is a faint smell of shit in the air.

'I love the smell of shit in the morning,' I mumble, with a nod to *Apocalyse Now*, as I creak up from where I've bent myself into the sofa. And it's a fitting reference too, considering the fact that everything feels faintly post-apocalyptic.

Gingerly, I walk towards the door entry system. It's still in the back of my mind that Mr. Snootles may have escaped from imprisonment at the cattery and somehow made his way back here, just so he can catch me unawares. As I pass the cinema-screen mirror, I note how bedraggled I look. Give me a couple of days, and I'll have the same saddlebags as Samantha. As it is, I have this big red mark on my face from where CLJ's discarded rattle dug into it and my hair looks like a tramp's. Indeed, my hairstyle can't even be described as bird's nest any more. Bird's nest would be a euphemism; there's so little order here that it now looks like a demolition site.

I press the button and a familiar face crackles into view. But it's not the familiar face that I'd been hoping for; it's not Samantha, here to collect the little one.

'Morning sleepyhead,' says Rachel. 'I thought you'd never let us in.'

'What time is it?' I grumble, through my poor, sleep-numbed mouth.

'Half nine,' says Rachel. 'We let you sleep as long as possible. Jack and I have been out for a nice walk so as not to disturb you.'

I feel a pang of guilt as I buzz her into the flats; Rachel must have had even less sleep than I had. But even so, this whole stupid baby-sitting weekend is her *idea,* so she should take the brunt of the punishment, shouldn't she? I sigh with frustration and wait.

When I let them into the flat-proper, Rachel doesn't let me peck her on the cheek. She doesn't make a big fuss about it, but by this small gesture alone, I know that we'll be having one hell of an argument later on. This knowledge is almost too much for my over-loaded brain, and I'm in half a mind to get the bawling-match out of the way now. After all, it's not as though we'll be bothering CLJ. Judging by the way *he* can shout; his ears will be pretty much immune to loud noises anyway.

Rachel deposits Jack in his cot in front of the plasma screen television and makes herself busy unpacking a couple of shopping bags that she has miraculously pulled from some kind of secret compartment in the pram. It's like the smuggling compartment in the Millennium Falcon, I reckon, and would make an excellent hiding place for any shop-lifted items that Boba Fett the Security Guard might be on the look-out for. For a moment, I think about letting Rachel in on my amusing observation, but the way that she's standing – that backs-to-me at all-costs stance – tells me that she's giving off all the wrong signals. In fact, she's pulsing out these lightning bolts of negative energy, which remind me of the emperor at the end of *Return of the Jedi*.

'Where've you been?' I ask, by way of conversation. I suppose that in some situations, my question might have been misinterpreted as the demand of a jealous lover, but Rachel knows me better than that. She knows I don't care. And I'm not sure that she cares enough about me to care if I care any more.

She ignores me.

'Any word from Sam?' I ask, hopefully.

Freeze-frame; Rachel stops, hand mid-way into the fridge and straightens her back; a defensive gesture if ever I saw one. Then, ever so slowly, she speaks: 'Oh, you'd *love* that, wouldn't you? You'd *love* it if I told you that good old Samantha was on her way back here this minute to get poor little Jack out from under your feet. *One night;* that was all she asked for, but the way you moaned and cried about it…'

'She hasn't called then?' I interrupt. 'I'd have thought she'd have called as soon as she got your message. Some concern she's showing, eh?'

Rachel slams the fridge door shut. The handle, which I'd spent so long lovingly super-gluing back on last night, promptly clatters to the floor. She turns to face me, anger burning in her cheeks.

'Samantha is trying her best with Jack,' she hisses. 'She is supposed to be away this weekend in order to recuperate. Just because she hasn't called back yet...'

Jack must have heard his name mentioned and bursts forth with a clarion-call of hoarse yells. I'd never known that babies could get hoarse before, but CLJ sounds as though he smoked a few packs of Camels last night. And with this new, husky voice of his, he seems even more likely to ruin my ear-drums. His yells seem to be ripping through the whole flat, virtually de-framing the prints on the walls.

'Look what you've done now,' I say, in triumph. It had been Rachel's hissing that had set the little bundle of fun off, not me; I've somehow landed myself in a better position than I've occupied for the whole weekend. It's a position from which I will have no qualms about launching a counter attack. 'He'll have us thrown out of the flats by the evening if he continues like this. The neighbours are already complaining. And I don't blame them. I *hate* that noise.'

Rachel stares at me for a moment, as though deciding which particular clause in my argument will be the first one she'll attack. 'Hate,' she says finally. 'You hate everything. You hate even inanimate objects like the door-buzzer. You sit in this flat all day long in your own little world, designing your stupid little computer games for stupid little stay-at-homes like you that can't handle the real world. This isn't *Star Wars* you know. I'm not Princess Leia and you're...'

'You're damn right about that,' I manage to cut-in. Bringing Leia in is a step too far, and she knows it, but before I can engage the heavy artillery, she's talking over me once again.

'In here, in your little galaxy far, far away, you don't have to care about anyone. You're just as much a little kid as Jack is...'

Jack starts to cry even more frantically at the mention of his name. I make sure that a wide grin is slapped right across my features. When I smile or laugh in the middle of one of Rachel's tirades, it's as though it pushes that final button, the one that launches her into full-on, light-speed rage.

'Look at you smiling,' she roars. 'You think you're so special… You think you're in a film or something. But the fact is; nobody would watch a film about you because nothing happens to you and you don't do anything!'

I simply smile, but already I fear that I may have unleashed a monster that I can't contain.

'It's not all about you,' she continues. 'Jack is not crying just to piss you off. The world does not revolve around you or the daft games you play. There is a world outside these four walls.'

There is a world outside the four walls, Rachel's right about that, and right now, it is banging on our front door with a frenzy that stops even CLJ from screaming. I give her that now *look what you've done* look, but she doesn't respond this time. She walks to the door looking broken – her shoulders all hunched-up – and I hear her talking in a soft voice to my neighbour from across the hall.

Rachel's phone is on the kitchen work-surface where she's left it alongside the half-unpacked shopping bag. Without giving myself enough time to think about the potential ramifications of what I'm doing, I pick up the thing and flick through the call register. Again, I don't do this with the green-eyed desperation of a shunned partner looking for proof; I do it with the cold-eyed righteousness which Rachel had previously trade-marked as her own stock reaction to *anything*.

With something verging on shock, I see that Rachel has dialled Sam's number on seven or eight separate occasions since her two calls from last night. None of these calls have been answered and there have been no return calls. For some reason, my eyes shoot round to CLJ in his cot and I wonder just what the hell is going on.

A second shock rips through my defences almost as soon as I've managed to start dealing with the first one. I suddenly realise that while I've been checking her phone, Rachel has slipped out of the flat with my neighbour; the one that always gives her those looks in the mirror when we happen to get into the lift together. Desperately, I race to the door and take a look out into the corridor. Everything seems quiet but I'm sure I can hear the low bass-tones of my neighbour's voice coming from his flat. He'll be trying on that 'shoulder-to-cry-on' hat for size, checking whether it's the kind of thing that might win Rachel over. I hover on the doorstep, wondering what action I can take. Part of me wants to take those three steps across the corridor and kick the prick's door down; part of me wants to go in, all guns blazing and rescue my princess. Part of me realises that if I do any of this, she will more than likely never speak to me again.

The more I think about making those three easy steps, the more I convince myself that it is a terrible idea. I've not been out for a good few weeks now and to break that vigil for something so trivial (in the great scheme of things) would be something I'd always regret. And besides, those three steps don't necessarily look easy any more. In fact, the corridor is looking more and more forbidding by the minute. I close the front door again and heave a deep sigh of relief.

Deep down, I think I have started to understand the fact that I am trapped. I am trapped within this adult flat and adult body and adult life and there's nothing I can do about it. The last time I talked to my old group of friends, there were only two of us that weren't already married, engaged or had children on the way. Conversation had become a minefield of honeymoon

locations and joint bank accounts. Over beers, some talked of
the fabled tax credits or of the extortionate cost of enrolling a
child in the local nursery. One day, I just decided that I didn't
want to be involved in such conversations any more. My job
as a computer game designer began to take on the key role in
my life. It was my one escape from the relentless pressure of
time. And if you thought that by my explaining all this to
Rachel, we'd have reached some kind of understanding, then
you've got another thing coming, buster. Because *those* are
the kinds of conversations Rachel wants us to be having. In
her opinion, they are the kind of long-term plans that we ought
to be making.

In the flat, CLJ is crying again and I realise that I can't
stand it any more. I pick up Rachel's phone again and dial
Sam's number. I press the damn phone against my ear and
drum my fingers on the cold, hard work surface that I know so
well.

'Come on, come on!' I breathe, listening to the unchanging
ringing tone nine, ten, eleven times... Suddenly Sam's voice
kicks-in and for a moment, I don't realise that it is her answer-
phone message.

'Hi, this is Samantha and Jack Richards,' she Jar-Jars,
'we're sorry that we're not here to take your call, but if you
leave a message after the beep, we'll get back to you as soon
as we can.'

A random image pops into my head: CLJ collecting Sam's
answer-phone messages and returning the calls, a cigar
chomped between his lips like some big-businessman. The
beep sounds loud in my ear and I almost jump, but manage to
compose myself enough to leave a message.

'It's Mark,' I moan. 'Please come and pick up your son so
that we can all regain a little bit of sanity.'

Sam's answer-phone offers me the option of re-recording
my message, but on reflection, the message that I've already

left pretty much says it all. She should come and pick up the little bastard before he ruins anything else. As an afterthought, I hand Rachel's phone over to CLJ and give him an encouraging smile. Perhaps if he tries hard enough, he'll be able to break it before the day is out.

I have a yearning for the sofa. I have a yearning to be reclining into it, logged-in to my game-network, forgetting all about the fucked-up situation that I've found myself in. I'm thirsty too, and a nice Corona with a quarter-lime would go down a treat. But to grab a Corona would mean confronting the wrecked fridge, and attempting to climb back onto the sofa would mean doing something about CLJ's body-bag which is slumped across it like an even more bloated Jabba the Hut.

Sighing, I grab the phone back from Jack and dial Samantha's number once again. Once again, the phone rings out and I'm forced to leave another bloody message.

'Look Sam; where was this contract that we signed up to which said that we were making some kind of swap deal? Jack is your kid and Sy Snootles is our cat. I think that everybody should go back to where they started. Come back to our flat and we'll get everything back to how it should be.'

This time, instead of clicking the phone off, I hold it over CLJ and record the sound of his constant crying for a good two minutes. *That should bring her back here sharpish,* I think, kicking the body-bag off the sofa and slumping down into the deep crevasse that it has left.

But I can't relax, not with CLJ crying like that. I check his nappy and offer him some food. I even try pulling some faces at him again. Nothing works. He's crying for the sake of it. In desperation, I unzip the body-bag again, hoping that somewhere within its folds, Samantha will have left some forwarding address for the health retreat or something.

It's as I'm checking the inside pockets that I find it; the object which instantly destroys my life as effectively as the

Death Star blows up Leia's planet, Alderan. But the object that I find is something far simpler than a man-made star-destroying planet-sized space station. It is a piece of paper, ripped from out of one of those reporter-style notebooks. It contains the sprawling hand of Samantha Richards. It is a letter and it is addressed to me. My eyes scan the page in ever-increasing horror:

'Dear Mark,

And I hope it will be you that finds this note and not Rachel. There is something that you need to know; something which I've come close to telling you on so many occasions. In a way, I think you know it already what I'm about to tell you. You've known all along.'

I feel the fear start to rise in the pit of my stomach. My fingers tremble as they grip the page, causing it to rustle a little. Because I already know what she is going to tell me; I already know that Samantha – pained, poetic Samantha – hasn't got it in her to keep the silence going forever. I read on, wishing that somehow I'll lose the ability to recognise letters and words; wishing that somehow the ink will lose definition; wishing I'd never found the damn thing in the first place.

'Do you remember that night at Jimmy's; the house party? You clearly didn't want to be there; it was plain on your face. You argued with Rachel and she stormed off into town. I could tell that some part of you wanted to go after her, but all you could do was stand by the window and stare out of that gap between the curtains. I could tell that there was some kind of battle going on inside you. You don't even go out at all these days, do you?'

I don't; and it's for precisely this reason that I don't. *Things* happen out there; things which are out of my control. Other people come into play, and with them, nothing is certain. Even now, as I read this poisoned letter, I can feel myself becoming infected.

'Anyway, you got very drunk at Jimmy's. Drunk enough certainly, that you could convince yourself that you wouldn't remember anything, and that there would be no consequences to your actions. And you'd always known how I felt about you, hadn't you?'

That much is true; I have always known about Sam and her crush. Even then, I'd known that I'd been playing with fire when I did what I did...

'There's no point in trying to explain what happened. All I know is that you were gone by the morning; back to your microcosmic world in the flat. You probably brain-washed yourself into thinking that nothing happened. It wasn't as easy for me, Mark. Not only did I have to face the crippling guilt of having done something so terrible to one of my best friends, I also knew, right from the start that I was pregnant. I don't want to go into all of the medical stuff that I know you hate, but I had to be very clever with dates and times in order that I could convince Jeremy that the baby was his. In the end, he worked it out. Jack couldn't have been his; he'd been away in the U.S on business at the time if you remember.'

I steal a quick look up at the door; perhaps I'm checking for Rachel's return, or perhaps, as is more likely, the mere mention of Samantha's ex has me quivering like a wreck again.

'Jeremy worked it out for himself. Probably everyone else has worked it out now, but you. Look at Jack. He's got your messy hair, your killer smile and that sparkle in his brown eyes. When he yawns he looks just like you; as though he's bored with the whole world.'

I try not to look at CLJ. I try not to check the veracity of her statement. Perhaps she knew I'd be like this, and that's why she felt the need to put it all in a letter.

'I love Jack; more than I ever thought it possible to love someone, I love him. I would do anything for him. And that's why I've done this. I can't cope with him. Not on my own. I can't give him the time that he deserves. But you can, Mark; if there's one thing you've got plenty of, it's time, isn't that right?'

Strangely, I find myself nodding my head as though Samantha is in the room with me. And in a way, she is; I can't shake off the image of that broken woman settling down at her desk and having to write this letter. At some parts, near the bottom of the letter, there are a few blotches; tear-stains which she's left as though they are the final, clinching proof of my guilt.

'I don't know how long I'll be away for, but I want you – and that includes Rachel – to look after Jack. I don't care if you tell her about us or not. I'm past the point of worrying about that. Jack is the most important person in all of this, and he shouldn't be punished for our mistakes.

And Mark? Don't try to call me. I plan to throw my phone off Mordal Bridge once I've dropped Jack off at your flat. It might ring for a couple of days, but eventually, the battery will run out.

Meet your son, Mark. I mean *really* meet your son.'

I crumple the paper into a ball in my sweating fist. This is my Darth Vader/ Luke Skywalker moment, just like at the end of *The Empire Strikes Back*. I can almost hear the haunting John Williams score in the background. But it's more than that, isn't it? It's more than a moment in a sci-fi film. This is reality, and reality knows just how to kick a man when he's down. It feels like the end of the world. I am not the hero of my own life, but rather the villain.

CLJ obviously feels the tension in the room and the way that my mood has darkened, for he chooses that very moment to let loose with another wild bout of screaming.

'I feel the same way,' I mutter, leaning over the cot, staring into those eyes of his which I recognise as oh so familiar now.

Numbly, I reach into the cot and pick him up. I'm unprepared for the weight of him, just like I was with Mr. Snootles earlier. His weight convinces me that he is more than just a collection of pixels; he is real.

Even in my arms, he continues to cry those great, heart-wrenching sobs of pain. Absently, I begin to wonder if there is *anything* I can do for this little… person.

'It'll be all right, I whisper, as much to myself as to him. Lightly, I start to jog him up and down a little, hoping that it will soothe us.

Rachel chooses that moment to step back into the flat. She has her head down as she enters, but when she looks up and sees us, a confused expression washes over her. She stares at us for a long moment; suddenly, CLJ feels like a piece of burning coal in my hands. I know that I must put him back in the cot before she realises the significance of this little father and son reunion. But I can't let go of him; he's still crying. I'm still needed.

Rachel steps further into the room, still staring. I know she's worked it out. I know that the truth we'd all buried for the past four months has now been shown to her. I try to give her a look into which is poured all of my own incredulity and fear. She *must* know… This is well and truly the end of us.

But then Rachel smiles. Perhaps it's on account of the fact that CLJ has just been sick on my arm or perhaps it is something deeper. At first, it is only a fleeting smile, which plays at the corners of her lips, but soon the full-on dimples are out and even her eyes agree; it is a smile of acceptance. When I smile back, it is a smile of gratitude and when CLJ starts to smile, he's probably smiling because we're both grinning like loons. It seems as though the world has suddenly flipped on its axis. I think that we're all thinking that despite everything, things might turn out all right.

I don't call him CLJ any more. Unbelievable as it may have been to my former self, I call him 'son'. It started with a slip of the tongue. For ages, I was worried that Rachel may have heard me, but soon I realised that none of us wanted to look that deeply into things. I suppose, deep-down, we were both so overwhelmingly grateful to Jack for somehow, against all the odds bringing happiness back into the flat that the events leading up to his arrival became a kind of blind-spot.

We don't talk about Samantha any more. Her phone has run out of batteries, just like she said it would, and we receive her weekly postcards without even passing comment. They are all from far-flung places like Fiji and Samoa. In the brief notes, she sounds happy. Occasionally, she informs us that soon she might be strong enough to come back and start her life with Jack again and we start to worry for a couple of weeks, but we haven't yet had to face that earth-shattering old face on the video link of the door entry system.

Jack's well, thanks for asking. 'Cat' was his first word, despite the fact that Rachel and I were both secretly training him up so that 'Rachel' or 'Mark' or 'Daddy' would win. Maybe Mr. Snootles played the game best by simply staying in the background and minding his own business, much as he had since Rachel had picked him up from the cattery on that fateful Sunday.

Jack looks more and more like me every day, and only now do I understand that look that I used to catch my father giving me when he thought I wasn't looking. He can shuffle around the place pretty well now, in that ungainly style that he's perfected and he likes to investigate everything. I suppose that in terms of his personality, he's nothing like me, but the way I've been in my time, that can only be a good thing. Still, we both enjoy it when I sit him on my knee and tell him amazing stories of space battles and space smuggling. I think we both recognise the fact that these stories are just for fun, nothing more.

Jack also loves sitting with me and watching the Gamorrean Guard juggling with his weights and we laugh at the fact that he's so poor at it. I've already convinced myself that Jack will not be one of his kind. Nor will he be a bus-stop man or a drunk or a moustachioed gasman. He's my shining hope for the future; my Luke Skywalker.

I suppose that in the end, we've all got what we want, and even though the whole thing is based on the most fragile of lies, we are happy. Rachel got the family unit that she wanted, even though it was only by default; I got to stay in the flat for the majority of all day every day as a stay-at-home husband; Samantha got to go back to her old life. Sure we were hiding from uncomfortable truths, and sure the equilibrium was so fragile that we thought we could shatter it with even the merest reference to the whole story, but we learned to hold on to what we had. We learned that in life, happiness only comes fleetingly, and sometimes you have to make do with degrees of happiness.

All of us live our lives making up stories to tell each other in place of the truth; all of us navigate haphazardly through life's asteroid fields, trying to stay on our somewhat shaky bearing. We live in fear of the croak of the buzzer telling us that everything we tried has been in vain. We make the most of what we have while we have it. And in this respect, I suppose that you could say that we've become normal again.

8

Miranda Winram

'One, two, three, four, five,
  Once I caught a fish alive.'
The words drifted into the room, a snatch of sound gradually diminishing and then cut off completely. I heard the words but did not move, I did not know how to.

I hadn't known the song before but the simple words linked themselves circularly, looping around my brain repeatedly. '...Once I caught a fish alive, one, two, three, four, five, once I caught a fish alive...' It wasn't the fish singing (of course); it was caught, hanging on the end of a line. But it was still alive – maybe it gets away? Or dies? Perhaps it could sing then. Six, seven, eight, nine, ten, what must have happened then?

Time passed. I opened my eyes, experimentally. Closed them. Prepared for the brightness. And opened them again.

A woman appeared sideways, opening a swing door just within my field of vision, turning in a practised move around the end of the door and simultaneously looking up from the clipboard she held. "Good morning Farah." She smiled. "How are you feeling today?"

There was no answer; I could see she hadn't expected me to offer one. I kept my eyes on her; I could not smile.

"It's great that you're awake today. I'm Deepa Partha." She came closer and stood with her face above mine, speaking slowly. She had dark skin, like me, with long black hair tied into a ponytail. "You've been unconscious for a day. You're in Mildenhall Hospital; we're a specialised unit for the treatment of burns. I'm the Consultant here, the senior doctor.' She gestured behind her. 'This is Jena; she is a nurse on the ward and is here to help look after you."

Jena, small, blonde, young, stepped forward and smiled as well, saying something, though I couldn't tell what. Tears filled my ears. I closed my eyes to stop them falling out.

It was later, another day? I had been awake for some time, eyelids masking the world. I was content just lying, drifting. Then I could feel someone come into the room. I opened my eyes, relaxed; it was the blonde girl.

"I've just come to check your drugs!" she said brightly. "They're good you know! When you're feeling a little stronger you'll be able to control them yourself, but right now I'm just making sure that you're as comfortable as possible." She twiddled with something behind my head, out of vision, a faint coolness washed across my face – I almost hadn't noticed the prickling sensation until it disappeared.

Jena checked her watch and signed a clipboard, then bent over me. I felt her hand on my arm and was comforted; my eyes closed again.

Dr Partha was here once more, smiling again. It seemed that everyone smiled here. She told me that I was doing well. I'd banged my head but that was nothing to worry about, that my face was burnt but the hospital would make it better. Her voice was like the Queen's.

I moved my index finger to acknowledge her; I wanted to move my lips but my face was frozen. I wondered how bad my face was. I tried to move my hand more, to gesture, to try and ask, but it was so very heavy. It didn't move as I asked it to. I knew all about that, about my body refusing to obey the screams of my mind.

"Your facial burns are severe." She was picking her words carefully, as precisely as her diction. "You do not have a great deal of skin left on your face at the moment. But skin is an amazing thing; it will heal, in time the scars will not be noticeable. You'll be beautiful again, don't you worry."

But you don't know, I thought, you don't know if I was beautiful before. Perhaps she thinks everyone is beautiful, that everyone is lovely.

The Doctor hesitated, seemed about to say something, then, "Your head may be a little sore where you banged it, but in a day or so that'll be back to normal. I'll see you again tomorrow; we'll have longer to talk then. Keep sleeping and resting in the meantime. You're doing well."

I lay back and closed my eyes; it was justified, I'd been told to. Daydreams, dreams, came quickly and I sank into them. I was running, with Zeb, through the trees. They were so green and the ground underfoot was spongy, forgiving. I could hear my shrieks, him calling me, speaking in our language, telling me he'd catch me. Zeb was older, he always caught me, but I didn't mind. Often he and our cousins chased me away, were not keen on a girl hanging around. I'd crouch on my heels, watching, hoping I could join them. I grew out of it, of course, when I was older, when Zeb sought my company and we became best friends.

It was unusual for there only to be two of us, it made us feel special, that it was us against the rest of the clan. Our mum had died having me and Zeb could remember her. She was a smell to him, and a feeling of being in her arms. When I was very little I used to get Zeb to hold me, to try and pretend. But it didn't work, however hard I tried to imagine her.

Our aunties took us in. While I was careful to be unobtrusive, not to cause offence, aware that we were intruders into our aunties' lives, Zeb was outspoken and rash. There only had to be a rule for him to want to break it, even if it meant disobeying my father. No one else *ever* disobeyed our Da. My aunties were at first tolerant and then dismissive – he was labelled a troublemaker. None of us went to school that often, we moved on too much, but he less than anyone. Our

Da didn't mind, it was an extra pair of hands, and in a family business that was never a bad thing. Until Zeb cheeked him, and he'd casually reach out and punch him, hard, and Zeb would go off for a few days. He always came back though. Until the day he didn't.

That was the mother of all rows; Zeb wanting to marry out. I'd met her, she was sweet, but they were both so young that I was as surprised as anyone. If they'd been left alone I reckon it would have blown over, but the aunties found out about her, wouldn't let it be. Zeb, typically, fanned the flames by announcing proudly that they were getting married. He was traditional at heart, I think. He left and never told me where he was going, never wrote.

I tried to think of something else, tried to finish the fish jingle from yesterday. We'd fished together Zeb and I. We'd never caught much, but occasionally we'd be able to provide tea. We fished until I was too old, until the aunties told me I had to start behaving properly.

I opened my eyes to make him go away. I was conscious of my body, could feel it pressing an outline into the narrow mattress. My hands moved, touched the edges, gripped them, loosely. As I tightened my fingers I could feel something in my left arm. A sideways glance confirmed it, a tube reaching down in that direction. I'd seen this on TV. My head moved, slightly, as my gaze followed the line down, and then, with some effort, returned to the same position, eyes glazed by the ceiling's glare.

The light was bright, fresh with a whiff of bleach when I next woke up. Jena backed in, wheeled around with her hands full, chattering away.

"How are you feeling this morning? You look lots brighter."

She came closer, looked at my face, noticed my fingers wiggling at her.

"Excellent. It looks really good."

Jena drew away and replenished the drip.

"You're going down to a lower morphine level today. But you can call for more pain relief at any moment by pressing this button."

A plastic bulb was placed gently in my hand, and she looked at me carefully to check that I had understood.

Dr Partha joined us in the room, and mirrored Jena's comments.

"Thank you." I surprised myself with the whisper of sound, barely moving my lips.

They smiled with genuine pleasure. Dr Partha paused, then spoke. "We have had a call from your husband, he has asked whether he can visit. In cases like this," she paused again, "we are cautious about allowing visits too early."

I didn't speak, could not communicate my thoughts.

Dr Partha was looking at me. "It is difficult to judge how the body will react to trauma on this scale. I think, until you are able to articulate your wishes more clearly, we will keep you quiet for the moment."

I tried to smile, felt my face immovable but a shard of pain cutting across my thoughts. I pressed the bulb.

Dr Partha returned later. After doing the, by now routine, checks on the clipboard, she sat on the seat next to the bed, yawning as she did so.

"I'm sorry," she turned it into a laugh. "I was up early this morning with an emergency. You're progressing well Farah, I'm really pleased."

"Great," I moved as little of my face as possible.

"It's an odd circumstance, but facial burns sometimes heal more quickly than others. The eschar," she glanced at me, "that's a scab, is starting to form already, and I don't think we are going to need to do any skin grafting; the deepest burns are quite contained in their area."

"Great," I said, again.

Dr Partha seemed to be in no rush to leave. I was glad; it felt companionable to have her sitting there. "My family come from India originally, we're Hindus," she was relaxed into her chair, casual in imparting this information.

I was interested, our family lore says that many generations ago we came from the Indian sub-continent. "Hmmm?"

"My father is a medic too – he came here as a junior Doctor – and my grandfather in India still practises, although he is 83 now. They are both GPs. I liked surgery so I decided to specialise. And," she glanced at me smiling, "it seemed a bit dull to follow the family tradition and be a GP as well."

I obviously was looking interested enough for her to keep going, although quite how I'm not sure.

"Burns interested me because of a tale my Grandmother told me when I was a teenager. There was a news story about suttee, a widow burning herself to death on her husband's funeral pyre, and Aka told me – with such horror that I can still hear her explaining it today – of the history of suttee."

I felt sick at the thought of someone voluntarily burning themselves to death.

"I've never heard it," I managed to whisper.

"In the north of India it was a reasonably common practise hundreds of years ago for the higher castes. It was outlawed almost two centuries ago, but there had been the very occasional news story of its recurrence through Aka's lifetime. She told me that burns were such a painful injury that she could not imagine many instances where the practise had been fully voluntary, that the majority of suttee widows had been forced to do it by their husband's family."

Dr Partha paused. "There were also, quite often, reports in the Indian press of wives suffering terrible burns while living in their in-laws' homes. Frequently it seems these women are very careless when frying the family's dinner."

I stiffened under my sheets.

"Aka was a great advocate of women's rights and she volunteered at a charity for destitute women, often widows thrown out by the husband's family." Dr Partha smiled at me. "It all made a great impression on me; I felt that working with burns was my calling. Although, of course, in England it is unusual to find burns as a result of abuse."

I was silent, my eyes blanking out her story.

"I'm tiring you."

She patted my arm, softly, checked I had the pain relief bulb securely in my hand, and gently left the room.

I woke to press the button several times that night, stark images searing my dreams, and woke with Zeb's name on my lips.

I was 15 when he'd dropped his bombshell, and I could not lie when I was asked if I had known about the girl. I didn't mind the blow from Da, I understood his loss. He had never hit me before, and he never did again. The aunties were more painful.

"I always knew that boy was bad."

"An outsider right from the start."

"No family feeling."

"Always causing trouble."

I had to listen until I thought I would scream and had no one to share my memories of his kindness and his love.

And then the aunties' gaze switched to me. I made their lives untidy, I was a reminder of a community failure. I could see that they wanted to tick me off, dispose of me. Our clan traditionally marry young, but to the right type. It's normally a family group known to us, that live like us, have the same customs, traditions. The same sense of honour. Marriages aren't arranged, so much as introduced. Of course if you've any sense you try to make your own decisions, to find someone before a choice is forced. But I was shy and did not have any sense. And, anyway, who is to say it would have made any difference?

I felt brave enough to try to touch my face the next day. I lay for a long time before I focussed on raising my forearm, bending my elbow and ever so slowly moving my fingertips closer until they touched, something. I could not feel them on my face, and my fingers told me they were in contact with a surface that wasn't skin. It was hard, solid, immobile. I grew braver, allowed the fingers to roam across my cheeks, my chin, even up and over my nose. In places the surface felt like a beetle's, it was smooth and slightly rounded, and then it became corrupted, bumpy and pitted. Like those flat layered rocks shelving out to the sea, with little holes and lines where pebbles have worn away at weaknesses. It was slippy, but then my fingertips would stall on a sticky section along a crack, seepage from the flesh underneath.

My face was vast; it took a long time for my fingers to work their way around it. I became much less tentative, even tried pressing lightly. That was not a great idea, it hurt, a lot, deep under the surface, and the pain spread from the first point, trickling outwards until it covered the whole of my head. My scab of a face would never look normal again. The salty self-pitying sting deep in the crevasses didn't stop me slipping back into temporary oblivion.

Hideous or not, I was undoubtedly feeling better. The bed was set with an incline for my head and shoulders when lying down ("It helps reduce swelling," Jena had explained). Once I had stopped feeling so utterly sorry for myself, I gradually worked my way into a better sitting position. The effort made my face burn a great deal more. I could feel blood pounding up against the scabrous surface, but I was happy with that. Surely it must mean that I was fighting and healing? I groped around for the control for the incline, increased it and sat back with my face painfully expanding and contracting. I took a proper, horizontal, look around the room, my room.

It was utilitarian, but clean. A locker sat in the corner to the left of the bed, white chipboard with two swing doors underneath and a tray on the surface holding packets of swabs and wipes. There was a sticker on it, disclaiming any hospital responsibility for valuables. The swing doors, through which I'd had slanting glimpses of the corridor, occupied the wall beyond it. To the right was a window, looking onto a new brick wall about two metres away.

It was wonderful. It was my space. I was happy to sit and look at it all with the pride of possession. I'd never had a room of my own before. I'd shared with Zeb when we were very young, then with my aunt and a female cousin. And then, of course, I was married. I breathed deeply, appreciating that it was only me that could hear, that no one else could know that I had breathed. Would not know if I stopped.

"You've worked out the bed then." Jena gave me a complicit glance. "You wouldn't believe the number of people we have to explain those controls to! Now, would you like the TV on?" She looked enquiringly towards me.

"Yes, please." Slurred, but recognisably words.

"Here's the remote." Jena stayed close to me to examine my face, softly tilting my head back and round. "Still no infection, good. That's what we have to be very careful about; it can cause havoc with burns."

"How long will I be here?" My whisper was firmer, although the intonation was still flat, my mouth trying to expel the words without disturbing the skin around it.

"It depends how long it takes for you to heal, but I think it will be at least one week more. Dr Partha will be here shortly; she's got a big round today. She'll be able to tell you better than me."

Gathering up the swabs she'd been wiping my face with, she left. She did, I thought, an amazing job.

"Jena mentioned that you were asking about progress; I'm

afraid that I can only counsel patience, it's too soon to say." Dr Partha stood at the foot of the bed. "You're making great steps. Now," her tone softened, "can you tell me how this happened?"

"I was cooking dinner, I slipped and fell towards the pan of oil."

"You were deep frying?"

"Yes."

"In an open pan?"

"Yes, it's how I always do it."

"Farah, I have to tell you, that I cannot imagine how you managed to sustain these injuries just falling towards a pan of oil. Your whole face went into it. And then you hit your head hard enough to knock yourself out."

I could say nothing.

Her voice was still gentle. "You can trust me, you know. If you need help I can get it for you."

There was nothing I could say. She let the silence lengthen and then breathed deeply.

"There is nothing to worry about, but you will have to speak to the police. The hospital has to inform the police if we feel patients may have been involved in suspicious circumstances."

"But I can't, that's not necessary." I felt panic. "They don't like us; I don't want to see them."

"They will be very kind, and very discreet, and I'm afraid that there is no medical reason to bar them from interviewing you now."

I gazed at the ceiling again.

"And your husband," the Doctor's voice tiredly went on. "Do you wish for me to tell him that he can visit now?"

I nodded, still unable to speak.

Jena brought me some books that morning, a good mixture of novels left by other patients. I loved reading, could always be found curled up with a book, unobtrusively in a corner. English was my favourite subject at school, my teachers consistently surprised by my work. "It's the words," I'd try to explain, "they are like magic."

Whatever my mood there was always a book to match it – exciting or adventurous or comforting. Tobe thought me dopey, getting distracted by a book and I had to be careful when I spoke to him. To make a conscious effort not to use words that I'd just delightedly discovered, that described something more precisely than I'd thought possible. Today, in my room, I could read whatever I liked. I picked up a book with a horse on the cover, a thriller, but for the first time ever was too tired to start it, even to read a page.

Tobe and the police arrived almost simultaneously in the afternoon. I woke to the sound of voices outside, my heart beginning to pound, then the doors opened and Jena came in with Tobe. She stood back and let him move forward. He didn't stop and stare; he'd obviously been warned what to expect. He came forward to the head of the bed, awkwardly holding some flowers, speaking quickly.

"Are you OK? How are you feeling? I've been dead worried."

I looked at him for a long second before speaking, "I am going to be fine."

"What?" He couldn't decipher the words, leaned closer. He did look worried.

"I'm going to be fine."

He sat next to me, put the flowers on the bed. "I love you so much. You know that? Don't you?"

I nodded. He couldn't see where to kiss me, I could see the indecision on his face, so he took my hand. I felt it burn as he bent the wrist to hold it.

"Farah, the police are here to see you as well. They would like to see you alone," Jena said.

"They can see her with me here," he hurried over a possible objection, "this is the first time I've seen my wife since she was injured – I'm not leaving now."

Jena tried to speak and he interrupted.

"I don't want her upset by them, they don't like our kind." He was clearly immovable.

To my surprise Jena didn't give in to him, she politely held the door and firmly told him he could return after they had been. He looked furious, clenched his fists, but eventually stood and walked out. "I'll be back as soon as they've gone babe."

There was one policeman and one policewoman. They had asked me about the accident several times by now, and I was tired again.

"I just slipped. I don't know how, it happened so quickly." I couldn't do this anymore. I closed my eyes.

They were speaking in low tones outside the room, but the walls were thin. "We'll talk to him as well, but there's nothing else we can do right now. She's clear on what she says happened. You might be wrong, you know?" There was an almost audible shrug. "We'll see about sending a community support officer to speak to her again when she's back at home."

Tobe was shaking my arm. I felt angry. I was asleep, and enjoying sleeping. I did not want to wake up. He persisted, and I reluctantly let my mind surface.

"You've been asleep for ages." It was a complaint.

"I am meant to sleep. It helps me heal." My tone was apologetic, if the words were not.

"How long are you going to be here?"

"I don't know." I looked at his face, hastily added, "They don't even know, it depends on how quickly my face gets better.'

"I need to go now, my shift starts soon. Do you need

anything? Can I bring you anything?"

"Perhaps," I considered, "some clothes? For when I can get dressed."

"I'll be back tomorrow. I hope," he hesitated, "you feel better soon."

The door admitted some childish voices as he left, the same nursery rhyme filtering through as the door slowly closed itself, '... Six, seven, eight, nine, ten, then I let it go again.' I smiled at the lyric, happy to know the fish's fate, and appreciated the silence as I regained my room. Despite the space it gave me to think. I picked up the book, held it high so that I didn't have to bend my head down to read it (that started the blood pounding around my face) and disappeared into it. A world of chivalry and people doing the right thing, and happy endings. That was essential. I'd read many of the classics, the 'literary' books, but for relaxation I always came back to those where goodness wins.

It was the same time, mid-afternoon, when Tobe came again, with a box of chocolates this time. I asked him to lift the flowers he'd brought last time from the corner behind me to the table by the TV.

"So I can see them. The cleaners move them you see."

They didn't – I chose not to have a reminder that the room was no longer mine now, but it was a lie that he wouldn't be likely to catch me out with.

"How are you managing?"

"Oh," he fidgeted, "good. I'm going next door for meals."

His mother lived next door, with his younger brother and his wife.

"I'm sorry. I'm sorry for being angry."

There was an unspoken world between us, a flimsy (what was the term Dr Partha had used?), eschar, over recent events that I was not going to test for strength.

"I know, that's OK."

He told me his family's news, and handed over cards that my aunties had sent. He'd already opened them. The rumour at his work was that there would be lay-offs soon, the company was not doing well, and it was unlikely that his casual work would become permanent. He had talked about staying put, when the family moved on, but it seemed that he would be rejoining his dad. He did not visit long, the machines, my face and the staff popping their heads round the door every few minutes made him uncomfortable.

I had another visitor that day, a lady, who knocked and asked if she might come in for a chat. She was, she said, Sarah, a hospital visitor, and I was the only one awake. She was a little older than me, early-thirties perhaps, and had wonderful clothes. The kind of relaxed tailored look that tells you how well regulated someone's life is, how cosy and safe they are. I could imagine Dr Partha wearing those kind of classic clothes. Beige and brown and cream. We chatted about my book, laid face down on the cover. I was enjoying it, gripped by the story from the word go. The author was one of her favourites, she said. I'd always ignored them in the library, thinking that they looked like men's books; what a waste not to have discovered them earlier I exclaimed! She laughed, and I did too, as the notion that there would ever be enough time to read all the good books in the world was ridiculous.

She asked about me, whether I had children, and quickly stepped into the silence when I didn't reply.

"I don't," she said. "It was one of the sadnesses of my married life. My husband desperately wanted children, a boy particularly, to carry on the name."

How did she know I wondered? She couldn't.

"That was when," she paused, took a deep breath, "he first hit me."

I felt furious that she had barged in to my room, that I had not invited her, that she had the nerve to come do-gooding to me. I looked up, my mouth full of bitterness, trying to choose the words that would cause her to leave immediately, but found the sounds stuck. She had tears in her eyes, was pleading with me silently not to reject her disclosure. We have all done that. Floated a line in front of a friend or acquaintance, a line we want them to follow, to pull on, to land the subject and to dissect it. To help. And, maybe I've been unlucky in my life, but on the occasions when I've thrown out that lure, it has never been grabbed. The moment would pass and I'd know not to try again.

"Tell me," I said.

"We met after college. My degree was in history, his in economics. We'd both moved to the City with our first jobs and were in the same graduate intake for a bank."

Sarah looked happy as she remembered, and I was intrigued by a life so different to mine. I'd never even had a job.

"For a while it was wonderful, I'd never felt like that about anyone before, and he was rich. His family were lovely, they welcomed me, and I enjoyed this new unconscious assumption that Christmas meant Klosters and August the Med." She looked embarrassed. "We didn't even have to struggle to buy our first flat – it was a wedding gift from his parents."

I didn't envy her wealth, it was just different. Her face twisted again and I realised it was pain she was feeling, not embarrassment.

"We hadn't talked about it before we got married, but we knew we both wanted a family." Sarah went on, more slowly now. "I was ambitious; I wanted to achieve in my career before having children, but he wanted everything then. He started highlighting anything negative I said about work, agreeing wholeheartedly if I worried about having done a good enough job on something, assuming for me that I wouldn't get promoted very far, that I didn't have it in me to make a success of myself in a tough corporate world."

I could say nothing; I had no experience I could console her with.

She smiled, wryly. "It's very easy to think you can't do things, especially if you have an alter ego telling you all the time that you can't. I agreed, in the end, that we should leave having children to chance, that if I got pregnant then I didn't have a great career anyway so it wouldn't matter."

Her eyes were wet and she apologised.

"I'm sorry, here you are, so brave with your proper injuries and I'm weeping over things that happened a long time ago." She smiled waveringly at me. "I don't think I'm as strong as you. I've only recently been able to talk about this at all, and I'm afraid that I'm not very good at it yet."

That someone else could see me as strong amazed me and that she was apologising for her pain felt very wrong. I murmured inarticulately.

"When I didn't fall pregnant, he started to blame me. He upped the amount of times he told me I was useless, and started to push me around. Just a little, you know? A push here and there, a shake if I was being particularly stupid, and then he graduated to proper punches. Just occasionally, when he'd come back from a night out, or had had a few drinks at home. I started to have to take time out from work, to cover up the damage."

"And then?" I wanted her to leave him now. For the happy ending to come soon.

"I couldn't face the world every day, I felt incapable, so I left work."

Even I knew this was a bad idea. She'd have no one else to listen to, no validation other than his corrosive comments. "You didn't tell anyone?"

"No. Oh, I tried to bring the subject up with his mother, once, when she noticed me wincing with pain. But she changed the subject, wasn't interested in a truth that she knew would be uncomfortable."

Sarah seemed wrapped up in her thoughts, was absorbed in her memories.

"How did you escape?" I noticed my choice of words with surprise.

"An old Uni friend came to visit. She was furious with me for having lost touch and determinedly came to stay for a couple of nights. It was luck that he was out for one of them. She'd had no idea what had been happening, and of course I didn't tell her. But she saw the bruises, heard that I wasn't working and saw me jumping out of my skin at any noise. She fed me a bottle of wine and asked me questions until she knew everything."

Expressions flitted across Sarah's face; I could see shame and embarrassment.

"Even then I didn't leave. My friend told me to, but I couldn't. What would I do without him, where would I go, how would I live? Who else would ever love a failure like me?"

She saw my intent look, could see that I was gripped.

"It took another year and a broken arm." She was wryly humorous and we both smiled. "My friend came to the hospital and, against my protests, took me away with her when my husband had gone home for the night. She did some research and made me contact a wonderful organisation for battered wives."

"And that was that." She made it sound easy for her.

"Not quite. I nearly went back to him several times because I knew he loved me."

"What stopped you?"

"I gradually met some other women at the hostel, and when they told me their stories I was so angry for them. Furious that they could let anyone abuse them like that. It was a shock when I realised that they thought the same about me. They made me realise where I'd let myself get to, that I was just the same as them."

Sarah laughed, in control again. "Battered wives! Makes us sound like fish, doesn't it?"

That tune. Why did they let the fish go?

Sarah's voice recalled me. "The people at Women's Aid were amazing. They gave me a home and helped me to find a job." She visibly squared her shoulders, sat up straighter. "That was three years ago, and I now have a life that I am in control of and that I feel confident in again. I've just started volunteering for them, and this is my first hospital visit. I want to be the friend to someone else that I was lucky enough to have."

She looked at me, at my face. I'd forgotten why she'd come to see me, was shamed by the reminder.

"The biggest thing in an abuser's favour is that they create a climate in which the victim feels she cannot turn to anyone for help, that there is no choice. And there is. There is always a choice. All the help you need is here."

My neck, my arms, my legs, everything, were tired from listening to her story. She pressed a contact card into my hand and got up to leave. I struggled to move my mouth.

"Thank you for visiting me."

She touched my hand, lightly. I tried hard not to be overwhelmed.

"If you are in the hospital again," I swallowed, "I would like it if you were able to visit again."

Sarah smiled. "I'll try not to cry next time! Oh, and I'll bring you another of that author's books. His earlier ones are better, I think."

She left me to think about my baby, the one that a Doctor had told me I could have. Perhaps I might be able to persuade Tobe to see someone. I slept then, at peace with hope.

I must be making progress, I thought, although the needle was left in my arm, the drip was disconnected and I was given proper food and tablets to take instead. Eating was slow, each opening of my mouth wide enough to get a loaded spoon or fork in cracked the precious new surface of my face, and chewing ground those edges together like a pepper mill. The only upside was that my face felt more mobile afterwards, the cracks and fresh wounds allowing my words to sound normal. I looked around my room; it must be deliberate that there was no mirror.

It was sing-song time down the corridor again. I liked hearing the children's voices,

'...Then I let it go again.

Why did you let it go?

Because it bit my finger so!'

I felt a peculiar satisfaction in hearing the ending, and I liked it. Well done Fish I thought, you set yourself free.

I was not in a great deal of pain – periodically, yes, when I ate or smiled too widely – but any sudden shocks like that that soon subsided to a dull thud of blood. I could, I decided, manage with less pain relief. The next time Jena came with the tablets I suggested that I take fewer.

"You're best off just to keep taking them for the moment," the easy smile, "No point being uncomfortable if you don't have to be."

I opened my mouth to speak, and then changed the words to agreement. I swallowed one and discretely slipped the other safely to one side. Perhaps I'd need it later.

"How long did you have to train to be a nurse?" I asked her, interested in her job. It seemed so varied, some parts were highly skilled, others very mundane, and yet her love for it, for me, ran through all her actions.

"I did it the long way." She looked up from tucking in bedsheets. "I wanted to get a job immediately so I could leave home, be independent, so I started work here as an assistant and did a part-time Pre-Registration course. They give you some time off work to help, but it's hard work, you barely have any free time with studying as well as working. Took me five years. Worth it though." She patted the sheets approvingly. "You're done, see you shortly!"

Sarah came again to visit, bringing the promised book. I'd finished the other one already, was looking forward to it. I liked very much that I had invited someone to visit me, to share the hospitality of my room, and that they had come. I was worried that she'd bring up things I wasn't keen to talk about, but she didn't. We just chatted. She liked coffee, I was tea all the way; we both liked the countryside; she was interested in local politics, I only ever bothered to vote for the Prime Minister. She was smart and in control, it was difficult to believe that she'd been the ground down person she'd described before. Until we moved onto books, then I caught a glimpse. She jumped and apologised when I disagreed with her praise for Thomas Hardy, and then realised what she'd done and blushed. I didn't comment, how could I? Anyway, I was transfixed by how clearly I'd been expressing my point-of-view; I'd never talked about books before in this way, and it was fun.

She asked me about my family. I didn't like to bore her, but she seemed really interested. I told her how we lived, the dominance of just a few extended families among my people, that the majority stuck to the old ways.

"It's a very male society in lots of ways, we have a strong tradition of honour and justice, and colourful revenge!" I was proud for a moment, laughing. "Women have to maintain that honour, for their own family before they marry, and then for their husband's family. Things are changing a little. Sometimes, if it's needed, a man joins with his wife's family, rather than the wife leaving to join his, but it's still unusual.

The old ways dominate, and if there is justice to be dispensed it's done by our elders; the families close ranks to protect each other."

"And do all the young people believe the same things, behave the same way?" Sarah was curious.

"There are a few who leave, every generation. My brother was one." I stopped. And then continued, telling Sarah his story, briefly.

"I don't know where he is now, or how to find him."

She was sensitive, changed the subject. "What do you mean by your own kind of justice?"

I felt uncomfortable; I'd already said more than I should to an outsider – our life sounded mediaeval when I heard my words bounce around my clinical room.

"The elders can pass judgement against someone, fine them or assign tasks if it's an offence that they are aware of."

"Like what?"

"Well, anything serious, like theft. Smaller disagreements are normally sorted out without the elders; they only get involved if it gets out of hand, but that's only occasionally."

"Like how?"

"A man was killed a couple of years ago in another family." I was conscious that this sounded bad, and hastily added, 'But it's only what happens in other groups, other societies. We just sort it out ourselves, that's all, without troubling anyone else."

"So, what happened?" She didn't seem like she was judging me, us.

"It was hushed up, an accident. The police were suspicious, they got involved despite the family efforts, but they didn't get anywhere. The elders banished the killer, even though it was not thought to be a premeditated murder. He is not considered part of our people anymore."

"And what about other things? If I had been one of your people, would it have made any difference to me, to the way my husband treated me?"

"No." I tried not to sound sad. "We are very supportive of each other, and women are meant to be respected, but what happens inside each home is considered the business of the head of the house. Just like your mother-in-law, most people would not have wanted to know because of the shame."

We left it there, returning to the safer, neutral, subject of books. She promised to keep supplying my fix while I was in hospital, would bring some of her other favourite authors in for me to browse. "Oh, I almost forgot to say, but your face looks like its started healing."

"I haven't seen it at all yet; I haven't a mirror."

Sarah looked at me and considered. "Do you want to look? I have one in my handbag."

I wasn't sure. Thought for a moment. Took a deep breath. "Yes."

I held the compact she handed to me for several seconds before raising it. Left to myself I would have chickened out, but I couldn't with someone watching, someone who thought I was brave.

My face looked like it felt, crusty, horrifying. A variety of shades of angry reds fading to softer browns near the edge. It was not me that I was looking at, but a blotch of a stranger. A new person that I needed to get to know. Someone who, looking at what I had become, felt very angry.

Sarah's voice was soft, breaking into my thoughts, "It's better than you think. Even just yesterday it was all far redder; it looked much sorer. I think the darker patches must be where the skin is healing and reforming underneath."

She was right – Dr Partha said as much when she and Jena came round in the early evening. Tobe was there as well, he'd just arrived when ward rounds began, bringing a bouquet of roses, and telling me how much he was missing me. He had always been great at buying flowers, it was a romantic side to him that I liked a lot. He didn't stay long, we chatted about not much, and Dr Partha's instruction to keep getting lots of rest released him almost immediately. "Love you, can't wait to have you back." He had brought me a bag of some clothes. I might, I thought, try getting dressed tomorrow.

"Once the new facial skin is starting to be revealed we'll be able to allow you home."

Dr Partha was peering through a magnifying glass at my skin as she spoke. "I want to make sure that it is healing just as it should before we let you go. Perhaps in two or three days. Now," she stood back and looked at me, "how is the pain?"

"Hm. So, so."

"Jena mentioned that you'd asked about the level of painkillers, do you want to try a lower dose?"

"No." I reddened slightly. "I think Jena was right, I'll stay with the two tablets for the moment. It is still quite painful sometimes."

Dr Partha nodded, and made a note, and Jena passed over the dose. I treated it as before, tucking the spare pill quietly away.

It felt odd to be dressed and walking around. I'd even, slightly shakily, ventured out of my room that morning, explored the corridors outside, and asked the nurse at the desk (I didn't know her) for a mirror. I felt pretty much well again, although I still seemed to sleep a lot. I propped the mirror above the washbasin, and stood in front of it, gazing at my face. It was itching. I ran my fingers over the surface, allowed them to stray to the edge, the almost shocking line between face and neck, where the solidity of my road-kill-face changed to no-longer-just-ordinary skin. That join was alluring, my fingernails almost absently slipped sideways, sliding along the edge, seeing if the scab was loose, if it would allow my nail a sliver of purchase. It did.

I couldn't ever accurately describe the feeling of release as that first bit of solidity flaked off and revealed new skin underneath. It was unnaturally pink, it looked nothing like my neck, but the knowledge that there was new skin, NEW SKIN! waiting to be revealed was amazing; I had not felt a happiness that intense before, a conviction that anything was possible. I think I had not quite believed Dr Partha when she'd said that I would start to heal so quickly. This demonstration that she was right, that something could grow from nothing, was revelatory.

Dr Partha made me jump guiltily as she came in while I was standing there, tapping my nails against the hard scab on my right cheek, trying to resist the temptation to keep working at it, to scrape as hard as necessary to reveal what lay underneath.

"Gosh Farah, be careful!" She came across to look over my shoulder in the mirror. The contrast between our faces was stark.

"Look," I pointed at my neck in the mirror, "new skin!"

"Yes, that's good." She peered closer. "It looks very healthy. But don't go too far with it. I know it gets itchy doesn't it?"

"Yes, but..."

"Well, trust me, the best way for the healing to continue quickly is to leave it alone. Don't pick at it!" She tapped my hand as I absently moved it towards my face.

"I know it's hard, but before you know it you'll have caused more damage. The area you've just been looking at was on the edge of the injury, the damage was much shallower. In places, here, and here," she was pointing to my cheeks and nose, "the burn was extremely deep. It was touch and go whether those areas would need grafts. The eschar on those areas will take many more weeks before they are ready to fall off and leave the new skin capable of surviving without protection."

"What will my face look like?" I was pleased my voice was calm.

"You will have quite visible scars to start with. They'll fade given enough time, but you should just be prepared." She was serious. "They'll be worse if you pick!"

I was sobered by her sternness and left the mirror to lie on the bed, trying to ignore the Delilah call of the itches. And the message they contained.

I was, (of course, how could I not be?) pleased that I was healing rapidly, but it meant that I had to face the outside again. Doing the simplest thing would involve people staring at me, asking questions. I could not even think of how to face my mother-in-law, my cousins. And I would have to, they would be there, around me as soon as I left the hospital. I was already embarrassed by what they would think, what the community would talk about. It was likely that I'd be blamed, that people would wonder comfortingly that it must have been my fault. And then there was Tobe. But I didn't have much choice.

Words from two days ago floated back into my mind. "There's always a choice."

There was one choice I'd thought about before, and then dismissed as cowardice, or just plain wrong. But, actually, I am a coward, cowed, and why not meet wrong with wrong?

Because there might be other choices.

What choices?

The ones Sarah had mentioned, the possibility of just leaving, starting again, creating a different life.

But it was different for her – she had a degree, a career, an obvious future.

She hadn't mentioned her family though; I'd assumed, reading between the lines, that she either wasn't in touch, or was too ashamed to tell them what had happened to her. And she hadn't had a posh job to go back to, she'd got an ordinary job in a shop, one that anyone could do, and lived in a hostel for nearly a year. She then started sharing a flat with another girl from the hostel. It was only then that she'd gone back to her professional world.

Perhaps I could train for something? Nursing maybe?

No, it was impossible, it was totally different, easier, for Sarah. She came from a background where women were much more independent. I had never lived alone, never survived outside my community; how would I possibly manage with all these people who didn't understand me? I wouldn't make friends, no one would like me because I was different. I'd no qualifications, I'd never even had a proper job. It was impossible.

My room surrounded me with calmness, space. Urged rationality.

To be fair, I corrected myself, I didn't have a lot of friends in my own community. I'd been shy when I first arrived to live with Tobe's family, and things had started going wrong between us quickly. It was impossible to confide in his cousins, to become proper friends with them, when their loyalty would always be with him first. I had, actually, always been totally dependent on him. And, again, trying to be reasonable, I did get on with Sarah, and she couldn't be from a more different background to me. I could join a book group, I could even try and find Zeb; that thought made me shiver with its enormity and move quickly back to the seesaw of my thoughts.

Sarah had had more incentive to leave – she'd been trapped by her husband, she'd been completely scared of him, he'd been violent constantly. I wasn't scared of Tobe. Sure he had a temper, but not all the time, and sometimes I did provoke it. He had not meant to cause this much damage; I could tell he'd been horrified by my face. I think it had made him think about things differently, in fact, I was sure that he'd be more controlled in the future. Tobe was a good provider, and his family were supportive. If we ever had tough times they would all step in to help – there'd never be any real material worries. And he loved me, he loved me to bits. I might not ever find someone to love me like that again. If we had children, that would make all the difference – maybe it could still happen? Maybe I could raise the subject again.

I drifted into an uneasy sleep, I was running, Dr Partha pursuing me across a car park waving a pregnancy test and then Tobe loomed over me accusing me of bearing someone else's child. He raised his arm to hit me and I handed him his baby, a scaly monster that smiled and stabbed a knife into his chest as he reached for it. I woke sweating. Jena was by the bed, taking my hand, speaking calmly to me, telling me there was nothing to worry about, to calm down.

It was two days later. I'd spent the long progression of hours troubled by the unremitting to and fro of my thoughts, the space I'd initially relished now would not let me stop exploring possibilities. I had reached no resolution, I did not know if there was one. One minute it was as clear as day that I should do one thing, the next another. The outcome, it seemed, would be dependent on which way the pendulum was swinging when I could no longer avoid making a decision, when I walked out of the hospital doors.

My injuries were setting the timescale, they had continued to heal, "solid progress" Dr Partha called it. The edge of my face was already shedding some of its eschar, proving involuntarily that I was ready to present the new me to the world.

Sarah had visited each day, and she didn't seem to mind that I was distracted, wasn't able to talk much. She told me about her job, her volunteering, her plans to get a kitten. We'd laughed, mocking our pretention, as I agreed that Henry James was a really great name for a cat.

Tobe had also come often. Uncomfortable in the institutional environment, his visits were brief, but he was obviously delighted that I was making such swift progress. And he was very pleased that I was coming home so soon.

Today I carefully packed my belongings into my bag, pushing the small envelope of morphine pills I'd hoarded into the inside pocket. I was sitting in my pink armchair when Dr Partha came in, accompanied by Jena. They were both a little more business-like and a little less chatty than normal, and Dr Partha spent longer than usual running some checks on me.

"You are fine, it seems." She didn't smile. "You need to arrange a series of out-patient appointments with the reception desk, to check on progress, but there is absolutely no medical reason why you can't go home now."

Jena handed me some pills with murmured instructions about dosage.

"Farah," Dr Partha was about to continue when Sarah knocked at the door and on Dr Partha's "Yes?" slipped in to join us.

Sarah beamed at me. "You're looking so much better Farah; I'm really pleased that you're well enough to leave hospital."

She walked over and I stood to hug her. I looked round at the three women in my room and swallowed hard.

"Thank you. It isn't enough, but thank you. I can't tell you how much I have appreciated all that you have all done for me. More than anyone else ever has." My eyes were awash, but I was calm. "And more than you will ever know. You're such special people, and I'll remember you always."

I looked around at them; this was the moment I'd been dreading. Blood pounded against my new face, my stomach felt odd and my mouth was dry. There was a moment's silence, and in it I could hear the children from the next ward

having their sing-song, I smiled as I heard the now familiar
verse.

'One, two, three, four, five,
Once I caught a fish alive,
Six, seven, eight, nine, ten,
Then I let it go again.
Why did you let it go?
Because it bit my finger so!'

The others had been silent with me, listening. I took one last
look around the room, already no longer mine, and took a
deep breath.

"My husband is coming to collect me."

I breathed again, concentrated on speaking calmly, could
feel the focus of three pairs of eyes.

"He is coming tomorrow. I would be most grateful if the
hospital could inform him that I discharged myself today, and
that you do not know where I went."

"I am so glad." Sarah broke the quietness. "You'll let me
take you somewhere safe?" I nodded.

Jena was grinning and blowing her nose, and Dr Partha's
face had relaxed; she was smiling.

She then stepped forward and held my shoulder's firmly.
"Farah, you are doing the right thing. You will not regret it. If
you ever need any further help, please just ask." Her words
were emphatic, confidence flowed through her healing hands.
"And I can assure you," she spoke more formally now, "that
the hospital takes the confidentiality of patient records very
seriously indeed. No one other than you will have access to
your details, your future appointments or to any other
information relating to you."

I stood and enjoyed the moment. This was what making my
own choices felt like. Terrifying. There was suddenly one
more thing I wanted to do. I reached into the bag and drew out
the morphine pills I'd secreted away.

"Jena, I didn't take these, and I don't need them."

I was no longer a coward and I would not take that way out.

Sarah picked up my grip, and held the door for me to precede her out of the room.

"We've lots to do." She said it with energy. "Lets get going!"

I took my first step forward, heading in the right direction.

About the authors

C. J. Carver

C. J. is half English and half Kiwi. She is the author of five
novels published by Orion, including CWA Debut Dagger
Award winning novel *Blood Junction*. She lived in Australia
for ten years before taking up long-distance rally driving. She
has driven London to Saigon and London to Cape Town, both
with all-female crews. Her story was inspired by a drive
through the remote Xinjiang Autonomous Region in China, a
beautiful area of wilderness that is home to countless gulags.

Rebecca Strong

Rebecca's parents are from Sri Lanka and moved to England
in the 1970s, where she was born in 1981. She is the author
of *Here or There*, published by Legend Press in 2007, which
follows eleven seemingly unconnected characters captured at
points in their everyday lives. Rebecca had a passion for
writing and language from an early age and studied French
and Spanish at University College London. She wrote her
story in 2008 while pregnant with her son.

D. E. Rhylis

D.E was born in Stoke-on-Trent, and spent her childhood
moving around Great Britain due to her father's job. She is a
self-confessed travel lover and has worked abroad as a head
nurse in Saudi Arabia. As a qualified nurse, wife, mother and
grandmother, she has a different perspective on life and death.
D.E. met her present husband while working abroad and they
married in America.

Mark Kotting

Mark was born and bred in London, and moved to Sydney for a while to look at the surf. He is the author of *Nappy Rash*, published by Wrecking Ball Press in 2005. He has written TV and radio comedy including two plays for BBC Radio *The Match*, 2007 and *Gulf*, 2008. Mark is a London Cab Driver, who once played second division Rugby League.

E. C. Seaman

Emma is Legend Press' only author to be published in all four collections in the Short Story Reinvented series. Having studied English at Oxford, she only began writing again a few years ago, having given up 'working on her first novel' to start on her second instead. She has been widely published and has won numerous short story prizes. Emma lives in Devon with her husband and two young daughters.

Guy Mankowski

Guy was raised on the Isle of Wight before being taught by monks at Ampleforth College, York. After graduating with a Masters from Newcastle University and a Psychology degree from Durham, Guy formed 'a Dickensian pop band' called *Alba Nova*, releasing one EP. After that he started working as a psychologist at The Royal Hospital in London, writing his story during any free moment he could get. Guy now works at a psychotherapy clinic in Newcastle. The setting and mood of the story was inspired by the front cover of the Tubeway Army album *Replicas*.

A J Kirby

Andy has published a large number of short stories in a variety of media, including print anthologies, magazines and journals, on-line and as downloadable pod casts. He was awarded third prize in the Luke Bitmead Writer's Bursary competition 2008, judged by a panel including best-selling authors Deborah Wright and Zoe Jenny. He is currently engaged in writing a sitcom. Andy lives in Oakwood, Leeds, with his girlfriend, and kitten, Eric, who provided inspiration for the cat in his short story.

Miranda Winram

Miranda lives in Yorkshire with a one-eyed dog and a black fluffy cat, neither of whom approve of her new habit of ignoring them and typing madly away at fictional stories. Miranda's story was inspired by her own brief stay in a Yorkshire burns unit and by the wonderful people she once met at a Sheffield women's refuge. It is Miranda's first published fiction.

Legend ⫘ Press
Independent Book Publisher

This book has been published by vibrant publishing company
Legend Press. If you enjoyed reading it then you can help
make it a major hit. Just follow these three easy steps:

1. Recommend it
Pass it onto a friend to spread word-of-mouth or, if now you've
got your hands on this copy you don't want to let it go, just tell
your friend to buy their own or maybe get it for them as a gift.
Copies are available with special deals and discounts from our
own website and from all good bookshops and online outlets.

2. Review it
It's never been easier to write an online review of a book you
love and can be done on Amazon, Waterstones.com,
WHSmith.co.uk and many more. You could also talk about it or
link to it on your own blog or social networking site.

3. Read another of our great titles
We've got a wide range of diverse modern fiction and it's all
waiting to be read by fresh-thinking readers like you! Come to
us direct at www.legendpress.co.uk to take advantage of our
superb discounts. (Plus, if you email info@legend-
paperbooks.co.uk just after placing your order and quote
'WORD OF MOUTH', we will send another book with your
order absolutely free!)

Thank you for being part of our word of mouth campaign.

info@legend-paperbooks.co.uk
www.legendpress.co.uk